LT LINES

Also by Kristen-Paige Madonia

Fingerprints of You

INVISIBLE FAULT LINES

KRISTEN-PAIGE MADONIA

SIMON & SCHUSTER BFYR

NEW YORK / LONDON / TORONTO / SYDNEY / NEW DELHI

An imprint of Simon & Schuster Children's Publishing Division
1230 Avenue of the Americas, New York, New York 10020

SIMON & SCHUSTER BFYR is a trademark of Simon & Schuster, Inc.
For information about special discounts for bulk purchases, please contact Simon & Schuster Special Sales at 1-866-506-1949 or business@simonandschuster.com.
The Simon & Schuster Speakers Bureau can bring authors to your live event. For more information or to book an event, contact the Simon & Schuster Speakers Bureau at 1-866-248-3049 or visit our website at www.simonspeakers.com.
Also available in a SIMON & SCHUSTER BFYR hardcover edition
Interior design by Hilary Zarycky
Cover design by Krista Vossen
The text for this book was set in Electra.
Manufactured in the United States of America
First SIMON & SCHUSTER BFYR paperback edition May 2017
2 4 6 8 10 9 7 5 3 1
The Library of Congress has cataloged the hardcover edition as follows:
Madonia, Kristen-Paige, author.
Invisible fault lines / Kristen-Paige Madonia.
pages cm
Summary: Callie struggles to come to terms with the disappearance of her father, but eventually chooses to believe that he has traveled back to the San Francisco earthquake of 1906.
ISBN 978-1-4814-3071-5 (hc)
1. Missing persons—Juvenile fiction. 2. Fathers and daughters—Juvenile fiction. 3. Time travel—Juvenile fiction. 4. San Francisco Earthquake and Fire, Calif., 1906—Juvenile fiction. 5. San Francisco (Calif.)—Juvenile fiction. [1. Missing persons—Fiction. 2. Fathers and daughters—Fiction. 3. Time travel—Fiction. 4. San Francisco Earthquake and Fire, Calif., 1906—Fiction. 5. San Francisco (Calif.)—Fiction.] I. Title.
PZ7.M26572In 2016
[Fic]—dc23
2014043981
ISBN 978-1-4814-3072-2 (pbk)
ISBN 978-1-4814-3073-9 (eBook)

For Chris and Porter
Every day you remind me that anything is possible.

How beautiful the ordinary becomes once it disappears.

—David Levithan, *Two Boys Kissing*

PART ONE

AFTER THE ORDINARY

My father disappeared on a Tuesday that should've been like any Tuesday, but eventually became the Tuesday my father disappeared. It was April 18, 2006.

"Chicken piccata," my mother said. "It's Tuesday." Because that's what we ate midweek back then.

It was the year I knew things would change. The summer before, I helped start a band as the drummer. On New Year's Eve, I got my nose pierced. SAT prep classes and cross-country running practice swapped places that spring with rock concerts and poetry slams. I hadn't told anyone yet, but I'd decided I wanted to study abroad. I wanted to go places where I couldn't speak the language, so I stashed my college catalogs under my bed and requested passport forms instead. I collected foreign-language dictionaries that I stacked in piles and stored on a shelf in my closet. Spanish. Turkish. Thai. It was the year we were supposed to go from teenagers to . . . not adults, exactly, but instead to that thing in between. It was April, and I was a junior, the last year before I had to commit to college or hold off, the last year before I was expected to decide exactly how the next four would go. A lot was supposed to change that year. But not my father. He'd never changed a day in my life until he disappeared.

Before, he did this: Awoke to his playlist of live concerts by The Who and the Stones and occasionally Stevie Nicks because sometimes, he said, a smoky, sorrowful love song is the best way to pull yourself out of your dreams. Coffee, black. One mug before and one mug after his shower, and he always, no matter what, ate toast with peanut butter in his pine-green bathrobe. A handful of raisins sprinkled on top. Quick change into dark-washed jeans, gray Vans, and a long-sleeved T-shirt because that was his favorite perk of his job—casual dress. Black wire-rimmed glasses and a small shot of orange juice while he organized his papers in his brown leather backpack. The juice glass was an antique, cut with a floral design from the twenties. We'd found the set when we cleaned out my grandmother's condo in Chicago after she died the year before. Besides her Italian recipe books and photo albums, the glasses were the only things of hers he brought home. Glass rinsed and on the drying rack. Brown leather watch, set five minutes fast. Puffy North Face vest, navy blue with a small hole next to the left pocket—a cigarette burn from a friend's Marlboro at a club in Chicago back when he was young. His forehead pressed against my forehead with toothpaste breath between us before he jabbed me in the ribs or plucked my ear. "Callie," he'd say. "Be good, all right?" Or maybe, "Stay out of trouble." A kiss on the nose for me, and then a kiss for my mother, too. Out the door, the sound of him locking it behind him. The 1BX bus, a direct shot to downtown San Francisco while he read *Wired, National Geographic,* or *Popular Science.* He worked in a high-rise corner office with a view in the morning and then at job sites around the Bay Area in the afternoon. Hard hats and soil samples. Backhoe digging. Water testing. Phase II site assessments. Meetings with people who wanted to build condos, who wanted to develop on top of land that had once been industrial buildings, and before that, a different kind of city, and before that, the Bay water.

My mother tossed the grated lemon peel and a handful of capers into the pan. "He's just late, that's all. No worries," she said. Her feet were still encased in her work shoes, the thin white skin of her ankles pinched and pink inside the leather heels she'd bought off a clearance rack that fall. She was infinitely tired. Too tired for what-ifs. My mother worked in the library at UCSF, and in the spring she formatted and archived dissertations for grad students so they could be bound and shelved for reference. Her eyes were often mapped in red, her fingers sliced with paper cuts.

It was dinnertime on a Tuesday, and he was not home yet. He was working late, she said. He was running late or moving slow. No worries. The bus probably broke down. The job site probably took longer than he'd planned for.

Before, I did this: Awoke to the alarm on my nightstand. The White Stripes playing from my speakers, a quick IM to my best friend, Beckett, and one full mug of water after I brushed my teeth, but before my shower. The mug, brought back from Portland when Beckett visited his cousin the previous summer, was chipped above the coffeehouse logo, and sat on the counter next to the sink in my bathroom. Shower, quickly, after my father had had his turn and before my mother took hers, as to avoid risking cold water. Bell-bottom jeans, gray tank top, long-sleeved shirt, and my red zip-up hoodie. Wet hair knotted into a sloppy bun. Lip gloss and a quick brush of powder on my forehead and nose. My nose, small and ski-sloped like my mother's—too small for my face, I'd always thought. Black mascara. My father's dark Italian eyes, my favorite trait. Small gold necklace—the only piece of jewelry from my grandmother that I took when we cleaned out her condo in Chicago. The cornicello, an Italian horn-shaped pendant worn to protect against the evil eye. Read and reply to IM from Beckett. Cup of coffee in the kitchen, lots of cream and sugar. Explanation to Dad that coffee is simply a device to consume lots of cream and sugar. Piece of toast smothered with butter. Cinnamon and sugar sprinkled on top after the butter has made the toast wet enough to turn the topping into warm brown goo. My forehead pressed against my father's forehead with toothpaste breath between us before he jabbed me in the ribs or plucked my ear. Me telling him, "I'm always good," and then the click of the lock behind him. The sound of my mother's shower ending as the water flushed through the pipes, and then her calling "Bus in five minutes!" from behind their bedroom door. IM Beckett from my bedroom. Blue Converse high-tops with my last name, Pace, on the left shoe, inked next to a drawing of square buildings, star-shaped snowflakes, and a lamppost—a winter cityscape graffitied during biology class. On my right shoe, a treble clef, a black arrow pointing up, a small guitar, and our band name, Nothing Right, sketched after school in Golden Gate Park. My mother in the hallway with a question about my math test. Me, mentioning band practice that night. My mother with a question about college applications. Me, rambling about something that happened at work the day before. The thumping of The Clash in my headphones and an open front door. Me, asking about dinner.

"Chicken piccata," my mother said. "It's Tuesday."

An hour after dinner, we called everyone we knew. Friends, coworkers, neighbors, poker-night players, and even the guy my dad bought bike parts from for his motorcycles. Forty-five minutes later we drove to his office, found it empty, and drove home. It took a million years to park the car because Wednesday morning was street sweeping, and every parking spot in every neighborhood close to our house was taken. Finally we found one, went back inside, and checked for phone messages. Again. Eventually, Beckett and his mom, Lori, came over. Eventually, we called the police.

Someone ordered a pizza with pineapple and ham—the leftover chicken was cold and half eaten in the pan on the counter. I cut my fingernails, let the clippings fly and scatter onto the hardwood floor. Mom changed from her work clothes to her sleep clothes, then back to her work clothes before the cops showed up. They talked to her and then they talked to me, but I didn't talk to anyone after I talked to them, not for a long while. The words were there, thick jumbled things like rocks or cement pooling in my throat, choking me. I don't know why, but suddenly words didn't matter. There was nothing to say, really. Beckett ate pizza, and Lori made tea, and the police took notes and wrote down some phone numbers and left.

Beckett said, "Maybe it's a joke. Maybe he's planning some kind of surprise. Things like that happen all the time, you know."

We sat in the kitchen at the small, square table, and our mothers sat in the living room on the other side of the wall. One of them was crying, but I couldn't be sure which.

"*Hidden Camera*, maybe. Or *Caught on Video*. I think that show still exists, right?" he asked. "I bet that's what it is."

I shrugged, pulled a piece of ham off the pizza, and began shredding the meat into tiny strips I collected on the placemat.

"Maybe he's helping someone. Someone homeless he saw on the bus. Or a kid who can't find his mom, maybe," he said.

It was almost midnight by the time I said, "I think he's dead, Beck. I know it. He's gone."

"That's impossible."

"He is. He just . . . He is. He must be. I can feel it. He's not here anymore. I can tell."

I knew that when the cops asked, "Was anything out of the ordinary? Did he seem strange before he left for work? Did he seem distracted?" they meant that he'd left on his own. The thing is, when a grown-up disappears, people assume they made a choice to go. He'd gotten tired or restless and went looking for something more. Something different. He'd been fighting with his wife, with his boss, with his kid. He had a mistress. He had a plan. He had a midlife crisis.

Here's what people assume: My father, Aaron Pace, decided to leave.

But here's what I knew: Before he disappeared, there was nothing unordinary about us. Until that Tuesday, we were a perfectly normal family. And he never, not in a million years, would have walked away.

CHAPTER TWO

Six Days After

I didn't go to school for the rest of the week, and the days moved by in a fog, watery and blurred beneath white noise. With each day that passed, I grew one day further away from him.

There was the search party, a group the city organized, which lasted through Saturday. About thirty people volunteered to scour the neighborhoods of San Francisco, but the last place my dad had been was his job site on Bryant Street in SoMa, and the search party didn't find much there but a homeless man who'd been hanging around the lot.

"Yeah, he was here," the guy said when the police showed him a photo. "But I was too, and I'm not supposed to be. As soon as he saw me, he told me to scram. So I did."

The job site was a vacant lot my dad's company was sampling before the construction crew was scheduled to break ground on a condo building, and nothing looked out of the ordinary when they'd gone to search the grounds. After combing the city for four days, they'd found nothing. The *Chronicle* ran an article buried on page 6, and the local news station covered it quickly on the evening show, prime time, but no one responded.

"So when do we start looking?" Beckett asked. "As in you and me, *we*."

It was Sunday, which meant we were tucked in the window booth at Squat & Gobble on Haight Street. I was drinking coffee, and he was polishing off Zorba the Greek: a gigantic crepe stuffed with cheese and onions and tomatoes, olives and eggplant and mushrooms. The cucumber yogurt sauce on top had warmed and run all over his plate, turning the heap of food into a white-covered slop that reminded me of roadkill in wintertime. I thought I might vomit, sitting there looking at his brunch and thinking of my dad. Broken bones and bruised skin, a collection of body parts in a backyard graveyard.

Beckett's dark hair fell over his eyes as he forked a mountain of food into his mouth. "The police stopped looking because they've got too much to do." He spit a little, chewed longer, and swallowed. "But clearly, you and I have nothing to do, so we may as well get to it."

"Clearly," I said, and he reached over and stabbed at my bowl of fruit with his fork.

"What?" he asked, catching my eye. "I'm a nervous eater."

Beckett and I had been best friends since fourth grade, when we ended up in the same math group because we were both terrible with numbers. He was kind of quiet, like me, but funny, too. He had dark hair, big dimples, and water-blue eyes. He liked art and film, while I liked music, but we both did best in history and struggled most in math. So we partnered up in class that year and waded through long division and fractions together, never looking back. Callan and Beckett. Beckett and Callan. We sounded like a law firm. In eighth grade, when he came out, I didn't bat an eye. In ninth, when I was six points short of failing Earth Science, he rewrote my final lab report and landed me a C plus. In tenth grade, I taught him how to drive even though neither of us ever got our own car, and that winter, after Andrew Parker and I broke up, Beckett and I spent three days camping down in Big Sur, playing cards, strumming guitars, and gorging ourselves on junk food and s'mores until the breakup didn't feel nearly as bad.

"Screw Andrew Parker," he'd said.

"Maybe if I had, we'd still be together," I said.

"It's going to be okay, Callie," he said over and over again, until eventually I believed him.

He was the kind of friend who wasn't going to let me sit

around and do nothing about my dad going missing.

"First we go to the job site. In SoMa, right?" he asked. "Since it's Sunday, we can check it out without worrying about other people being around."

I imagined searching the area and finding his brown leather backpack. Finding his navy-blue vest. Finding a shoe, or scattered white teeth. But the police were already done looking, and if we didn't keep searching, nobody would.

"We'll find him," he said, and then, "'Let every sluice of knowledge be opened and set a-flowing.'"

"Madison?" I asked.

"Please. John Adams."

He'd been obsessed with quoting American presidents since we were freshmen, and mostly did it in times of distress.

"Let's get a move on," he said. "Come. On."

I picked up my mug, knowing I'd need the caffeine. I hadn't slept well since Tuesday. "One more cup of coffee," I said, and he said, "You're the boss," because I had the earlier birthday. I was already seventeen.

The job site was a sprawling lot enclosed by temporary construction fencing, and there was a gate at one end with a padlock and a sign that read NO TRESPASSING.

"This is amateur stuff," Beckett said as he mangled a section of fencing so we could crawl underneath.

The site looked exactly how I'd expected: lots of dirt and debris, a bunch of trash, and a handful of banged-up construction vehicles scattered around. There was an old wall at one end of the lot and a wood frame with a brick chimney about thirty-five feet tall propped in place by support beams.

I knew from my dad that most of the sites he tested were originally used for industrial buildings or warehouses, and I told Beckett so. "See?" I said, pointing to the remnants of a concrete foundation wall. "That's left over from the building they probably just tore down. My dad's company will come in and sample for toxins. Lead and that kind of thing. And then the new owners will build some crazy high-rise condos here."

We walked past piles of rubble and scraps of metal.

"But this," I said when we got to the chimney and wood frame, "this is being saved because it's important. It must have some kind of historical significance, so they have to keep it intact. They'll use it in the new building design."

"Badass." Beckett ran his hand over the brick as dust and dirt crumbled under his touch.

I watched him wander the lot, kicking up dust while he walked. At my feet I noticed a glint, a quick but sharp flash, and when I bent down and brushed the dirt away, I lifted a small piece of glass from the ground. A perfect piece of clear cut glass, jagged on one side but smooth on the other two. It looked like part of a bottle. Or a vase. A water pitcher or fancy soap dish; a wine bucket, maybe. Like it had been there a million years just waiting to be scooped up. So I pocketed it. I wanted to take something from the job site because part of me felt like it had taken something from me.

My dad brought me to one of his job sites earlier that year. He'd been working for his company since I was a kid, but it was the first time he'd invited me to one of the dig locations.

"Mostly my sites are like giant dirt boxes," he told me.

"Appealing," I said. We were at the kitchen table. Small shot of orange juice for both of us. I didn't start drinking coffee until that winter.

"But this is different," he told me. "Meet me down there after class. You can take the 12 bus. It'll be worth it."

I met him at the corner of Folsom and Spear after school, where he was directing a job in the middle of downtown. There were cranes and backhoes and work trucks strewn around the lot, and I hovered by the fence gate, not sure where to go. And then he spotted me. He hugged me close, dropped a hard hat on my head with a smile, and handed me a safety vest. Then he tugged me inside and began showing me around. We walked the site as he introduced me to coworkers and construction guys, but I could tell he was in a hurry, anxious to get me to the center of the lot, where eventually we stood at the edge of a giant hole at least two city blocks wide and twenty feet deep, watching as his dig crew sifted dirt and set up markers and orange flags below us.

"This bigwig firm hired us a few months ago," he told me. "They want to develop a six-hundred-and-fifty-unit condo complex," he said, and I said, "Okay," not exactly sure what we were looking at. Besides a hole.

"But look what we found," he said. He was proud, I could tell, but I couldn't tell why.

So I looked harder.

I watched a handful of men and women in hard hats and bright yellow safety vests move beneath us. They used shovels to carve away dirt and clay while others shadowed them, taking photographs.

"It kind of looks like a giant dirt box," I told him.

"Look closer, kiddo."

I shifted my backpack on my shoulders and leaned forward a little. It was September, which meant warm weather and yellow light pouring off tall office buildings downtown, reflecting on the streets. Somewhere nearby someone was using a drill rig, filling the air with dust and a pounding like a jackhammer amplified a thousand times. I shook my head, squinting into the dirt pit. I wanted to see what he saw, but I couldn't.

"Keep looking," he said. "Just wait." And he hooked his hands on either side of my backpack so I could lean farther into the cavity of space.

Gradually it came into focus. I drew in my breath, not trusting my eyes but mapping it out in the ground. Thick wooden timbers outlined the side of a hundred-and-fifty-foot-long ship. The bones of a boat.

"Probably dates back to 1849," he breathed. "It's a ship from the Gold Rush."

"Here?"

"You got it. Last time they found one was in 2001, in the Financial District. The archaeologist thinks there could be up to seventy-five of them buried in the city. Ships making the journey during the Gold Rush. Once they arrived, they'd sink them or anchor them in the Yerba Buena Cove and leave them to rot because they didn't have anywhere to put them. Hundreds of boats beached and abandoned. Just like that. Deserted."

"I don't know where that is," I said. "The what? The Yerba Buena Cove?"

"It doesn't exist anymore," he said. "It got filled in during the 1850s. At one time the bay came all the way up to Montgomery Street." He explained that Yerba Buena was the original name for San Francisco and how, initially, parts of the city were built on water lots and wharfs or on rickety piers.

"Most of it had fallen into the bay by 1857," he said. But eventually the cove was filled in properly, and the shore was built up and expanded. "Huge loads of rocks were brought in," he told me. "Dams were sunk, and they poured concrete into the bay, all the while pumping out water."

"Weird," I said. "The Financial District used to be water?"

He nodded. "And certain parts of the cove served as sites to sink the ships."

"So this was one of those?" I asked. "This was a junkyard?"

"A Gold Rush ship graveyard," he said.

He was always doing that: seeing things as being more mysterious and important than most people saw them. It was one of the things he did best.

Inside the hole, a crew shifted a piece of timber, gently tugging it into place before a photo was snapped.

"But look," he said, so I did.

I could see the massive section of a ship lying on its side in the middle of the city. But only part of it.

"There's no bow on the boat," he said. "It's like it just disappeared."

It had been his favorite job, that Gold Rush ship, and afterward I understood why he liked going to work so much. I also understood how extraordinary it was to do something for your job that made your heart race, and it was after that visit to the site that I began thinking about holding off on college. There was nothing I'd done in school that made me feel the way he felt when he discovered pieces of history underground, and I figured there was no reason to spend all that money and time on college until I had some idea of what it was I wanted to study.

. . .

"My dad loves this stuff," I told Beckett when I was next to him again, walking the lot in SoMa.

"Yeah?"

"Yeah. Loves it like you love Zorba the Greek," I said.

"Loves it like I love presidential quotes?"

"Yep. And Fellini films," I said, thinking of all the movie marathons at his house during winter break.

"He loves it like I love chocolate?" he asked.

"Like I love playing music," I said. And then, after a pause, "Like I love hearing my dad in the kitchen cooking bacon and eggs when I'm still kind of asleep on Saturday mornings."

I shoved my hands in my pockets, and next to me Beckett said, "We're going to find him, Callie."

"Says who?"

"Says me. And here's the thing. This whole fatalistic mood thing you've got going on—it stops here, okay?"

I shrugged and kept my eyes on my feet, but he kicked my Chuck T.

"Look at me," he said, so I did. "This pessimistic doom-and-gloom thing you're rocking? That's not you. I know it and you know it, so you might as well cut the bullshit."

He was right; it wasn't really my style. When my grades started slipping during my sophomore year, my parents told me I'd have to give up my after-school job working for Lori as a metal apprentice for her jewelry business. But I liked my job, so I worked like crazy to raise my grades, asking for extra-credit assignments and offering to rewrite papers I'd gotten rotten scores on. I stayed after school for super-annoying group tutoring sessions and helped organize a field trip to the Aquarium of the Bay to nudge my C plus in Bio to a solid B minus. And eventually my grades were good enough for my parents to let me start picking up shifts again the following semester.

I was stubborn, always had been. It was one of my favorite traits I'd stolen from my dad.

Like when I announced I was starting Nothing Right and quitting track the summer before my junior year, my parents told me I couldn't bail on my commitment to the team. So we made an agreement that if I kept running, I could also be in the band. I ended up managing to do both just fine.

I didn't like to be told what to do, didn't like to have decisions made for me, and I usually found a way to line things up the way I wanted, no matter how hard I had to work for it.

"But it feels like he's gone. Like I can tell he's . . ." I tried to find the right words. "I can tell he's not here anymore. I just know it."

"Well, no shit, Sherlock," Beckett said. "He's not *here* here." He motioned to the empty lot. "But he's somewhere. And you have to believe that. Otherwise, us searching for him is a waste of time," he said. "And I hate wasting time."

On the other side of the fence, a group of boys with buzz cuts hovered by a parking meter. A girl on a skateboard skidded by, and they whistled at her until she flipped her middle finger at them as she faded out of view.

"Are you in?" Beckett asked. "Because if you don't buy into the fact that we can fix this, then we won't be able to fix this."

But he was my father. And that meant I was part of him. Which meant him being gone was the same thing as part of me being gone, too. We had to fix it. There was no other option.

"I'm in," I said. "All in."

I had to be.

CHAPTER THREE

Seven Days After

The next day my mom made me go to school, which was pretty brutal since people hear about things super-fast in high school no matter if they're true or not, proven or false. I overheard a girl with a high-pitched voice gossiping in the restroom as I sat in the stall, and a boy with dreadlocks three heads in front of me in line in the cafeteria speculating about my father, neither one knowing I was there. And in the crowded hallways, when words weren't even audible things, I felt the rumors in the vibrations of their bodies, the kids who stared and those who looked away, those who stopped me to say they were sorry and the cliques that scattered when I passed by.

The whole thing was ridiculous: the fact that the world continued to go on—pop quizzes and homework, pep rallies and tryouts for A *Chorus Line*—that the world continued to exist even though my father was gone.

When I got home, I found Mom at the kitchen table. Not reading or doing the *L.A. Times* crossword or flipping through cookbooks like she sometimes did. She was just sitting there. Doing nothing. And it was only four o'clock.

I dropped my backpack in the doorway of the kitchen and pulled off my headphones, killing a sad, bluesy song, the music trancelike and sluggish, just how I felt.

"You okay?" I asked as I slid into the chair across from my mother, which was a pretty absurd thing to say. Dad had been gone seven days, counting the day he vanished, which I did.

Mom was forty-five, two years older than my dad, but she looked younger than that—everybody said so. She was skinny, like me, and had dark hair that she wore long, and I'd heard some of the college kids call her "the sexy librarian" behind her back when I stopped in at the university and saw her at work sometimes. But on that day she mostly looked tired, with dark circles tucked under her eyes and parted lips that lay as lifeless as a rag doll's.

She was a researcher, the kind of mom who used recipes and studied *Consumer Reports* before making any kind of purchase. She wrote long lists: to-do lists, shopping lists, lists of goals at New Year's, short- *and* long-term. She liked to be organized, prepared, and in control, and Dad going missing didn't fit any of those categories, so I couldn't imagine how she was supposed to survive it. I worried about her—about the shift in her routine, the sound of muffled sobs at night when neither of us were sleeping, the way she seemed to drift through the house, a vacant, spaced-out energy trailing her since he'd been gone.

She didn't respond, so I got up, put the teakettle on, and pulled out mugs and a box of ginger lemon—her favorite. When I sat back down, I said her name, and she snapped out of it a little, but not like normal. She didn't cock her head and squint at me with a half smile, didn't ask how school was or offer me something to eat.

"What time is it?" she said instead.

"Four," I told her. "Did you leave work early?"

She shook her head no, but said yes.

That morning, when my alarm clock beeped and I turned it off and rolled over, she'd been standing in my doorway.

"Monday," she said. And then, "One foot after the other, I guess. It'll be good for you to go back to school. It's Monday, after all."

That was it. As if the day explained exactly when I was supposed to shower. If I showered before she did, like usual, the water would be too hot, since my dad hadn't gone first. But if I waited until after her turn, the whole timing of our morning routine would've been off, making me inevitably late for the bus. As if the day of the week, the simple word *Monday*, might fix the fact that I'd have no one to watch eat peanut butter toast with raisins, no one to talk with while I sipped sugary coffee, waiting for the caffeine to buzz me awake. As if *Monday*—the plain sound of it, two syllables, one, two—as if the word changed the fact that there'd be no one there that morning to rub foreheads with.

And then she said, "Up. School today," and left me listening to her footsteps moving down the hall, and then into their bedroom, and then, eventually, to the kitchen, where she poured cereal, one bowl for her and one bowl for me. Bloated O's like buoys floating in the milk while we talked about the weather until it was time for me to catch the bus for school.

"What are you going to tell people?" I asked when we were both standing at the door. It was her first day back at work, too.

She shrugged. "Nothing," she said. "Anything. I'm not sure. The truth, maybe?"

But that was the impossible thing—there was no truth to tell. No facts. No explanations.

"It'll be good for us both," she said, and leaned in to tighten the shoulder straps on my backpack. "To get back to doing the things we do." She was in her work clothes, her reading glasses perched on top of her head. "I know it doesn't seem like it, but getting back into a routine will help."

I nodded and figured she was trying to convince herself just as much as she was trying to convince me.

"It's going to be terrible," I said, then a pause. "Will we be okay?"

"We will."

I raised an eyebrow.

"We're tough, remember? You and me," she said, forcing a smile. "Tough as nails."

"Tough as superheroes," I told her, playing along. "Or rock stars. Biker chicks, maybe."

"It won't be so bad," she said. "I promise." Then she pulled me to her, the hug made awkward by the backpack, but strong and sturdy still as she said "It won't be so bad" again, and then, finally, "I love you, baby, now go," before nudging me out the door.

The teakettle hummed softly because my parents had bought one of those ear-friendly things built to not make you go deaf, so I got up and fixed the tea. It was the time of year when my mother often left early for work and came home late at night—dissertation deadline season. I worried she'd backed out that morning and called in sick instead. That maybe she'd call in sick forever to avoid having to explain this thing that had happened with no explanation. I didn't blame her. I knew if I had had the option, I'd have called in sick to school indefinitely. Called in sick to life, maybe.

"I've got band practice tonight," I told her, thinking I might be able to perk her up with an argument. The mere fact of Nothing Right's existence bugged her, and she especially didn't like it when we practiced on weeknights, but she just nodded. "The band," I said, nudging her mug of tea toward her. "It may go late tonight. Like, real late, maybe."

She nodded again, her eyes looking at the mug but also looking far away.

We lived on Broderick, in an old Victorian that was tall and skinny like a fence post, and I heard the bus pass in front of our place. I imagined the driver following her route up my street, stopping on target, turning like clockwork. Same way every day, day after day, with no surprises.

"Mom," I said, louder. And then, just to see her reaction, I smacked my palm on the table between us.

"It was his turn," she said finally, which meant absolutely nothing to me, so I waited. She drank from the mug, put it back down. Lifted it back up.

"His turn, what?"

"With the band. I didn't want you to do it, remember?"

It was July when we started Nothing Right, and I was supposed to be training extra hours for track in the fall, not starting some band in my friend Madison's basement. I should've been studying SAT prep books, not rock band documentaries. Being a drummer wouldn't round out my college application the same way being on Student Council or being in the school musical would have. It'd be distracting, Mom said. It would divert my attention from the things I was supposed to be concentrating on: SATs, college catalogs, and the extracurricular school-endorsed activities I'd already committed to. But I liked that no one I knew—no girls at least—played drums. That we'd be starting something from the ground up, me and Maddie and Rabbit building a band out of nothing. I liked that there weren't any rules, no prerequisites required to form Nothing Right. We could make it up as we went along, try one kind of music, then change our minds if we wanted to. There were no lines we had to stay inside. I'd played in the percussion section back in elementary school, when we were required to participate in the school band, and I'd always known I belonged behind a drum set. That's where you were really in charge. And something about being behind the drums again seemed necessary. It felt like something I was supposed to do, the One Thing that summer I was meant to focus on.

They'd argued over it—that weird and unfamiliar muffled rise and fall of my parents' voices behind their bedroom door the night I asked for their permission. They didn't argue much, never yelled or bickered like a lot of parents I knew, and I'd stayed awake listening until the conversation faded and I heard them turn off their light on the other side of my bedroom wall. In the morning, they announced I'd be allowed to play drums in the band *and* I'd continue running track in the fall.

I asked my mother, "His turn, how?"

She picked at her cuticles, tugging the skin of her ring finger and then bringing it to her mouth to tear the hangnail with her teeth. I'd grown up watching her do this, whittling down her fingers one by one when her nerves were shaky. She'd never been the type of mother to get manicures; she'd chew the nails away before they were long enough to file.

"My parents fought a lot when I was a kid," she said as she wiped her hand on a napkin on the table, the red bleeding and spreading on the white ply like paint. "And when your dad and I started dating I told him I'd never do it, never be the kind of couple that argued. He wasn't a fighter anyway, but it was a good rule to set from the start." She shrugged. "Money and kids. Those are the two reasons married people fight. So when you were born we started taking turns. If we ever *really* disagreed about a decision we had to make for you, we alternated between who got the final say. It was his turn when you asked about starting that band."

It didn't surprise me that Dad was the one who let me do it, not really, though it was funny to think they'd worked out a system like that, a structure in case they weren't sure what to do with me. I always figured parents, my parents at least, knew exactly what they were doing.

She finished the tea and pushed her chair back. "Don't make it too late, okay?" she said, and then she was gone. I listened to her drifting through the house and up the stairs.

I stayed at the table for a while and took care of my homework. I'd been carting that piece of glass in the pocket of my zip-up hoodie, and I pulled it out, rubbed my thumb over the smooth sides and then along the jagged part, just to see if it'd bring blood. It was designed like our juice glasses, but instead of flowers it had vines. Ivy, maybe, I couldn't be sure. I liked that, a plant instead of a flower—less girly. By then I'd memorized each swoop of the pattern, ingrained each rise and arc in my mind, my fingertips endlessly moving inside my pocket as I rubbed them over the glass while I watched TV, rode the bus, and pretended to listen in class.

I needed to run. I needed to let my mind fall into the rhythm of rubber on pavement, of inhale and exhale, of blood swooshing between my ears. I had a few hours before band practice, so I laced up and caught the Divisadero bus to Fell Street where I could start my route in the Panhandle and loop through Golden Gate Park. It was my favorite spot to run, an 8.67-mile loop that was guaranteed to clear my head. I windmilled my arms like they taught us in gym class in grade school and rolled my neck, listening to my popping bones. And then I folded myself down and placed my palms on the black asphalt, feeling the stretch of fibers and tendons in my back, my legs, my shoulders. I always started at twelve, not ten or twenty, but twelve, counting down and breathing steady, a dozen even inhales and exhales before I began. And then I took off.

Fell Street leads into the park, and I liked to veer north so that I'd run by the Conservatory of Flowers and past the de Young museum—which had just opened back up the year before—and out toward Stow Lake. That end of the park was warmer than the area near the ocean. The route was the perfect balance of flat expanse and hills, and with each stride, each pounding of foot against pavement, I felt my mind unraveling and stretching out until there was nothing but me and the park and the sound of forward movement. I passed Lloyd Lake, the water level low but blue and clean, and then the Disc Golf Course where college kids and hippies tossed Frisbees into chain-link baskets hidden among redwood trees. A handful of Goth girls from school sat on a picnic bench—some of them reading paperbacks, some of them playing cards—but I just kept going. Down by Middle Lake, north again at the fork, past the windmill near the Beach Chalet, and finally out to the water, where the air was cool and wet. My lips tasted like salt and my body buzzed with that good kind of ache that meant I'd pushed myself. I couldn't catch my breath, couldn't slow it down, with my heart thumping so fast and my legs getting shaky, but I felt better than I'd felt in seven days. Seven days.

Practice started at seven, which really meant seven thirty because Rabbit, the bass player, evidently didn't know how to tell time. Ever. We played at Madison's house on Fulton near USF, and her mom let us use their basement because she taught night classes to grown-ups who were trying to learn English at a community center in the neighborhood. Maddie opened the door with that expression I'd been looking at all day at school, that I-don't-know-what-to-say-to-you face, but I felt a little better after my run and didn't want to talk about my dad.

So I said, "Come on, don't look at me like that," and walked right past her and headed for the basement.

She had some bottles of water and a super-size box of Raisinets on the coffee table downstairs, next to a bowl of popcorn sprinkled with garlic salt. Like always. The walls of the room were papered from ceiling to floor with posters of shows from the Fillmore that she'd been collecting since middle school. When a concert sold out, they usually gave away a print for free, and she had saved a slew of them from all the years of going to see bands with Rabbit and me.

I dropped my bag on the floor and turned up Sleater-Kinney on the radio—one of my favorites since I'd started drumming again.

Straight to the drums, I picked up my sticks. If I looked at Maddie too long, with her watching me through those worried eyes, I might break down. The key was to keep distracted, to push back at that tornado ripping through my gut and to drown out the sound of all the what-if chatter buzzing through my brain. So I started drumming. The set was the only worthwhile thing Maddie's dad had left behind when he left them, but by then she'd already begun guitar lessons, so it was mine for the taking when we first starting playing.

"I'm guessing you don't want to talk about it," she said. She sat on the coffee table, cross-legged, and pulled the bowl of popcorn into her lap, plucking out the pieces with the most seasoning. Like always. "You don't have to do that," she said. "That thing when you act like nothing bothers you." She opened a bottle of water and took a swig. "We've been friends for a long time, Callie. You know I'm here if you want to talk it out."

I shook my head and tapped the snare drum, warming up as the crisp clicks of the beats matched the music from the speakers. And the more I played, the further away the sound of that girl gossiping in the restroom at school became. The we-feel-sorry-for-you stares in the hallway grew dimmer with each thump, and the image of the bright blood staining my mother's napkin began to seem less sharp.

But Maddie kept going: "It just makes me sad, is all," she

said, and sighed. "You not being able to talk about it with me."

"It's not that I'm not *able*," I said, the double stroke roll catching the rhythm of my words somehow. "There's just not much to say. He was there in the morning." Right, right. Left, left. Right, right. "Everything like normal. And then he never came home." Left, left. Right, right.

"I bet you talked to Beckett about it," she said.

This was an ongoing thing, the thing about Beckett. I'd been friends with Maddie first—we met at a roller-skating party right before first grade, an event the school organized the last week of summer so the kids and the parents could meet each other. We were assigned to the same teacher and sat at the same table in class, inseparable, but then we got split up in second grade. I was pretty devastated at first, certain I'd never make friends in the new class of kids. But then I did make friends, and Maddie and I just kind of drifted apart. We had a handful of play dates and some shared snacks at recess by the swings on the blacktop, but we went to different middle schools and weren't really close again until freshman year. It wasn't any-one's fault. We landed in the same high school, though, assigned to four out of seven periods together, including homeroom, and it turned out that we also lived in nearby neighborhoods after Maddie and her mom moved when her dad took off. But by then Beckett was my best friend, which was fine; they got along okay. But every so often she'd say something like "I bet you talked to Beckett about it," and I knew it still kind of bothered her that I was better friends with Beckett, even though she'd known me longer.

But she always meant well, and I'd never want to hurt her feelings, so I added, "I appreciate it, I really do. But I feel like it's all I've been talking and thinking about since it happened. It's kind of exhausting. I just sort of want to play music tonight. And not talk about it."

Rabbit showed up at seven thirty. He was two years older than us but stuck around and enrolled in City College after he graduated so that he could help take care of his grandmother. He lived with her in Chinatown because his parents had a hundred other kids and had asked Nai-Nai to take him in when he started getting into trouble during his freshman year of high school. Not the too-many-hours-playing-video-games kind of trouble like most boys that age, but the drinking-booze-and-smoking-weed kind of trouble. Nai-Nai put an end to it instantly, and he'd ended up a straight A student in AP classes. Rabbit was straight-edge now, and smarter than most kids I knew, and he was the best bass player we could think of when Maddie first decided we should start a band. A real band. A band that practiced regularly and booked gigs on the week-ends. Not that we had yet, but still. She and Rabbit hooked up sometimes, an on-again, off-again kind of thing, but mostly I just ignored that part.

So we played.

Maddie was on lead vocals: She played guitar and dressed like Laura Ingalls, but somehow sexy with ripped tights and brown leather lace-up ankle boots, and she had this smoky 1920s kind of voice. She rimmed her brown eyes in black liquid liner, and she cocked her hips left to right or swayed them slowly in little figure-eights, depending on the mood of the song.

We played covers first, songs by Modest Mouse and the Pixies, then we played our own songs—not as good, but getting better each time we worked at them. We took a break around nine, and Maddie and I sat on the couch and watched Rabbit pull out his yo-yo and roll the Sleeper, Walk the Dog, and the Forward Pass, because that's what he did with his hands since he went straight-edge and quit smoking weed and cigarettes. Maddie had already told him about my dad, and he asked what he could do to help.

"Blog post?" he said.

He was into that kind of stuff, so I told him to post away. Whatever he liked. Whatever he thought might make a difference. "Your guess is as good as mine," I said. "We've gotten in touch with every single person I can think of," I told him. "No luck. No hints, even."

After Beckett and I had searched the job site downtown and deemed it full of absolutely no useful information whatsoever, we'd gone back to my place and made a "Missing Person" poster. Which made me feel like we were looking for a lost dog, not my father, but Beckett swore it might help. AARON PACE: WHITE MALE. FORTY-THREE YEARS OLD. SIX-FOOT-ONE(ISH) AND DARK BROWN HAIR. LAST SEEN WEARING JEANS AND A NAVY NORTH FACE VEST. WEARS BLACK WIRED-RIMMED GLASSES. Then we'd scanned in a photo of him from my mom's birthday that year.

He'd thrown her a party for her forty-fifth, even though she'd sworn up and down that she didn't want to celebrate, but in the end she'd loved the whole thing: the rooftop sculpture garden at SFMOMA, the dirty martinis, the three-piece jazz band, and the shrimp and grits. My dad went all out and asked everyone he knew to help in some way. Lori did the flowers and strung the lights. Dad's buddy from grad school was cousins with the sax player in the band, and she cut him a deal on the gig. The art teacher at my school, Alex Hunt, was a friend of my parents and offered to take photos. It had been a whole big thing, one of the best nights I could remember, and we'd used a picture of my mom and dad posed in front of one of the sculptures for the poster. We had to cut out my mom—which made me feel kind of rude, since it'd been her party and all— but it was a clear shot and he looked exactly like he always did: dark hair messy. Mouth a little open, like he was just about to say something we were all waiting to hear.

We put the flyers in all the good spots we could think of, though the sight of his picture posted on coffee shop bulletin boards next to advertisements for guitar lessons and private yoga classes made me feel pretty sick. I'd gotten used to the sweating already; it came in waves and without warning, seas of heat drenching every inch of me, even when I didn't realize I was thinking of my dad at all. But seeing those flyers taped to grimy lampposts and graffitied brick walls brought on a kind of nausea I never could have imagined. I powered through it, though, and we plastered the streets as best as we could, but neither Beck nor I had a car, so we didn't have a way to hang them anywhere outside the city.

"You could drive me to the East Bay," I told Rabbit. "To post flyers. Maybe tomorrow after school?"

He spun Skin the Cat. Rock the Baby. Three-Leaf Clover. "You got it," he said. "Consider it done."

We made plans to put up the posters in Berkeley, Oakland, and Alameda the next day; we'd stick them in cafés and on lampposts in El Cerrito and Walnut Creek and San Leandro.

Next to me, Maddie said, "I could come too," and I told her, "Yeah, that'd be good," thinking that maybe if we made it into some kind of group outing, I might be able to ignore the real reason we were doing it.

And then she added, "There must be something else we can do. Something you haven't tried yet?"

And maybe there was. Maybe there was Some Great Thing, some plan I hadn't come up with that was better than the police and the phone calls and the posters. Everyone kept saying it would be okay. Give it some time. The cops were doing everything they could, we just had to be patient. But as far as I could tell, there were no real clues. Nothing but dirt at the job site. Nothing but normal everyday stuff in his bedroom, ordinary things in his office, and typical work messages in his e-mail accounts. We'd checked everything we could think of to check and had found nothing. And still they said, It'll be fine, you'll see.

"I'll let you know if I think of anything," I said. And then I said I wanted to play a few more songs.

During the weeks that followed, I went to school. I hung out with Beckett. I went running, and I practiced with Nothing Right. I tried to talk to Mom as best as I could, but it was dissertation season, her busy time, so she wasn't around the house all that much.

And the days passed, feeling like slow motion and fast-forward at exactly the same time.

CHAPTER FOUR

Thirty-nine Days After

Graduation happened about a month later, the Friday of Memorial Day weekend, and ours was the kind of school where all the kids attended, even if it wasn't your year to walk. My mom and I met Beckett's family at the ceremony in the football stadium, and afterward Beck and I milled around, watching while the parents talked and the graduates set off firecrackers. It was a cloudless day, warm and dry, and I sported a strappy green dress Maddie let me borrow. I stood with Beckett, but I watched Andrew Parker and his cousin Ryan talking with a group of senior girls from the soccer team. They were shouting and roughhousing, trying to impress the girls, I figured.

Next to me, Beckett said, "You're gaping," and I said,

"I'm not," and he said, "Well, you shouldn't be. He's a spoiled jackass, Callie. Move on."

Andrew and I had ended up in the same elective that semester, Art History, and the week before, after our final exam, he'd stopped me on our way out of class.

"Think you did okay?" he asked, and I nodded.

A group of kids moved past us and into the crowded hallway, but I just stood there. Cement footed. So ridiculously awkward as he lingered by the door and shifted the straps on his backpack.

"I'm sorry about your dad," he said. "I always liked him."

Dad and Andrew had this friendly kind of banter thing they did when Andrew hung around at our house. The whole thing with Andrew didn't last long—four and a half months—but when we'd been whatever it was that we were, Andrew came by our place a lot, and he and my dad hit it off pretty well.

"You still playing in that band?" Andrew asked, and I said, "Yeah."

The first bell rang, but we just stood there.

"I heard you guys are playing Julie Hess's party after graduation," he said, but I shook my head.

"Not us."

Julie Hess floated rumors about asking us to play, but in

the end she'd gotten her cousin from Seattle to come down for her party—he played in some lame boy band that called themselves Browbeater.

"That's too bad. I was hoping I'd get to see you play," he said, which surprised me, since he'd never shown much interest in my drumming back when we were dating.

Then the second bell rang, and he reached out and did this weird thing: He took my hand, lifted it, pressed his palm against mine, and then laced our fingers together. I looked at our hands, his with that dumb copper ring he always wore and mine with the thin leather bracelet I'd bought from a hippie kid in Golden Gate Park. Then he pulled me toward him.

Before Andrew Parker, my friends would have described me as determined and focused, cautious maybe. But then Andrew, for some reason I never figured out, started paying attention to me, offering me rides home from school and showing up at my track meets. And when we were together, I caught myself acting like someone else, someone carefree and courageous. He took me to restaurants and I ate food I'd never tried before, like real sushi with those little orange fish eggs on top. We went Jet Skiing in Sausalito, even though I'd been afraid of those kinds of adventure sports. He talked me into sneaking out in the middle of the night to meet him at the park, and he even convinced me to skip track practice a handful of times and hang out with him and his friends in the Marina.

And then he asked if he could be my first. I'd seen the films and read the books, knew nothing would be the same after we did it, but that's what part of me wanted—for everything to change, for something big and monumental to finally happen to me. I thought on it for a long time and eventually decided I was ready, or ready enough, and that he was the right person because he was different. He was better than any of the other boys I'd dated, and he made me feel important; he made me feel fearless. So I told him I would, and we did that awkward but exciting thing when you start imagining how it's going to go, when you start planning it and letting yourself picture the lighting in the room, the music in the background . . . all that skin on skin.

But before I had the chance to go through with it, Lisa Stone from the track team caught him making out with some girl in a café in the Mission. The whole thing was ridiculously lame and straight out of an after-school special. The argument; the denial; the claiming she was just a friend, a friend of the family, a girl he'd met on vacation who was in town, visiting the city. It was totally cliché.

After all that worrying, after the pros and cons I'd cataloged in my head and the eventual decision to give him this important part of me that I could only give away once, after all that planning and imagining us being together in that way, I realized I'd never actually known him at all. It was embarrassing. Mortifying, really. So I broke up with him before he could break up with me, right before winter break. He told his friends it was the other way around, and I didn't bother to correct him, not even to Beckett. Because the truth was, it wasn't Andrew Parker that broke my heart, it was the lie—this huge scam about love and trust and the possibility of being connected, *really* connected, to another person in that more-than-just-friends way. Which got me thinking that maybe lots of things we'd been told for so long were just cons too.

Andrew dropped my hand from his. "I'm sorry," he said before he turned his eyes to the ground. "I'm just really sorry, Cal."

Maybe about my dad, or maybe about all the rest of it too, I couldn't be sure which, but for some ridiculous reason I almost started crying. Right there in the Art History room, with the rest of the school scattering to their next classes. So I tucked my hands into my pockets, stared at the floor too, and just shrugged.

"See you around, I guess," he said, and I said, "See ya," and that was it.

I watched as Ryan and Andrew and the girls from the soccer team drifted into the crowd, moving between bodies in graduation gowns and parents taking photos. "He's not a jackass," I said to Beckett. "He's just a normal boy, I guess. That's all."

"Whatever," he said. "So, we need to talk. I've made plans for tonight."

Every year since sixth grade, Beckett and I spent the evening of the last day of school in Alta Plaza, a small park at the top of the hill in my neighborhood. At first we'd just hang around talking about our summer plans and how glad we were that school was over. Then, after freshman year, we started bringing artifacts from the previous school year of things that reminded us of experiences we were glad were over. Like our Trig final. And the script for the high school musical our parents talked us into trying out for. Or the photo of me sporting that bad haircut with the bangs sophomore year. We'd sift through them, swapping embarrassing memories, and then we'd bury them somewhere in the park. The year before, Beckett invited Alan Nelson, the boy he crushed on that spring, and we hung around playing cards and trading stories until eventually Alan and Beck wandered off on their own and Beckett finally, after all that time, kissed a boy. But afterward, Alan turned awkward and started arguing with Beck over nothing, and I ended up feeling like the worst kind of third wheel. After that, we vowed never to bring along people we wanted to make out with. So I figured that was our plan. Alta Plaza Park. Just me and Beckett and a shoe box full of memorabilia I was ready to put behind me.

"Obviously, we're not going to Julie Hess's party," he said.

"Obviously."

"Screw Julie Hess's party, right?"

"You got it."

"But I'm switching it up this year," he said. "Big Basin redwoods. We're going camping tonight."

Nearby, our mothers stood with Beckett's dad, who was talking on his cell phone. Beckett's dad did something with money and numbers and banks in one of the tall buildings downtown, something we didn't really understand but seemed to require that he use his cell phone often, and in public. They didn't know I was watching, but Lori reached over and put her hand on my mom's arm, who looked more tired and thinner than usual. She said something, and Lori said something back, and Mom looked at the ground. Even from where I was standing, I could tell she was close to tears, and I worried that Lori might not be any better than I was at knowing what to say to make my mom feel less miserable.

"Our moms already talked it over and said it was okay," Beckett told me. "You know, because we're, like, four years old and all."

My mom caught me watching her then and waved with this slow, faint flick of her wrist. A half wave. And even with all that sadness, she still looked beautiful.

"And I invited Thing One and Thing Two," Beckett said, motioning to Madison and Rabbit, who were nearby but not paying attention to us because they were too busy flirting. Maddie had one hand on her hip and the other hooked through Rabbit's belt loop, and he was nodding like whatever she said was the most important thing he'd ever heard. "The bigger one's driving," Beckett said, because Rabbit was the only one of us who had a car.

Big Basin was south of San Francisco and about half an hour outside Santa Cruz, and when Nicole Wolfe got pregnant our sophomore year, everybody said that's where it happened. That's the only thing I knew about the campground, since I'd never been there.

"There'll be marshmallows and chocolate," Beckett said.

"I don't do ghost stories," I told him.

"Point taken."

I looked at our mothers again, and a wave of nausea rolled over me as Lori dug through her purse, fished out a tissue, and handed it to my mom, whose shoulders were shaking like branches in a storm.

Beckett caught me watching them. "It'll be good," he said. "To blow off some steam. You could use a night away, I bet."

"I guess."

"Trust me," he said. "I promise this is the perfect way to end the school year."

We planned to leave the city around three, which gave me plenty of time for lunch with Beckett and my mom and Lori at our favorite café downtown: gigantic spinach salads with grilled salmon; bowls of tomato soup, since it was usually cool enough in San Francisco in the summertime to eat soup; warm bread and whipped sage butter.

On the drive home from lunch, my mom scanned the radio stations, dodging reports on the war in Iraq and an NPR discussion about the effect iTunes was having on brick-and-mortar chains like Tower Records. Eventually, she just turned it off, and I stared out the window. I doubt that she'd meant to, but somehow we ended up driving right by the job site. There it was, the last place my dad had been seen. But it was different: A row of portajohns hugged the fence on one side, and all the leftover parts of the original building were gone except for the old brick chimney, which had been built into the shell of the new condo high-rise they were constructing. There was a huge crane lifting and moving steel beams and one of those spinning trucks mixing concrete, and the place was crowded with guys in hard hats and safety vests.

I rolled down my window and asked Mom to slow down. "How'd they do all that already?" I mumbled, and then it hit me. It had been over a month since Beck and I went to the site. Thirty-nine days since my dad went missing. And all I'd done was hang some lame flyers.

What had I been doing all that time?

● ● ●

Back at our house I changed clothes and packed for the night, even though I was in a rotten mood and didn't feel like going camping anymore. I slammed drawers shut, kicked open my closet door, and threw my backpack on the floor when I was finished filling it.

"Are you okay?" Mom asked from the doorway.

I didn't realize she'd been there, watching. "Not really. Are you?" I asked, angry that she'd let me get away with it, that she'd let me wallow and sit around doing nothing. Angry, too, that she hadn't tried harder to find him either. Thirty-nine days and no leads. It was ridiculous.

"Sure, I guess," she said as she brought her finger to her mouth and started chewing, which made me feel bad for snapping at her like that.

Then I remembered that just like Beckett and me, she and my dad had their own rituals on the last night of school: an early dinner at Annie's Bistro, a small restaurant in our neighborhood. They'd walk down Fillmore afterward to look at books at Browser's and to buy a bottle of wine from the market. They'd be on the couch, sleeping usually, by the time I'd come in from the park, their legs intertwined under the blanket because our TV room was always just a little bit cold.

"It'll be okay," she said, the words repeated over and over again the past month while we'd sat around like zombies, going through the motions.

It crossed my mind that if she didn't know how to make things right, and I didn't either, there was a good chance the world might never feel normal again. It was that thought that scared me the most.

"I thought I'd get a head start cleaning the house tonight."

"That sounds so depressing," I told her, and sank to my bed.

"You're right. It does, doesn't it?" she said with a half smile. "It sounds miserable." She sat down next to me.

The university gave her the week off after Memorial Day every year, and she used the time for spring cleaning and to catch up on her reading before she began her summer work sitting at the circulation desk.

Eventually I said, "I'm sorry. To be leaving you alone. I know you and Dad usually . . . ," but I couldn't finish the sentence, as the words got stuck in my throat.

"It'll be okay," she said again. "Give me a call if you get the chance. Beck's bringing his phone?" she asked, and I nodded.

He was the only one out of our friends who had his own cell, so he got stuck sharing it on trips like that.

"I don't have to go," I told her. "I could stay home. We could make dinner. Or order in."

"Right. Because hanging out with your mom would be a wonderful way to celebrate the end of the school year." She nudged her shoulder against my shoulder.

"I wouldn't mind," I told her.

"I know you wouldn't. But we both know Beck would have a fit," she said, which was true. "It's okay. Really, I'm fine, baby," she said. "Now get out of here. Be safe and be home in time for dinner tomorrow."

Rabbit drove his old Volvo wagon and we coasted south, with Maddie riding shotgun and me and Beckett in the back.

"Girls in the back," Rabbit said to Beck, because sometimes he acted like a moron, but we knew it was just for show.

Beckett rolled his eyes. "'Words wound,'" he said. "'But as a veteran of twelve years in the United States Senate, I happily attest that words do not kill.' You're a loser, Rabbit," he said, and then, to me, "Lyndon Johnson."

We drove through San Mateo, Redwood City, and Palo Alto, moving down Highway 101 through the weekend traffic. Eventually we stopped in Saratoga to fill up on gas and get last-chance rations. I bought pistachios, Beckett got dental floss, Rabbit said he didn't need a thing, and Madison got a jug of water, a bundle of firewood, and a pack of batteries. The closer we got to the mountains, the better the air smelled: heady like redwoods, and spicy like those Asian restaurants in the Inner Richmond District.

"I'm glad we're doing this," I told them when we were back in the car.

"I know," Beckett said. "And there's more, too. Tomorrow

we're taking you to the MOMA. There's this history exhibit up, and I figured it would be fun if we went. All of us," he announced.

We stopped at the park entrance for maps and to pay the cost of camping for the night. We checked out our assigned spot and took some photos of the redwoods while the light was still good, and then we set up our tents and gathered sticks to start the fire.

Beckett and Lori had always liked to camp—it was kind of their mother-son thing—so he had all the good equipment, like an Easy Cooker camp griddle, lots of those canvas folding chairs with the cup holders, and a tent that was big enough for the both of us. Maddie was in charge of the food, and Rabbit brought the fun stuff, like a deck of cards, Travel Yahtzee, and bocce balls. We began getting things ready for dinner just as the sun was setting: grilled cheese sandwiches with tomatoes, garlic salt, and sliced avocados.

I snacked on pistachios and helped prep the food while Rabbit played a new song he'd been working on. Next to me, Maddie heated up the stove, a large portable griddle built into a wood frame and hooked to a tank of propane. At the next site over, someone slammed a trunk shut while someone else started laughing. They sky was turning that pastel-colored palette that made you feel grateful but a little bit sad, too. Dusk has always been my favorite time of day.

"You do this a lot, huh, Beck?" Maddie asked, and Beckett nodded from his crouching position by the fire pit as he arranged the wood and tucked the newspaper under the teepee of sticks he'd built.

"We go at least a few times a year," he said. "Me and my mom. My numero uno."

As an only child, Beckett and his mom were closer than him and his dad for a million different reasons. His dad worked downtown, while Lori's jewelry studio was set up in their garage, making her kind of a stay-at-home mom, so she spent more time with Beck. He liked art and creative things just like Lori did, while his dad liked numbers, which Beckett was always terrible at. The list went on and on, but I also always wondered if he wouldn't have been as open about liking his mom best if his dad had been a little nicer when Beckett first came out.

I was an only child too, but it was because my parents couldn't afford to stay in the city if they had more than one kid, and they always said there was nowhere else in the world they wanted to live. And when I thought about it, I realized that if someone had asked me, had forced me to pick between the two, I would have said I'd always been closer with my dad—that I liked him better, even—for no real good reason that came to mind. There'd been something between us that was different than the relationship between my mom and me.

I loved them both, of course, and it was kind of screwed up to even think about it that way, but if I had said "my numero uno," it would've been Dad that I meant.

The grilled cheese sandwiches were perfect, and we played gin rummy until it was too dark to see the cards, and then we played music on the guitars Rabbit and Maddie brought. Cover songs Beck could sing with and new ones we'd been working on at practice, and as it got later, we started making them up on the spot, dumb stuff that didn't make sense but still kind of sounded good. And then Beck pulled out a half-full bottle of whiskey he must have lifted from his parents and said, "'When the president does it, that means it is not illegal.'" A pause. "Richard Nixon," he said, "but it sure worked for Clinton, too."

"I bet it was the Nixon interview with David Frost," I said, and Beckett said, "Nerd," and smiled. Even in the dark, I could see his dimples, like commas, one on each cheek. That's how he got away with most stuff.

"With Clinton, it was pot, you know," Rabbit said. "Please tell me you didn't bring weed, Beck."

Beck shook his head no. "I'm not a total hoodlum," he said. "Well, not yet, at least." The dimples again.

"I'm not going to give you the 'This Is Your Brain on Drugs' talk," my dad said once, using his fingers to mime the quote marks. I was fourteen, and our middle school principal had mailed a letter to every student's family after a bunch of kids got caught getting stoned in the restroom at school. "But I will say that I think you're a smart kid. And that's a good thing, being smart. It's also not a given. Staying smart, that is," he told me. "You have to make good decisions to make sure that you *stay* smart. Brain cells and all that."

I'd nodded, embarrassed to be talking about drugs but trying to bear it.

"But if you're going to do it, if you're going to try it, just don't be stupid," he said. "Make sure you're somewhere safe, and don't do too much of it. Don't do it too often," he said. "Not often at all, actually. If ever. As in hardly ever, if you try it. And only when you're safe." I knew he was doing his best, but it was super-awkward and I'd just wanted the conversation to end. ASAP. "And always, always, always give me a call if you think it's gotten out of control," he said. And then he left it at that.

The fire was going strong as we sat in a circle, leaning toward the light. It suddenly felt late, but we kept at it, roasting marshmallows and taking turns stoking the flames. Rabbit had Maddie's feet in his lap, one hand on her legs and one hand spinning the Gravity Pull. By the time Beckett opened the whiskey again, he was talking about Fellini. He told us Fellini had failed his military exam. Fellini had enrolled in law school but never attended a class. In the end, Fellini only had a high school degree.

"Who does that?" he said. "Who goes to law school and doesn't show up?" He took a swig from the bottle and tried to pass it over to Maddie, who shook her head no. He skipped Rabbit and handed it to me, but I put it down at my feet.

"I'd do it," I said.

"Do what?"

"I mean, not the law school part. Law school is impossible to get into. But the school thing in general."

Beckett said, "What are you talking about, Callie?" and next to him, Maddie shifted in her camping chair.

Beckett and I had made a plan about the school thing back when we were freshman and he'd visited his cousin in Portland for the first time. He would go to the Art Institute, and I would go to Portland State University or Reed College. Portland was undoubtedly where we wanted to be. It was small but cool, and it had a hip art and music scene. We both liked the rain, that dismal gray-sky thing that helped you write gritty songs or make great art. Plus, it was close enough to our families that we could see them when we wanted, but far enough away that they could never do a drop-in. But I never told him about the conversation I had with my parents when I'd first signed up for the SAT test.

"In-state," my dad said. "We want you to go to the best school possible, but California has a slew of fantastic programs right here, and you won't put yourself into debt that way. No one wants college loans if you can help it."

But I hadn't found a school in California that interested me half as much as Portland had.

"Seriously," Beckett said. "What are you talking about, Cal?"

"The whole college thing," I said slowly. "I'm just not sure I'm going to do it."

"Give me that bottle back," he said, reaching for it just as Rabbit said, "Here we go."

"Don't be ridiculous," Beck said. "Of course you're going to college. In Portland. With me."

I could tell by the rise in his voice and the slowness in mine that there was no way the conversation would bring about anything good. But I had to get it out because saying it out loud meant that I was serious. It meant the foreign-language dictionaries in the back of my closet were more than just a weird habit or a wish.

"I'm not, Beck. I can't. I've been researching this international program with Habitat for Humanity instead. So I can travel." The website said the host country covered a lot of the costs for volunteers, so I figured the program would be pretty cheap. Cheaper than college, at least. It would give me the chance to explore other countries and cultures in a way that going to college wouldn't. And skipping town, getting as far away as possible from the city that stole my dad, was the best idea I'd come up with in a long time.

"That's such a cop-out," Beckett said, and he leaned toward me, glaring.

"My parents can't afford to send me to Portland," I told him, and he said, "Liar," but I shook my head. "It's true. They said so themselves when I started researching schools. This isn't my fault."

Maddie said, "Come on, you guys," but we talked right over her.

"You're full of shit," he said, louder.

"And you're acting like a drunk," I told him as I leaned for the bottle, but he was too fast. "You're not listening. There's nothing I can do."

"Give me a break," he said. "Nothing you can do? Who are you?" He shook his head, rolled his eyes. "Lately you've become this . . . this pushover," he said. "Like a zombie. I've never seen you act like this, so complacent. I'm actually embarrassed for you, you know, Callie?"

"You don't know what you're talking about."

"Of course I do," he said. "The Callie I know, she'd make sure she went to Portland if she really wanted to."

I tried to tell him again. Out-of-state tuition was too

expensive for my parents and the Habitat program would give me the chance to travel before I had to commit to college, but he wouldn't let me explain.

"We had a plan, Cal," he said. "It's like ever since your dad . . ."

But I stopped him. "Careful, Beckett," I said. "I'm serious."

"Relax, you guys," Rabbit said, but I couldn't slow things down.

I kept thinking of the thirty-nine days that hadn't changed a thing and the way Beckett had just sat there and done nothing too. He was my best friend; he should have called me out, should have snapped me awake, not watched while I went through the motions. What was *he* doing those thirty-nine days?

"It's like you're giving up. Just quitting. Like you're not even *you* anymore," he said, even though it didn't make any sense to say it like that.

Of course I wasn't me anymore. How could I be? My dad, my favorite grown-up, had upped and disappeared without a trace.

"It's like you just don't even care anymore," Beck said before he swigged another shot of whiskey, his eyes red and watery. "We put up some posters, Callie. That's it. Are you kidding me?"

We both had our hands wrapped around the bottle then,

tugging back and forth while I tried to ignore what he was saying. He was wrong. I hadn't quit looking for my dad, I just hadn't figured out how to start.

"You're a moron, you know that?" I said, pulling harder on the bottle. "Who are you to judge?" Tears trailed paths down my cheeks. Hot and unexpected. "It didn't happen to you. You don't know what you're talking about."

He jerked the bottle toward him, but I had both hands on the neck and yanked it back, stubborn. And then, inevitably, the whiskey bottle slipped from his fingers and flew toward my face before either of us had time to stop it.

After we cleaned up the campsite and put out the fire and watched Maddie and Rabbit head to their tent, we slunk into our sleeping bags and Beckett rolled toward me, his chest against my back as he draped his arm around me and pulled me close.

"I'm sorry about your face," he said.

"You were right. I haven't tried hard enough," I said. "You know it's been thirty-nine days? How did that happen?" I rubbed my nose on the small, scratchy camping pillow Beckett had brought for me. "I miss him," I said.

"I know you do."

"Like crazy miss him. All the time. I tried to pretend it wasn't really happening at first. And now I'm worried it's been too long, that there's no way to fix it," I told him.

His hand found my hand in the darkness and he squeezed. "We can start again. *Really* start looking," he said, and I nodded. "We'll make a game plan. Make a detailed list of people to call and places we can look. I promise it'll be okay, Callie." Then he rolled away from me onto his back and whispered, "I'm sorry about the whiskey. And about your face. I'm pretty sure I just gave my best friend a black eye."

"Worse things have happened," I told him.

But he groaned. "Bill Clinton: 'It wasn't my finest hour. It wasn't even my finest hour and a half,'" he said.

CHAPTER FIVE

Forty Days After

In the morning, I ran. I got up before everyone else did, slid on my tennis shoes, and took off through the redwoods. It was early and a little bit cold, which helped to shake my sleep haze. I broke through my headache with each strike of foot against trail, and I worked my way up the hills, shaded by a thick canopy of tree branches. It was foggy and damp, but the spicy smell of the woods worked to sharpen my thoughts and focus my breathing. I pushed back against Beckett's words, against the sound of my mother crying softly on the other side of my bedroom wall every night since April 18.

"I'm glad you found something like that," my dad said once when I'd come in from running in our neighborhood, my

T-shirt damp against my back as I stood in front of the house and watched him working on his motorcycle on the sidewalk outside the garage.

"Something like what?" I leaned into a stretching lunge, my breath slowing but my skin still hot and prickly from running the Pacific Heights hills.

"Something you can use to get out all that . . . that teenager-ness." He eyed me from a crouched position by the back tire of his 1988 Ducati. He had three bikes, but this was by far his favorite. It was a red-and-black 750 Sport, and even though it gave him the most trouble, he said he'd always liked it best because he bought it the spring he and my mom found out they were pregnant with me.

"Teenager-ness?" I said. "I'm pretty sure that's not a word."

He picked up a wrench, looked at it and then at the bike, and dropped it back on the pavement. "This may come as a surprise to you," he said, "but I actually remember what it's like to be a teenager. It really wasn't all that long ago when it happened to me."

Behind me, on California Street, a bus buzzed by and someone honked their horn. It was the weekend, a Sunday maybe, and the sidewalk was clogged with people walking dogs, jogging in pairs, and rushing to or from the bus stop. A group of kids moved past a pair of older women in church clothes on the other side of the street. It must have been early fall, September or October.

"I don't believe it," I said, my eyes teasing him. "You? You were a teenager once?"

"And it was awful. I mean brutal stuff, those years. Acne and trying to fit in. Being short for my class, not athletic enough. Working for good grades but trying to seem cool at the same time. God knows no one likes the smartest kid in the class." He picked up a different-size wrench and began tugging on a bolt near the tire.

"Nuh-huh," I said. "Smartest kid in the class is inevitably bottom of the food chain."

He nodded but rolled his eyes. "And hormones. What a mess. The hormones were out of control."

"Gross, Dad."

He laughed, and behind us my mom opened the front door and called, "What are you two doing out there?"

"I'm just saying it's good that you have something like running when you need to clear your head. When you need to burn off some of that—that teenager-ness," he said. "It's good for you."

"You guys getting hungry?" she asked from the top of the stairs. "I've got baked mac and cheese in the oven."

"Be right in, baby," he said to my mom, and then he looked at me again. "All I'm saying is that I'm proud of you,

Callie. You're a good kid, which makes me feel like your mom and I might actually be okay parents."

I nudged his gray tennis shoe with my blue tennis shoe and smiled. "You got that right," I said.

Back at the campsite, Beckett and Maddie were breaking down the tents while Rabbit loaded up the car with the coolers, the cooking equipment, and the guitars.

"Look what the cat dragged in," Rabbit said when I showed up.

"You okay?" asked Beckett, and I nodded.

"Sure, I'm okay," I told him.

"Really? Because you kind of look like you got your ass kicked last night," Rabbit said, and Maddie said, "Rabbit, leave it be," as she ducked out of her tent and began plucking the tarp clips off of the aluminum poles.

"I don't know what you're talking about." I put my fingers to my eye then, tender like. I could tell it was a little swollen, and, judging from the look Maddie gave me, ripening into my first black eye.

"You two," Rabbit said. "If I weren't one hundred percent sold that you were one hundred percent gay, I'd blame it on sexual tension."

"Gross," Beck and I said at the same time.

Rabbit was sitting on the hood of his Volvo. "But I can tell it's a brother-sister thing," he said. "I'm the same way with my siblings. They drive me nuts when we're together, but I miss them like crazy when we're not."

I helped clean up, and then we loaded back into the car and headed north, me and Maddie in the back this time, Beckett up front.

"First stop: grub. I need food like a fish needs water," Beckett said.

"Second stop?" Rabbit asked, and Beckett said, "MOMA."

"On a holiday weekend? It'll be packed." I was tired—I figured we all were—and nothing sounded worse than a crowded museum. I wanted a shower. A long, hot one. I wanted my bed and the sound of my mom puttering around the house while I napped under the bay window in my bedroom. That was the best part of summertime—afternoon naps.

But Beckett shook his head. "You, my friend, get no vote. I already bought our passes online, so we won't have to wait for tickets," he said. "This is my thing. The thing I picked to kick off summer break," he told me. "Besides, it'll be good to *not* think about all the crappy stuff for while." And then: "Just for today. Tomorrow we'll start looking for your dad all over again."

• • •

We went to the Grove on Mission Street and ordered from the chalkboard menu on the wall above the counter: pot pies, hummus-and-cheese plates, and BLTs. There was a hipster behind the register in skinny jeans and a Sonic Youth T-shirt, and Beckett used the band as an excuse to flirt with him while we waited for our food.

"It's like, punk meets indie meets avant-garde, right?" he said, and leaned toward the kid on the other side of the counter. "The best combination by far."

"Absolutely," the boy said back. "I could listen to that album all day long."

It was crowded, but we scored a big wooden table by the window and settled in: hot coffee in hand, sunlight on the bench seat, and the buzz of the city on the weekend. The Grove was one of my favorite cafés in San Francisco. Next to us, a couple shared a bottle of white wine and read paperbacks, the girl sporting blue dip-dyed hair and a strapless sundress, the boy in rocker jeans and a bow tie. And for a minute — just a quick one or two, with the windows open and the sound of street traffic merging with the hum of café conversation — for a minute it felt like things could be normal again.

"I reek of campfire," Maddie said as she pulled her shoulder-length hair into a ponytail.

"Better than morning-run sweat," I said. "He's really making us go straight to the museum?" I asked, looking at Beckett as he scribbled something on a napkin for the guy behind the counter. "I think showers first would be in everyone's best interest."

"When the man makes up his mind . . . ," Rabbit said, and shrugged.

"It's a historical exhibit about the earthquake," Maddie told us. "You know. For the hundredth anniversary."

We'd spent a week studying the 1906 quake in history class that spring, and most of the newspapers had done some kind of feature or another in April, so I was surprised I hadn't heard about the exhibit at the MOMA.

"Mission accomplished," Beckett said when he sat back down. "Digits shared with the hot hipster at the register." He smiled. "What are we talking about?"

"The exhibit," I said, and someone at the front of the café called our number for the food, so Rabbit slid out from behind the table.

"I'm on it," he said, heading to the counter.

"It's called 'A Disaster in Pictures,'" Beckett told me.

"Sounds uplifting."

"No, it's like, history stuff. Before-and-after shots of the earthquake compared to now. It's supposed to be really good," he said.

"Okay, okay, we'll go," I said, and then, getting more serious, "Thanks, Beckett. For the camping trip and the museum tickets. It's been a good weekend."

"Minus the black eye, you mean," Maddie said.

"Minus that."

"You should check yourself out in the bathroom," she told me. "We might need to move you to vocals. Put you front and center. You look super-hard-core, bruised up like that."

"I could never do vocals," I told her. "That's your gig. No one owns an audience like you do," I said, and she smiled, the pink rushing to her cheeks.

Once things got going with Nothing Right, my dad started asking questions.

"When can I hear you play?"

"Not yet. We're still in the warm-up phase."

"Well, what style is it? What genre?"

"It's more complicated than that, than just one genre. We're kind of like the Smiths. Or Nirvana, maybe, with Cat Power vocals. I don't think we believe in labels, really."

"So who's the front man?"

"Front man? No one, like, calls it that, Dad."

"Well, who writes the lyrics? Who's the leader?"

"There's no *leader*. Maddie's on vocals. She writes the melodies, and Rabbit's on bass."

"But the drummer establishes the pace, right? The tempo of the music?"

"Yeah, I set the tone through the rhythm," I told him. "I'm

the one that finds the feel of the song and sets everything up."

He'd nodded. "I get it. You stay tucked behind the drum kit, but really you're taking the lead with no one realizing it." He smiled. "You control things, but you don't need the spotlight. Noble. I like that. My silent warrior," he said.

I shrugged, but looking back, I realized he'd found the right words to describe my role before I did.

The food looked amazing when Rabbit brought it to the table, and I was suddenly so thankful for school being over, for the summer stretching out ahead, and for Beckett's promise to help me start searching for clues about my dad. He had to be somewhere, and I knew that wherever he was, he'd be looking to find his way back to us.

"We eat, and then we roll," Beckett said. "It's almost noon."

But Rabbit shook his head. "We should make that game plan," he said. "That list you guys were talking about last night."

I looked at Beckett and he looked at me, thinking of the conversation in the tent.

"What? We were camping," Rabbit said. "It's not like tents have walls. Come on. It's not eavesdropping when we're sleeping outdoors."

So Rabbit got another napkin and borrowed a pen from the counter kid after we'd finished eating. At the top he wrote, *FIND AARON PACE*, and underlined it.

"We need to establish a baseline, so we can develop a systematic and efficient method to examine all the potential Where-did-he-freaking-go? options," he said. He was taking Intro Business and Psychology 101 that semester at SF State, and I watched as he morphed back into the student I'd known in the AP classes we both took the year before, the student who got Maddie's attention in the first place.

"Have you personally called all of his coworkers?" he asked me, and I shook my head, so he wrote: *(1) Coworkers.*

"We can probably find his office directory online or by calling and requesting it. Then we can divvy up the list alphabetically. It's easier for people to shaft you on e-mail, so we'll have to get the telephone numbers," he told us. "Like I said, a system."

The coffee-boy–crush stopped by our table and put a mug down in front of Beckett. "Another latte," he said. "You know, in case you wanted a second one. It's on the house."

They did that funny smile thing you do with someone you think you'd like to get to know better, and then he walked away.

"Good God," Rabbit said. "Get a room already. Okay. Have you found that homeless guy the police talked to?" he asked, and I shook my head again.

Next to me, Maddie said, "Good call. I bet he'd be more likely to give us information than the cops. We should definitely talk to him if we can find him."

Rabbit wrote: *(2) Find the Homeless Guy Who Was Probably too Paranoid to Tell the Cops All of the Truth.*

"How about your garage? He hung out there a lot, right? Working on his bikes?" he asked, and I nodded. "Have you snooped around down there?"

I shook my head and said, "What's wrong with me? What have I been doing all this time?"

Rabbit wrote: *(3) Get Nosy in the Garage.*

And Maddie said, "You've been grieving," but then must have immediately regretted it, because she rushed right into, "Not grieving. That's the wrong word. You've just been in shock, is all. Like, trauma shock, maybe mixed with a little denial."

"I've been an idiot, is what I've been," I said, but all three of them shook their heads no.

Beckett said, "Look, it's been a few weeks. No big deal. You sunk down into your weird, dark rabbit hole, did your whole misery and anguish whatnot, and now we're pulling you back up. Onward. It's fine. Today we play, and tomorrow we start with the list Sherlock Holmes over there is plotting. It's fine," he said again. "We're on it. Now let's hit the road before I bail on this whole museum thing and do something humiliating, like throw myself at that barista."

The SFMOMA was within walking distance, and when we got there, Beckett went to pick up our tickets while we stood in the gigantic atrium and people-watched the weekend crowd.

"Let's motor," he said when he found us again.

Photography exhibitions were usually on the third floor, so we headed up the staircase toward the circular skylight that cast light throughout the main building. I hadn't been to the MOMA since my mom's birthday, when that photo of Dad and her was taken, and maybe Beckett guessed I was remembering that night, because he nudged me and said, "It's gonna be fun. I promise." And then, "Just relax."

Since it was the weekend, the museum was filled with families, college-age students from all the art programs in the area, and other teenagers like us just looking for something to do. The exhibit was mounted in a series of side rooms that connected to one another like a maze, and we checked the time on our watches and decided to meet an hour later in the café if we got split up.

We started together in the first room but soon drifted apart, each taking a different amount of time with each set of pictures. But I liked it better that way, seeing the art at my own pace.

Each display showed two photos: on the left-hand side, Image A, a black-and-white shot of a place in San Francisco taken within the last few years, mostly 2003 or 2004, and, on the right, Image B, a photo of the exact same location taken just after the 1906 earthquake and fires. The left side duplicated the viewpoint of the right exactly, only almost a hundred years later, and under each photo there was a caption listing the location or some kind of descriptive detail about the picture, followed by a date and medium information. The photographer, Mark Klett, called it a rephotography project and an examination of our relationship to time and change. His statement at the start of the exhibit said, "The past, the present, and the future lie uncomfortably close together in a curve of probabilities; and they are not necessarily connected by an implied linear flow." He believed the project demonstrated that an anticipated future is never guaranteed by the flow of time in any one direction, which took me forever to wrap my head around. No particular future guaranteed. Time flowing in any direction, an infinite number of possibilities.

There was a constant murmur in the gallery, but the voices of the visitors became white noise once I started paying attention to the art. Some of the photos were what I'd expected: shots of buildings like Grace Cathedral in 2003, pristine and symmetrical, and then, next to it, the shell of the church, piles of wood, collapsed arches, and half-broken windows. There were pictures of parks in the city that, after the quake and the fires, became refugee camps, with draped white tents and makeshift shelters with men on horses riding about. Some photographs were small, and you had to get close to see the details, and others were panoramic, and you had to stand back to view the whole scene. There were photos that showed cracks, actual splits in the ground, running right through the city, with holes like caves you couldn't see the bottom of—I didn't like to look at those too long. I recognized my neighborhood and our cars and trees and bushes on street corners in a modern picture, shot south from Alta Plaza Park. And then, in the blurry one on the right, empty sidewalks except for a handful of horse-drawn carriages. How strange and startling it must have been to see the land crack open and the buildings turn to dust on a random morning that shouldn't have been different from any other.

And then I saw it. IMAGE 8A: "MOVING CAR, SACRAMENTO STREET NEAR POWELL, 2003." On the left, a shot down the hill toward downtown—a moving truck parked on one side of the street with its back hatch open and a small car, next to it, driving uphill. It was a familiar scene, the street corner where the number 1 bus dropped me off when I took it from my neighborhood to Union Square. It could have been one of my teacher's cars driving up that hill, could have been a family I knew from school moving their stuff out of the van and into a new apartment. I'd looked downtown from that exact spot countless times.

And, on the right side, IMAGE 8B: "UNTITLED (VIEW OF FIRE DOWN SACRAMENTO STREET), 1906." A picture of the same street corner, the downtown a smudge of fire and black clouds. Instead of cars and vans lining Sacramento Street, people in chairs watched from the top of the hill as the city burned below them. My breath bottomed out as I studied it, the folding chairs lined up like a movie theater's, the men and women in dark clothing, some with hands raised to their faces, shielding their eyes from the sun, maybe; others with fists on their hips as they looked at the smoke and flames. The shock must have stolen their breath away—having to watch the city they lived in and loved burn to ash before their own eyes.

And there in the corner, tucked into a sliver of the image that was either underexposed or double-exposed, I couldn't be sure which, was a blurry silhouette of a man. Dark hair. Small glasses, a profile as familiar to me as if it were my own. A man I couldn't look away from.

A man with the face of my father folded into the shadows of a photograph from 1906.

Suddenly, there was nothing but me and that photo, the museum having fallen away. His nose, I was sure of it. My father's slight frame and worried mouth, his face tilted downward.

PART TWO

THE UNRAVELING

Image 12B: "Untitled (Produce District, Washington Street), April 18, 1906." Cellulose nitrate negative, 87 × 146 mm irreg.

He smells oranges first, the spicy citrus of summertime and brilliant bright juice leaking from the fruit. Oranges first, and then fire.

The man pulls himself to his feet, his legs shaking as if he's run miles to get here, to this street pulsing under soot-black clouds of smoke. Washington Street—it's early, not long past sunrise, and he hears the ocean, though he's certain he must be miles away. He hears water and voices too, screaming words he can't decipher. His eyes dart across the roads as his heart picks up speed—the corner of Washington and Montgomery, much too far from the Pacific to hear it as loudly as he does. But then he sees it as the dust shifts: a gaping trench, six feet deep and half-full of water, cut right through the middle of the street, heaving and ripping the earth in its path. On the opposite side of the corner, a warehouse lies crumbled on the pavement as spears of asparagus, bruised pears, and fist-sized oranges tumble down the road, slashed and oozing at his feet, the fruit scattered and riding waves through the pavement.

Like marbles, small pieces of a child's game.

He snaps his eyes left and right, trying to make sense of the water and the torn-open concrete, but his mind is blank. It's the headache, the pulsing behind his eyes and the confusion of sand and smoke. And the screams. His heart sprints like a locomotive through a tunnel as he tries to understand these city streets broken by water and fire.

A wholesale grocery on Clay Street burns. The flame is fast as the man stumbles through the wreckage of fallen walls and sections of sunken pavement. He moves west, away from the water, which has become an unpredictable thing as it pours through the city. Packs of dogs nip and bark in the distance, and the noise of shouting blends with the shattering of falling objects: bricks and glass and wood. He stumbles, wipes his palms on his trousers, and watches the flames from the grocery spread to a neighboring meatpacking company. He quickens his pace, and his breath hastens with each moment. Under his breastbone, his heart thrashes, the pulse like an aria rising toward the tragic culmination of an opera. A pack of horses bolts down the street with no riders, the animals frantic and loud as he dives out of the way.

At the fire station, the wall of an adjoining factory collapses as the firemen scramble out front, yelling while they watch the two buildings collide—the air pops and crackles while the alarm shrieks. The heat spreads, clotting the streets, and he longs for the water he ran from, for the ice of it on his legs and his arms, for the way it would numb his skin and cool his fibers. The thumping rises from his chest to his ears as he staggers west, instinctively following the sound of voices and a rumble of . . . what, he's not sure.

And then a strange quietness falls over the area.

He thinks of church. And funeral prayers.

A group gathers on the sidewalk, some with their cheeks streaked with tears and others expressionless, their faces like poorly wrought sculptures with no sense of life.

"Earthquake," he hears one woman say. "I've never felt anything like it."

The man approaches them, wary. "What's happened?" he asks.

"Earthquake," the woman repeats as she adjusts her broad-brimmed hat. "Didn't you feel it?"

"I don't remember a thing," he says.

"You're one of the lucky ones, then."

CHAPTER SEVEN

Forty-two Days After

In the summer, Before, I did this: Tuesdays and Thursdays, work for Lori from nine thirty in the morning until three o'clock for twelve dollars an hour. The days I didn't work started around ten(ish), coffee for breakfast or no breakfast at all. Out to meet Beckett at Squat & Gobble or Ben and Jerry's because, in the summer, ice cream qualified as breakfast. Amoeba Music at the top of Haight Street, then a straight shot into Golden Gate Park to Hippie Hill to watch the hula-hoopers and musicians—the drummers were long-haired or dreadlocked or buzz-cut, big African djembes clasped between their thighs; kettle drums and bongos and tambourines too. Sometimes we'd bring paperbacks—historical biographies or books by Kurt Vonnegut or Edmund White, George

Saunders. Maddie would track us down, the three of us, then, and sometimes Rabbit, depending on whether he and Maddie were on-again or off-again, visiting the de Young Museum, the Japanese Tea Garden, or the Botanical Garden because it was free. Music in the afternoons at the Park Chalet or Stern Grove. Or maybe we'd skip the park and head to North Beach instead. City Lights bookstore and the Stinking Rose where we'd eat roasted garlic, baked Brie, or garlic hummus until we couldn't taste a thing. Home by five, or maybe six. Maybe not at all: We'd sleep at one another's houses instead. Share toothbrushes and T-shirts and sweatpants because we were too old to plan and pack for sleepovers. Kid stuff. We were simply crashing at friends'. On the weekends, I'd wake to the sound of my dad's motorcycle revving in the garage beneath the kitchen. Coffee first, then him handing me a helmet before kissing my mother on the cheek. Us moving north, me clinging to the bike with my legs, my hands at his waist, tucked inside the pockets of his coat as he drove, halfway holding on to him and halfway not while he moved us out of the city on his Ducati or his Suzuki or his Yamaha. I'd close my eyes sometimes as we moved over the Golden Gate Bridge and imagine the millions of fish and plants and sunken ships beneath us, a world all its own I'd never see. We'd leave the fog behind as we stopped in Tiburon or Point Reyes for lunch. Crab corn chowder or grilled cheese. On a good day, on some of the best, we'd go all the way to Sonoma. Bring my mom back a bottle of dry red for the two of them to share that evening once we, all three of us, were sprawled on chairs and carpet and couches in the living room, watching the History Channel if Dad won, or an old black-and-white classic with Clark Gable or Jeanette MacDonald if Mom got to pick.

In the summer, After, I did this: followed Rabbit's list of ways to find my father.

"'Things don't turn up in this world unless somebody turns them up,'" Beckett announced when he sat down at the table. "James Garfield. Now let's get to it."

We met at Martha's coffee shop on the corner of California and Divisadero in my neighborhood on Monday, and the place was packed, since everyone was off from work for the holiday. Rabbit brought the list of phone numbers for employees in the San Francisco branch of my dad's company, and he'd divvied up the names onto separate pieces of paper, so each of us had our own group to call. I had A through F.

"We call in the afternoons, after lunchtime," Rabbit said. "Starting tomorrow, when everyone goes back to work."

Next to him, Maddie picked at her towering piece of crumb cake, the powdered sugar clinging to her fingertips. "Let's start with the big picture," she said. "What are we thinking? What are the options, in terms of what might've happened?"

The small metal table rocked back and forth when Rabbit flipped his sheet of employee phone numbers over—G through M—and wrote: *Possible Explanations of What Could Have Happened*, underlining it in blue ink.

"Kidnapped," Beckett said, and Rabbit wrote it down.

"What do you call that?" Maddie asked. "When it's not a kid?" She cupped her mug between her hands, thinking. "Hostage. That's it. When it happens to adults," she said, and took a sip of her chai-tea latte.

"Abduction," I said. "It's called abduction."

Rabbit wasn't the only one who'd been doing research since the camping trip. After we got back from the museum on Saturday, I'd tried to put that photo out of my head and told myself I'd been seeing things through tired eyes. So I'd spent that night and the whole next day studying missing persons' websites and reading testimonials and police reports too, looking for clues. But the idea of someone taking my dad seemed completely improbable, and in the end, all I could really think of was that man in 1906. It was ridiculous. And impossible. Not to mention completely insane that I'd even given it a second thought. Sci-fi stuff, Hollywood blockbuster story lines, and the smart part of me knew it, no questions asked. But still, I couldn't get it out of my mind. Time-jumping and black holes—that's what I thought of when I imagined where he might be, which was pretty much all I'd been doing.

"It's not like we have lot of money," I said. "For ransom, I mean. I don't know why anyone would target my family."

Rabbit scratched out *Kidnapped* and wrote: *Abduction*. "It does sound a little unrealistic," he said, "but we're not ruling anything out yet."

At the counter, a man in his thirties with tattoo sleeves and a messy ponytail started grinding coffee beans, and I had to lean in closer to hear Beckett talking.

"How about mugged?" he asked. "Mugged and left somewhere. Or drugged and dropped off at a hospital after they took all his stuff," he offered.

And Rabbit added *Hurt and Abandoned* to the list, and then, in parentheses: *Call Hospitals*.

"This is depressing," I said, envisioning my dad stumbling stoned through an emergency room, confused, in one of those white paper gowns that doctors make you wear.

"Sorry, Cal," Beckett said, and under the table he reached over and squeezed my knee.

The police called the hospitals the night he didn't come home, but I agreed to try them again the next day. I'd call them every day for forever if I had to.

"Or maybe"—Rabbit slowed down and looked at me, apologizing with his eyes—"maybe something like temporarily insane? Mental confusion? Disorientation? Maybe he had some kind of breakdown," he said.

But my dad didn't have a history of anything like that.

"We should check homeless shelters," Rabbit said. "Just in case something like that happened and he ended up at one."

So that went on the list too.

I moved my hand to the piece of glass in the pocket of my zip-up hoodie as we sat in the café, rubbing my thumb over the smooth, flat surface of the slick side while they talked. Their suggestions were possible, more possible than him being stuck in some bizarre time-warp past dimension thing, but my gut kept telling me none of their ideas were right.

My father's family was one of the first to settle in San Francisco after the Gold Rush—one of the forty-niners from Europe, according to my parents—so while I knew we'd had ancestors in the area forever, the photo of that man doused my insides with cold chills each time I thought of it. I knew not to trust it, wasn't that naïve, but it looked just like him. In the picture, he was wearing a black suit, like all the other men, and really they all looked the same, but still. . . . Small wire-rimmed glasses. Seeing that picture felt like a cold wind sucking my breath away, emptying me out and stringing my nerves tight. And part of me knew the photo meant something, even if it didn't make sense yet.

I sighed and said, "Twenty-three thousand one hundred and seventeen adult males were reported missing in California in 2005."

"Jesus," Maddie said. "Really?"

But Beckett was shaking his head and stopping me before I got the chance to keep talking. "Don't do that, Callie," he said. "It doesn't help. Your dad's different than anyone I know. Always has been. Some people are just good people, and he's one of them. Bad things don't happen to good people," he said, which we all knew was a lie. So he added, "Okay. Sometimes they do. But this isn't permanent. We're going to find him. You'll see."

I nodded, trying so absolutely hard to believe him, to believe in Some Great Thing that we could do to bring my dad back from wherever he'd been taken to, but all I could think of were those miserable statistics. And the man in the photo.

And then no one said anything for a while and just looked into their mugs of coffee because there was only one other option not on Rabbit's list.

That he'd left on his own.

I cast the thought away, certain and faithful that disappearing was something that had happened *to* him, not something he'd chosen.

It was cool and drizzly when we left the café, each with our own To Do list folded and tucked in a pocket or purse. That afternoon, Maddie planned to go online and make a list of homeless shelters for us to visit later that week. I'd been assigned to call the hospitals, since I was the only one related to my father, and medical people don't give information to non–family members. Beckett would search the archives of the *Chronicle* and the SFGate for police reports of anyone who'd been charged with mugging or abduction in the last twelve months, and Rabbit would keep brainstorming ideas in case there'd been something we hadn't thought of. We'd keep each other posted if anyone found anything, and otherwise meet the next night back at the job site downtown to search for the homeless guy who had talked to the police.

"It'll be easier to track him down after five o'clock," Rabbit said. "If he's still in the area, I bet he goes there at night after the work crews leave. It's probably a good spot to sleep. Quiet, maybe."

Something about the thought of going back there turned my stomach, the coffee and cream and sugar sloshing around with that butterfly feeling, but I nodded. We'd meet there at seven, after I was finished with my shift at work and we'd all had time for dinner.

When I got home, I grabbed a glass of water from the kitchen and headed toward my room, calling for my mom. The house smelled like cleaning products, the lemon scent drifting through the air, and in the hallway I noticed vacuum tracks etched into the long carpet runner. My parents' bedroom door was open, so I dipped my head in and called out again; Mom had the radio playing, that station where they read old classic novels, her favorite, and I caught sight of the balls of her feet barely hanging out of the bathroom door that connected to their room. Scrubbing the floor, I guessed.

"I'm back," I said, once, twice, three times before she finally ducked out of the bathroom and turned down the little radio alarm clock on her dresser.

"Did you say something?" Her rubber cleaning gloves were still on, and she wore cutoff jean shorts and my dad's ratty House of Blues sweatshirt from Chicago, the one with the ripped collar he'd had for a million years and mostly wore when he worked on his bikes.

"Just that I'm home. I'm here," I told her.

She nodded, said, "That's good. I'm just finishing up." She leaned on the doorframe. "You okay?" she asked, and I shrugged.

It was a question we'd been asking each other a lot. Ping-ponging it back and forth, but never really answering.

She'd taken to sleeping most nights on the couch in the living room downstairs. At first I thought she was doing it so she'd hear him as soon as he came back: She'd hear the lock click open and would be there, waiting, when he came home. But when I kept finding her there in the mornings, I realized it was because she couldn't bring herself to sleep in their bed alone. As she stood looking at me and peeling off those huge yellow gloves, the side effects were clear. The puffy blue-brown pockets under her bloodshot eyes were still there, always there. And she looked more tired than I'd ever seen her look before. He'd been gone forty-two days by then, and we were both barely hanging on.

"What about you?" I asked. "Are you okay?"

She shook her head. "It'll probably get worse before it starts to get better, you know?" she said as she moved toward me. She brought her fingers to my face and lightly skimmed the half-moon bruise around my eye. In the morning, it had been that rich navy-purple color, and tender still, but the swelling was gone. "Never would've imagined you sporting a black eye," she said.

"An accident," I said, repeating what I'd told her when I'd gotten home from the camping trip. She was good enough to let me get away with leaving it at that, or maybe just too tired to press me. "The house looks spotless," I offered. "You must be exhausted."

She shrugged. "Campus is closed for Memorial Day, so I spent the day cleaning. There's something strangely therapeutic about scrubbing and vacuuming."

"I'll take your word for it," I teased, but I knew it had always been like that for her. Whenever she was stressed or trying to work something out in her head, she cleaned. Cleaning and nail biting.

I tried to think of something else to say, something normal and mundane, even—anything to compete with that local car dealership commercial humming from the radio. I tried to remember what we talked about before my dad went missing, what kinds of conversations we had when we'd make dinner or run errands together, but it had become hard to remember anything before April 18.

"Is band practice going well?" she asked, beating me to it.

I nodded. "I think we're getting better," I told her. "Don't get me wrong, I don't expect *Rolling Stone* to come calling anytime soon, but we're figuring it out. I think we're getting better," I repeated.

"That's good," she said. "I'm proud of you, you know. For working so hard at it."

It was something my dad would have said. His words on her lips spread goose bumps across my skin, and a lump settled in my throat.

"Hey, there's this thing next week," she told me. "A reading and discussion at Books Inc. An autobiography by one of the Little Rock Nine, one of the first students allowed to attend an all-white high school. *Brown versus Board of Education*," she said. "A civil rights memoir."

We'd do that sometimes—go to events at local bookstores.

I always liked listening to the readings, and she enjoyed meeting the authors and learning about their research and the writing process.

"I thought you might be interested," she said. "I thought we could go together?"

A small and silly thing, but still. An attempt to help fix the strangeness that had built up between us in the weeks since my dad disappeared.

"I'm in," I said. And then, "Do you need anything? Want me to make you a snack or something?"

She shook her head. "Just a little bit longer," she said nodding toward the bathroom. "Then we can pick through some menus and order in if you're hungry."

And then I was in my room, a medium-size space with three bay windows facing the street and walls lined with white crown molding, which I've always loved. I turned my computer on, shed my hoodie on the floor, and noticed, right there on my bed, a large yellow envelope with the Habitat for Humanity logo and return address stamped in the left-hand corner.

It was wrinkled and weathered—had gotten lost in the mail maybe—but there it was. Finally. I'd requested it a few months earlier, after spending hours on their website and deciding I wanted information about their International Volunteer Program, even though I had to be eighteen to volunteer. I liked the sound of their emphasis on multicultural environments and the fact that the host countries helped cover the costs of housing and transportation.

But mostly I liked the idea of doing something different and of going somewhere completely unlike where I'd always been. I wanted to try new kinds of food, to hear the unfamiliar sound of a foreign language, to learn about different styles of music and dancing, customs and traditions I'd never known. I'd scanned the photos and read the descriptions online, and decided that this was exactly what I needed: something different. I'd requested the catalogs before my dad went missing, before I knew everything was about to change anyway.

"Junk mail, or did you request it?" my mom asked from the hallway, nodding toward the envelope I held in my lap as I sat on the bed.

After the talk about not being able to afford out-of-state schools, we didn't say much at home about colleges until I registered for the SATs. Then it was kind of all we talked about. The guidance counselor encouraged students to take the test early in the spring so there'd be time to retake it if anyone needed to. Our mailbox and coffee table filled with catalogs from schools in California, and dinner conversations were geared around campus perks and credit options. I played along, and part of me was interested for a little while, but the other part of me had already begun collecting dictionaries and watching documentaries about Paraguay, Peru, and Belize.

"*Not* junk mail," I confessed and ran my hands over the envelope.

She sat next to me and said, "I see."

At first it'd been about the Portland thing, about being told what I could and couldn't do, and about my plan with Beckett being taken away from me. But then it became bigger than that. I'd spent twelve years inside a classroom, and I wanted something different. I wanted to travel and to live out of my backpack, to study cultures and customs completely unlike my own.

"I just thought it'd be good for me to research other options."

"Options other than . . ." Her voice trailed off, and I finished for her: "Other than college."

I took the SAT test on April 1, but April 1 was seventeen days before my dad disappeared, so when the results arrived a few weeks later, they didn't seem all that important anymore. Even though I'd done well, well enough to land me an acceptance to any of the Cal State schools, at least, neither of us had the energy to make a big deal about it.

"Is this about Portland?" she asked, and I shook my head.

"Not really. Maybe at first, but not now."

"It's because of your dad, then," she said. "Because everything feels so. . . so tentative? I know it's been hard, Callie. It's been an impossible few weeks. But I don't think that's a reason to change your plans."

"But they weren't my plans," I told her. "The college plans were never mine. Not since I found out I'd have to stay in California, at least. I've been thinking about this for a while," I said. "Since long before . . . before the thing with Dad."

"But it's the first I'm hearing of it," she said.

"I know, and I'm sorry about that," I told her. It was a crappy thing to do, to throw one more thing at her like that. The timing couldn't have been worse, but I also wasn't willing to give up on the idea. Stubborn, like my dad. Even though I knew she'd be disappointed, I had to be honest.

"You're just tired," she said. "And upset about your father. It's only natural for you to rebel in some way."

But I was shaking my head. "That's not fair. And it's not true, either," I said, recognizing the whining in my voice and trying to control it.

I was seventeen. Old enough to make my own decisions.

"I mean, yeah, I'm tired. Tired of not knowing and of wondering about the what-ifs. And of course I'm upset. But that has nothing to do with me not wanting to go to college right away." I was standing by then, so she stood too, putting us eye to eye. "I've thought it out," I told her. "This isn't some spontaneous thing."

"Explain it then," she said. "Tell me. I want to understand."

I told her I didn't see a point in spending money on classes if I wasn't sure what I wanted to study. Instead, I wanted to learn about the way other people lived in different places. My life in San Francisco had started to seem so small, and I figured that traveling overseas and working in a program like Habitat for Humanity would help me decide exactly what it was I wanted to do in the long run. I figured it would be good for me.

My mother had strong opinions once she made her mind up and an innate fear of impulsiveness. But like Rabbit, she was systematic and precise, which was why she was so good at her job in the library. So she said, calmly and carefully, "We're not going to make this decision right now."

And I nodded. It sounded fair enough to wait it out and see if she'd come around. She'd have to, because my mind was already made up.

The next day I went to work. Work, for me, meant catching the bus to Beckett's house and taking over Lori's jewelry studio in their garage to help prep her designs. She created one-of-a-kind jewelry that she sold in small boutiques throughout the city, and most of her pieces used hammered metal, stones, sea glass, and fragments of coins or cultural relics that she collected when she traveled. She made two trips a year to places like Jordan and Egypt and Tunisia to purchase materials, and though I'd never tell my mom, looking through Lori's photos and hearing her stories swelled my wanderlust that year. I was the only person who worked for her, and she scheduled my hours so that I was in the studio during the times she did business stuff in her home office or booked meetings with boutique owners. Sometimes she'd be in the garage too, but more often than not, I worked alone.

She let me bring my iPod, and I spent my shifts pressing sheets of Argentium silver and gold-filled metal. I drilled freshwater pearls, and clipped and shaped wires, pulled strands of beads apart, and strung other groups of beads together. I organized pieces of turquoise and onyx in different jars, depending on their size and weight. Once every few months, she'd collect her work from boutiques—the jewelry that hadn't sold yet—and we'd stand in her kitchen and clean it with ammonia, assembly-line-style, so she knew the jewelry was being displayed in its best possible form when she returned it to the shops. She was a hard worker and she kept me busy, but it was the kind of work I liked. No computers and no numbers. I got to work with my hands and spent a lot of the day on my feet, listening to my favorite bands and thinking up new songs for Nothing Right.

It was my first day back at work after everything that had happened with Dad, so Lori was there waiting when I arrived to go over the list of tasks I'd need to finish during my next few shifts.

"Sweet Callan Pace," she said when I let myself into the garage through the side door. "How are you holding up?" she asked.

Lori had known me just as long as Beckett had, and she and my mom were almost as good of friends as Beck and me. This worked in and against our favor depending on the situation, but it was nice when I went to work because it meant I didn't have to explain my bruised face or give her an update on news about my dad. She already knew there was nothing new to report; she'd been at the house the day before, dropping off a potato-and-broccoli casserole.

"Never thought my kid had it in him to dole out a black eye," she said. "The first fight he gets in, and he hits a girl. Figures." She smiled. "I'm sorry it happened that way."

We talked a little about the camping trip, me not mentioning that I wasn't going to Portland even though I was certain Beckett had told her. And her not mentioning the liquor bottle and why the black eye was the perfect manifestation of what she'd always told us: We shouldn't drink, because drunk people do dumb stuff. I hooked up my music while she finished organizing the materials I'd be using for the day, and then she gave me my Post-it note of things to do and ran through a quick explanation of anything that wasn't quite clear.

"Beck's still sleeping because evidently he's become one of those things. What is it called? A teenage boy," she said, and rolled her eyes. "But he's got strict instructions to let you work, so I think he made plans for the afternoon."

I nodded like I didn't already know that he was slated to

meet Madison at the library at noon, where they planned to check the newspaper archives and Xerox the missing-person poster so we had copies to leave at all the homeless shelters when we visited them.

She eyed me as I sat at my workstation, organizing strands of pearls.

"You never answered," she said. "Are you holding up okay?"

I felt her eyes locked on me. "Sure," I said.

She kept standing there. Watching. "Sure," she repeated. "Depending on your definition of 'okay'?"

"I don't know what to say," I told her. "It's like everything was fine and made sense, you know? And then it just stopped. Making sense, I mean. I'm trying to figure it out and pick up where the police left off . . . but I guess I'm worried that I've waited too long."

I fought the tears that had been finding me so frequently during the past weeks. I'd never been a crier, never one for big emotions, heart-on-your-sleeve kinds of things.

"It's okay, you know," she said. "For you not to have the answers. You're just a kid, Callie, and this thing that's happened *doesn't* make sense. Not at all."

I looked at her and then I looked away. At the stained carpet and the light-pink pearls.

"It's not your fault," she said. "And you have to do what makes you feel better. If searching for him is it, that's fine. But it's also good to give yourself permission to stop searching when it wears you out. You're just a kid," she repeated. "You can't let this define you now. He would have hated that, you know?"

I nodded, but I didn't buy it. Of course I couldn't stop searching. It was the only thing that made me feel like myself, the girl who was stubborn and determined, relentless. Stopping would mean I'd given up—it would mean he was never coming back.

CHAPTER EIGHT

Forty-three Days After

It was clear out in SoMa at the job site except for a wisp of gray at the edge of the sky announcing the end of the day. Just about seven o'clock and quiet in the city.

"This feels familiar," I said when Beckett dented the fencing so we could make our way into the lot again.

He'd brought Jay, the coffee shop kid, which annoyed me a little even though Jay seemed nice enough in the car ride over. He was two years older than Beck—eighteen already—and was saving money for tuition at the Art Institute of California, where he'd start culinary classes that fall. He had good taste in music, as far as I could tell—was sporting a Velvet Underground T-shirt that day—and he seemed pretty genuine when he told me how sorry he was about my dad. So I breathed deep and counted backward from twelve while I reminded myself that Beckett deserved to be falling for someone new, which is exactly what I guessed was happening as I watched them flirt in the backseat of Rabbit's Volvo. I decided to be less annoyed with Jay for being there and less resentful that Beckett was distracted by the idea of starting some kind of relationship with Jay while I was in the midst of trying to find my father.

I slid my hand into my pocket and felt the piece of glass there, warm from my body heat, as we stood by the fence, getting our bearings.

"Looks a little different now, huh?" Beckett said.

Over a month's worth of construction had been done at the job site, and the place felt hectic, with all those machines and vehicles crowding the grounds. It was easy to imagine the pounding of the rigs during work hours and the burn of dust and sweat in your eyes after a long day of transporting, measuring, and building.

"You stop hearing it eventually," my dad told me once when I asked him if the noise of the drills and machines ever hurt his ears and if he got headaches after a long day at work. It was the last time he'd taken me back to the ship graveyard, his favorite site of all. We went that afternoon to watch them haul out the final pieces of the boat, and we stood at the edge of the hole as the archaeologists in their hard hats and neon-colored vests scurried below us.

"Like how I don't hear the number 1 bus on our street anymore?" I asked, and he nodded. "Or Mom sometimes. When she's calling to get me out of bed on Saturdays. Sometimes I just don't hear her."

"Ha!" he said. "Nice try."

"I know what you mean, though," I told him. "The honking horns at night? Normally, I don't even notice them when I'm in my bedroom. But if I actually pay attention, I can hear them perfectly clear. Loud even," I said.

"Exactly. It's amazing what you can get used to. Humans are remarkable creatures, Callie. The things we can endure and the way we adapt. Don't you forget it."

The sun threw shadows on the ground, and the temperature was dropping as evening pushed its way through the city streets. I let go of the glass and zipped up my hoodie.

"Let's just look for that homeless guy and get out of here. This place has the vibe of a B-grade horror flick," I said.

Beckett and Jay set off in one direction and Maddie and I started off in another, while Rabbit stood by the fence, shooting snapshots with his camera for "documentation of all the crap we see." There was a beat-up white van and makeshift shelter on the far end of the site, by one of the drill rigs, a strange little tent thing I hadn't noticed when my mom and I drove by on graduation day. It didn't take long to spot a body there, a shadow in a camping chair.

Maddie called for Rabbit when she saw it, which also got Beckett's and Jay's attention, and we all crossed the lot toward the man.

"You're trespassing," he told us when we were close enough to hear him. "Says so right there." And he hitched his thumb to a sign tacked to the construction fencing behind him.

"You are too, then," Rabbit said.

He nodded. "Got that right. Every day for the last six months."

He was older than us but younger than our parents—mid-thirties maybe—and his hair was tangled and sun-bleached, and long enough to reach the collar of his black hooded sweatshirt. He had tied one corner of a ratty green tarp to the fence and the other corner to the frame of his chair so that he had a flimsy kind of tent shading an area where a blue sleeping bag and a blanket were stashed. There was also a small rusted camp stove and a pot crusted with something that looked like beans. Or corned beef hash. A spoon and fork lay on the blanket, next to a gallon jug of water.

"Smoke?" he asked, holding out his pack of Reds, but Rabbit and the rest of us shook our heads no.

Jay reached out and took one, though.

"Thanks, man," he said. Jay was slimmer than Beckett, more bones and doorknob shoulders, but they looked good standing next to each other.

Jay and the guy lit their cigarettes with the guy's pack of matches, and the rest of us just kind of stood around with our hands in our pockets and our eyes to the ground. We hadn't planned much further ahead than (2) *Find the Homeless Guy Who Was Probably too Paranoid to Tell the Cops All of the Truth.*

"It's going to be a good one," the guy said from his chair as he waved his cigarette in the air, pointing over our heads at the beginning colors of the sunset sky.

We all turned, looked, and mumbled "Yep" and "Sure is," wondering who was going to take the lead. I eyed Maddie, who mouthed "What?" and shrugged; then she eyed Beckett, but he was too busy eyeing the swoosh of black ink revealed each time Jay brought his smoke to his lips and the sleeve of his T-shirt slid upward. None of us had had the courage or the commitment to get tattoos of our own, and in a matter of five seconds Beckett's new friend became that much more intriguing.

But our attention shifted when the man in the chair said, "Something I can help you kids with? I'm kind of trying to unwind here, and you're rattling my nerves."

Rabbit grabbed the reins and started talking. He said we were looking for some info about a man who had worked on the construction site, then he took out the flyer, unfolded it, and handed it to the guy.

"Her dad," he said motioning to me. "He's MIA, is all, and we're trying to track him down."

And then, just to ride out the idea that the guy might trust us more if we were one hundred percent not involved with the police, I added, "The cops gave up looking kind of quick, so we're searching on our own. We're not, like, sharing info with them or anything. We're not reporting back."

He nodded, inhaled, exhaled, and inhaled again while I counted from twelve down to three before he spoke.

"He's your dad?" he asked, and our fingers brushed lightly as I took the flyer back and handed it to Rabbit. "You wanna tell me why you think *I* would know something about it?"

He was teasing us and wasting time, which annoyed me, but I had to play along. "When it first happened, there was someone here who told the cops he'd seen him."

"A homeless guy," he said, and he ran his eyes up my body, starting at my navy blue Chuck T's and working his way to the top, lingering on the gold Italian horn pendant. "A homeless guy, like me."

"Just a guy," I said, holding his gaze. "Was it you? Have you seen my dad before?"

He nodded, finally, but I couldn't decide if I could trust him or not. "I seen him. But that's about all. He was coming

in and I was going out, just like I told the cops. That was it."
He dropped the smoke into the dirt and stamped on it with the
heel of his black rubber clog, and that's when I saw the brown
leather backpack tucked under his chair.

My heart raced like I'd had the wind knocked out of me
and had just come to, like I'd only then opened my eyes and
couldn't remember anything from before.

"That," I said when I'd caught my breath. "Where'd you
get that bag?" I asked, pointing.

Beckett was next to me by then, holding me up by my
elbow a little because I must have stumbled, knees buckling
slightly. He said, "You okay?" to me and then, to the man, "Is
that yours? That bag there?"

The guy tugged it out between his legs and hoisted it onto
his lap. "This bag here? It's mine now. I found it a few weeks
ago."

"It's his," I breathed. "I'm sure of it. It's my dad's."

The guy made us pay for it, of course he did. "Finders,
keepers," he told us, and then asked us how much cash we
had. He dumped the bag out and sifted through the contents,
taking the spare change, the BART ticket, the April/May issue
of *Wired*, and the half-empty pack of gum—anything he could
sell or use. And then he made us empty our wallets and pay
for the bag and what was left: a pad of yellow Post-it notes; two
empty Cliff Bar wrappers, crunchy peanut butter, my dad's

favorite flavor; a tube of Chap Stick; an unsharpened pencil with my father's company logo stamped on the side; and his ripped transfer ticket for the bus, dated April 18, 2006. There was no wallet, but that made sense, since he'd always kept it in his back pocket, not his brown bag.

I was crying by the time he handed the backpack over, the tears hot and fast and my hands shaking when I snatched it from him and hugged it to my chest. But it didn't smell like my father, as I'd hoped it would. It mostly just smelled like sweat and leather.

Between the five of us, the guy got forty-seven dollars. He said he'd found the bag lying by a backhoe in the dirt a few days after he'd seen my dad. That was it. He said he didn't tell the cops about it because he found it after they'd talked to him, and he sure as hell wasn't going to go calling the police to tell them he was sleeping in the lot again and had found some backpack with nothing good inside but some snack bars and a magazine.

"I didn't think that much about it," he said.

We were quiet on the car ride back, me thinking that nothing had changed with the discovery of the bag, not really, and then that everything had changed all at once. My father had been there, but we'd already known that. But he also dropped the backpack, as if he'd been taken by surprise or had wanted to leave some kind of clue behind.

"Not that we ever thought it, but finding the backpack does mean he didn't, you know, like, leave on his own," Beckett said eventually, breaking the silence. "If he was going somewhere, there'd be no reason for him to abandon it at the construction site." He was sitting on the other side of Jay, who rode between us in the back. "He would have wanted it. He wouldn't have just left it there."

The bag was in my lap, my knuckles white as I clutched the leather with one hand and pulled out the contents with the other. The yellow Post-it notepad was blank, every sheet of it, and the tube of Chap Stick was blunt and mint flavored, his go-to kind. The unsharpened pencil with his company's logo was covered in lint and had probably been sitting at the bottom of the bag forever. And then my fingers found the ripped transfer ticket for the Muni bus dated April 18, 2006.

April 18, 2006, right there at the top. The first number reading 7:00 a.m., always, and the diagonal tear cutting through the 4:00 and 5:30 time slots. It was proof that the last bus my dad took was late afternoon—at least the last one he took when he was still carrying his backpack. From his office to the job site, his final stop of the day before he planned to come home, I guessed. I imagined him first on the bus, sharing the seat, since it always got crowded late in the day, and then at the site, his backpack slung over his shoulder. Meeting with the head of the construction crew, or maybe arriving after they'd left, him walking the site alone and finding, eventually, the homeless man camped there.

And then my mind scattered, splicing together images of the struggle that might have happened, the argument between the two men.

"That guy. He has to know more, right?" I asked no one in particular.

Beckett was the first to answer. "Maybe. I don't know, though—he seemed pretty harmless. I mean, don't get me wrong—making us pay was a dick move—but he didn't seem violent," he said. "Not the mugging-and-robbery type. Too lazy and stoned for that. But what do I know?"

"I agree," Jay said. "He seemed more like the aid-and-abet type, not the initiate type."

I looked out the window and rolled my eyes, and maybe Rabbit caught it in the rearview mirror, because he said, "We'll follow up, though, Cal, don't worry. Let's think on it and see what else we can find, and then we can track the guy down again in a few days. See if he's feeling more generous with his information."

"We can always call the cops if you want," Maddie said from the front seat. "It's up to you. Technically, he was in possession of evidence, right?" she asked.

And Beckett said, "Absolutely. In fact, we should really turn it in—the bag, I mean. If it's evidence, the police should have it."

But I shook my head. "I want some time first. To think it over, like Rabbit said." The backpack was the first piece of my father I'd found since he disappeared, and I wasn't about to give it up so quickly. "The police haven't done anything to help out so far, so why would they start now?" I figured the cops had given up looking for my dad by then; we hadn't heard from them in weeks. "Let's see what we can come up with before we involve anyone else."

"It's up to you," Maddie repeated, and she turned and caught my eye with one of *those* looks.

I looked away, shoved all my dad's belongings back in the bag, and counted backward from twelve. It had been hard enough to stop crying at the site, and I didn't want to start up again. Rabbit had counted the money while Maddie helped me to the car, whispering, "Shhh, it's gonna be fine, Cal, you'll see." Beckett was clearheaded enough to give the guy his cell number in case the man thought of anything else, any small detail or snippet of conversation from the day he'd run into my dad, but I figured we'd never hear from him. He wouldn't bother, didn't have access to a phone, probably. It didn't matter to him whether we found my father or not.

"At least we have proof he was there. And I think we can assume he left the site abruptly, and maybe not by choice," Rabbit said, trying to turn the backpack into something that could tell us something important.

"I'm not going to tell my mom, either," I said once Rabbit parked in front of my house to drop me off. "I don't see what good it'd do. Not until we have more time to think it over." Heads nodded, and I sighed as I opened the car door. "I know this isn't how we're supposed to be spending the summer. But"—my voice caught in my throat as I pulled the backpack closer to my chest—"but I'm thankful you guys are doing this. That you're helping me," I told them, and then I shut the door and let myself into the garage to stash the bag in a box under a pile of magazines beneath a folding table. I'd keep it there until I could decide exactly what finding it meant.

She'd said, "I bet he's no more missing than he wants to be," that girl gossiping in the restroom during that first week I'd returned to school.

And I'd thought I had let it slide. But then the nightmares started, and I heard it OverAndOverAndOver again every time I slept. Her words echoed behind black-and-white images of a ship underground, my father becoming a vapor or a blur, an outline of limbs slipping down a black hole, a sinkhole, a sink drain, a storm drain—slipping out of reach. Like a broken-down déjà vu spliced apart and pasted together with picked-over imaginings and interludes. I saw backpacks under trees at Hippie Hill, next to rusted tambourines, dented life-less instruments lying on the ground. Abandoned buildings, broken windows, trains battered and derailed. I heard voices and the trembling vibrations of wind and firestorms. The settings were never the same twice—never the same monsoon or mudslide or earthquake scene—though the man was always slipping away somehow.

And the girl's words, the consistently tapped timing in her voice, like a drum: "I bet he's no more missing than he wants to be," she said.

In the morning, I woke thrashing and sweaty, queasy, as the cordless on my nightstand rang incessantly, while Maddie's number flashed on the screen.

"Hey," I said, and she said, "'Morning, sunshine."

Above me, light pushed its way through my blinds, and I listened to the street noises seeping beneath my bedroom window. A bus tugging on its wires. A dog barking somewhere nearby. A man calling to a woman, who shouted back, "Buzz me up—we're running late!" And I could tell, from the sound of nothingness inside the house, that my mother had already left for work.

"What time is it?"

"Early," Maddie said. And then, "Well, not that early. It's ten."

It'd been a fitful sleep, and after three mugs of chamomile tea, I'd called it a night but spent most of the dark hours tossing and turning, bound by thoughts of my Habitat application, that broken piece of glass, and the homeless man at the construction lot. And, always, of the man in the photo. The image tugged at me until it became a beating thing, like a heart, pulsating and relentless there in my memory.

"I've got until noon, right?" I said and rolled over, closing my eyes as I cradled the phone to my ear with one hand and slid the other under my pillow where the sheets were cool. We'd agreed to meet at the library that afternoon to post more flyers around the city: in cafés, public parks, libraries, and locker rooms at the YMCA; on bulletin boards at grocery stores, on lampposts, and at bus stops. Anywhere they would let us put them up. I should've been spending my morning calling names on the employee list from Dad's office, A through F, but I'd been in bed fighting the nightmares.

"No, you're fine," Maddie said. "Noon at the library on Larkin. But that's not why I'm calling." A long pause, and I imagined her sitting on the front steps of her house people-watching and scratching down lyrics in her red leather note-book. Brown lace-up prairie boots, a long skirt, and tank top. That's usually where I'd find her, mornings in the summertime. "You know Isaac Thompson, right?" she asked, finally.

Everyone knew Isaac Thompson. Kind of. He was in our year in school and was the son of a dot-com-boom business-man named Philip Cory Thompson who always, at least in the newspapers, went by all three names. Isaac went to the same elementary school as Maddie and I did, and he'd been sweet and smart and a little bit quiet, but everybody had liked him. And then his parents split up when we were in fourth grade. He and his mom moved to Paris, where she worked as an art buyer for a small gallery, and he became a Vespa-driving, espresso-drinking hipster in skinny jeans who knew about all the good books and Euro bands before anyone else did. That's how we'd imagined it, at least. He visited his dad every summer for six weeks, and occasionally there'd be an Isaac Sighting, which we'd aptly labeled I.S.s.

As in, "I.S. at the AMC on Van Ness this weekend. He saw *Hustle & Flow* by himself, then left on his skateboard."

Or, "Not affirmative, but possible I.S. on the Fillmore bus today. He's grown his hair out. Not gross hippie long, but, you know, cool and shaggy and kind of hanging in his eyes long. He was wearing a leather cuff and flip-flops."

Each summer we'd speculate if he was going rocker or artsy, if he was leaning toward outdoorsy or emo. We'd wonder what kind of food he had access to that we didn't, whether he thought in French now or still in English, and if American History was an elective instead of a requirement where he went to school. Sometimes he'd show up at a party or we'd run into him at a concert, but mostly Isaac Thompson existed in our minds as the one that got away. For all of us.

"Yeah, I know Isaac Thompson," I said.

"Are you sitting down?" she asked.

"Horizontal."

"Good. Because you're never going to believe this."

She started by saying that obviously, looking for my dad was our absolute top summer priority. "Obviously," she said. "But I also know the only place you're happy now is sitting behind that drum kit. I can tell. So you need to make sure you make time for it. You have to keep doing the things that make you happy, Cal," she told me.

"Okay," I said, trying to follow her ramblings. "What does this have to do with Isaac Thomson?"

"I'm getting there," she said. "So will you?"

But I was groggy and hadn't been able to keep up. "Will I what?"

"Keep playing with Nothing Right?"

The truth was, I'd never really thought about quitting the band when my dad went missing. If anything, I'd used it as a distraction, fuel for my denial or whatever it was that had happened during those thirty-nine days when I'd done practically nothing about him being gone. She was right—it was one of the only things that made me happy since he'd disappeared. And I felt rotten about that—guilty and a bit selfish, too. But I also knew that my dad would have hated it if I'd given up drumming; he was the one who allowed me to do it in the first place.

So I said, "I'll keep playing. I think I need Nothing Right now more than ever," realizing how true it was. "Seriously, though, what does that have to do with Isaac Thompson?"

Isaac Thompson was back in town, and that summer he'd be turning seventeen. Evidently, Philip Cory Thompson wanted to throw an epic party for his son, and since he used Beckett's dad for some kind of financial planning thing, he knew that Beckett and Isaac were about the same age. So he'd talked to Beckett's dad, who talked to Beckett, who was put in charge of recommending bands for the party. And out of the list of recommendations, Philip Cory Thompson picked Nothing Right. Or Isaac did, I guess.

"You've got. ToBeKiddingMe," I said.

And Maddie said, "I know. I thought Beckett would want to tell you himself, but he was super-official and secretive and stuff. He didn't even want to take credit for it. He gave Isaac's dad Rabbit's number and told him Rabbit was the manager," she said. "And Isaac's dad called Rabbit, who just called me, and obviously I called Beckett, but he was all modest and said he didn't really have anything to do with it. Which is totally a lie, but kind of sweet too. He said we got the gig because word was getting around about us. Because we were good and we deserved it."

"I. Love. That. Kid," I said, and Maddie said she did too.

And then we talked about how much we loved Beckett's

dad and the coincidence that Beckett's dad worked with Isaac's dad. Isaac Thompson's seventeenth birthday party would be our real first gig. Isaac Thompson. His party on Pacific Avenue, where all the monstrous-size homes are, homes with views of the bay and the Golden Gate Bridge like you'd never seen views before. Catered, Maddie said.

"Cocktail dresses and ties, too," she said. "All out. They want us to play from eight until midnight, *and* they're actually going to pay us. Like, real money, Callie. Not much, but still." She said she still couldn't believe our very first Nothing Right gig had been booked by Philip Cory Thompson for Isaac Thompson's seventeenth birthday party.

It was the best thing that had happened in forty-four days.

CHAPTER NINE

Image 3B: "Untitled (Baggage salvaged from the Valencia Hotel, Valencia Street), 1906." Cellulose nitrate negative, 135 × 78 mm irreg.

The city is burning. He tastes it when he licks his lips as thirst pumps through his body. A deep breath as he steps over a woman, lifeless, her skirt pooled around her knees and exposing a flash of pale white skin. He bends to straighten the fabric and then hurries onto the sidewalk so a horseback rider can pass by. The man's stomach clenches, and he imagines the dead woman as a mother, beginning her daily errands for a family waiting at home, perhaps.

At the bottom of the street he sees fireworks and makes his way there, thinking it some kind of SOS or the site of a relief organization that can explain this senselessness. The colors spray the sky, and he imagines Fourth of July parades as the air lights up with red, white, and blue flecks.

He counts backward to slow his breath, twelve to zero as he walks. His fingers and toes sting like needle pricks, and he wonders if he may be hurt after all. An internal wound from a fall, an injury he can't remember but must have occurred just before he awoke in the street. The soot and fumes have clouded his mind, he thinks. And the thirst, the dehydration. Dizziness washes over him, and when he arrives at the source of all that noise and color in the sky, he finds a fireworks factory near Market Street exploding and burning to ash.

There are bodies in the street blanketed in grit with copies of the morning's *Chronicle* dropped over top, the cover story a review of an opera performed the night before. A set of high-heeled pumps and black silk stockings stretch out from under the newspapers. Next to them, oxfords, the husband's perhaps. The points of two-toned spectator pumps and a pair of laced-up ankle-high boots. Bile thrusts upward from the man's belly, but he looks away and swallows steadily, with a one-two rhythm. Behind him bricks fall from buildings, and he steps lightly, dodging debris as he moves south.

A wounded teenage boy limps toward him, a long gash on his arm, the blood clotted and dark as black paint. He holds a derby hat in one hand, left shoe on, and right shoe missing. "Are you hurt?" the boy asks.

The man shakes his head; he has no visible wounds. A

racing heart, the sweating palms and cold chills—these are trivial compared to the damage he has seen.

"The boardinghouses south of Market, then," the boy says. "Valencia Hotel collapsed, only a few blocks down if you're willing to help."

Help: He can do that.

"They need axes and saws," the boy says. And then he moves on, shouting, "Can anyone help?" his words echoing under the sound of wind.

The Valencia Hotel is a four-story building that has telescoped into a single level, and there are men and women in the streets crying, What's happened? Has anyone seen my husband? My daughter? My friend?

The morning sun is replacing the gray, and he checks his watch: six o'clock.

"I can help," the man says, his voice dry and grainy but loud enough for heads to turn.

There is a gentleman in a black suit and bowler hat who seems to be in charge. "You?" he asks the man. "You're not hurt?" His name is William, and they quickly shake hands.

"No. I can help."

"The building sank," William tells him. "Most of those in the lobby and café escaped before the collapse." His voice is steady, as if he has been practicing the words, or perhaps repeating them with each new volunteer. "The fourth floor, though—it literally dropped to the ground. I watched the patrons on the top story step onto the street as if the roofline belonged right there on the pavement," he says, motioning to his feet. "I've never seen anything like it."

William's eyes are mapped in red, from sleeplessness maybe, or from the smoke, and the man thinks of blooming pink and white flowers yawning open under a winter sunlit sky.

"We need help digging," William says, and holds out an pickax.

"I don't understand what's happened," the man says, taking the tool. "I can't seem to remember how . . ." His voice fades out.

William nods. "Just dig and pray," he says softly, bowing his head toward the piles of debris at their feet.

CHAPTER TEN

Forty-eight Days After

The phone calls to my dad's coworkers went mostly like this:

Dial. Ring. Go.

"Mister Crawford? This is Callie Pace, Aaron Pace's daughter. I think you worked with my dad before he—uh—before he—disappeared?"

I'd close my eyes and try to think of anything but what the words meant. Missing; lost; misplaced; omitted.

A pause on the end of the line, a deep breath or a sigh. "Sure was sorry to hear about your father," they'd say.

Which struck me as premature, as if whatever it was that had happened was irreparable and complete. Part of the past. And I hadn't given in to that. I believed that he was out there, somewhere, alive and fighting to get home. I refused to consider the possibility that he might be dead. Just considering it, even slightly, would have felt like giving up, like I had abandoned him.

But then they'd typically follow with, "I'm happy to help, but I [insert polite but vague explanation as to why they don't have any information regarding my father. For example: "I didn't work directly with him much, and I wasn't around the day he disappeared." Or: "I wasn't assigned to any of his projects, and if truth be told, I didn't really know him all that well."] We've been thinking about you and your mom, though, his friends here at the office. We sure feel bad about what happened."

End call.

Repeat: Dial. Ring. Go.

End call.

Repeat.

AndOnAndOnAndOn.

On Sunday, my mom and I headed to Books Inc. for the author event with the woman who was part of the Little Rock Nine. I'd learned about the group of students back when we studied the civil rights movement in history class years earlier, but something about seeing the author, one of the actual people who was chosen to integrate the high school, made it seem like the incident hadn't happened all that long ago.

The book event was being held in the back of the store, by the children's section, and my mom and I got there with enough time to grab hot chocolates from the café next door and to stake a claim on seats toward the front.

"More people than usual," my mom said once we settled into the chairs.

I'd snagged a book from the table where the author would sit and sign copies after the reading and discussion.

"Tell me something," Mom said. "Anything. Talk to me about work. About Beckett. About what kind of trouble you two have been getting into." She cocked her head with an "I know you" look. "Tell me something interesting."

In front of us, the author and a high school–age boy who worked at the store emerged from a set of doors in the back and moved behind a tall table, which had been set up for the woman to use as a podium. She was gray-haired and wore a plain blue dress, and when I did the math, I figured she must be sixty-four years old or so. I looked at the black-and-white photo on the cover—a fifteen-year-old version of her clutching books to her chest as she and a young boy stood on the steps of the school, in front of a set of armed guards. She was there in the store, but there on the page, too. It was like bringing the past and the present into one place, the high school–age hero and the woman who survived to write the story, the woman with shaking hands, adjusting her glasses.

Next to me, my mother said, "Come on, Callie," as she put her hand on the book, nudging it aside. "Tell me what's going on with the band, maybe?"

So I did. I told her about the call from Maddie, the gig at Isaac Thompson's house, and about actually getting paid and all the practicing we'd need to do before the party. "I hope that's okay," I said.

She nodded, said that as long as I kept training for track and didn't bail on my responsibilities to Lori, it was fine. "It's a big deal, right?" she asked. "Your first performance."

"Gig," I said. "Our first gig."

"Exactly. And that's a big deal. I'm impressed, Callie."

The boy started talking then, welcoming us, thanking us, thanking the author and whatnot. Then the writer took over. She talked about *Brown v. Board of Education* and how forty-nine years ago wasn't really that long at all. She told us about the telephoned threats and the rogue police, the mobs and firebombs and, eventually, her indestructible faith. She read a bit from the book, stopping here and there to fill in the story with a memory or anecdote about one of the other nine.

"We were transformed into warriors," she said, her gaze seeming far away. "We should have been planning sweet sixteen parties instead." A sigh.

Behind me someone shifted in their seat, and at the front of the store, a telephone rang.

"It's funny. The way you don't always get to pick what you become. Reluctant warriors," she said. "That's what the press called us. Reluctant but set on an unwavering battlefield, a political firestorm. We rose to the occasion," she told us. "We found tenacity and courage when we needed it. We changed into the people we needed to be. I believe everyone does, eventually."

I figured that's why my dad liked studying history and finding old relics at his work sites—to be reminded that often, remarkable things happen to normal, everyday people, events after which nothing will be the same and those people will be forever transformed.

"Look how much the world has changed since then," the author said as she gestured to the cover of her book.

Afterward my mom bought me a copy of the memoir, and I stood in line to have it signed with the rest of the crowd. I was thinking of the author, of course, but I was mostly thinking of the 1906 earthquake photo. And of my father, always of my father, too.

We'd picked Wednesday as our homeless-shelter day, which turned out to be almost as terrible as the phone calls, except for the fact that by the end of it, we felt pretty grateful for all the things we had, like a home and food on the table every day.

"'Speak softly and carry a big stick,'" Beckett said when we were off the bus and hoofing it to the Haven, our first shelter of the afternoon. "Theodore Roosevelt."

"Bet that was the speech about the Monroe Doctrine," I said, remembering a U.S. History lecture from sophomore year.

"Your guess is as good as mine," Beckett said as we followed Maddie and Rabbit, turning the corner on Eighth Street.

Out front, three large men and two women sat on the steps smoking. They clutched cigarettes and white Styrofoam cups, and one woman whistled the Oscar Mayer wiener tune as we walked past.

I'd spent a few weekends at a local soup kitchen as part of a community service project through school, but I'd never just shown up at a shelter when there wasn't an organized event with grown-ups telling us what to do. It wasn't that it felt unsafe, but something about seeing all those people with nowhere else to go made me nervous.

We planned to visit nine locations after we'd weeded out the ones that only took women, families, or teens, and we averaged twenty to thirty minutes at each place, depending on whether or not it was mealtime. But even though most of the folks were nice enough, it was clear that no one cared much to talk to a bunch of kids. At the Haven, a twenty-four-hour facility that gave out meals to the homeless, they told us guests at the center had to be registered through the city; they mostly fed seniors with chronic medical conditions. And it kind of went like that every place we visited. We'd talk with someone in charge and find out that, for one reason or another, the odds of my dad being there were slim to none. Some places let us poke around, but a lot of places cited privacy policies and sent us on our way.

I noticed patterns. Clusters of folks played cards at folding tables in the main rooms of the centers, and groups of women on couches talked as their toddlers argued over toys at their feet. Teenagers watched daytime television or took turns on a community computer, checking e-mail, maybe, sports scores or job listings. Some people hugged doorframes and watched the rooms suspiciously, while others read newspapers and magazines, working crosswords. I wondered how they got there— how they went from not being homeless to having nowhere to go. I'd seen panhandlers and street kids all my life, had handed out spare change at bus stops and leftovers in carry-out boxes to people hanging around in front of restaurants, but being at the shelters was different.

By the fifth stop, I crashed, drained and disheartened, so I stayed out front while Beck, Maddie, and Rabbit scoped out things inside. I dropped my bag on the cement steps, tired from shouldering it all day—the flyers, my book, my iPod, pens and sunglasses, my house keys and wallet, change for the bus, and my drumsticks, too. I'd gotten into the habit of carrying them with me wherever I went. It was June, which meant fog and cool winds in the city, so I zipped up my hoodie and sat on the steps. Ever since the photo exhibit, I'd been reading every book about the 1906 earthquake I could get my hands on. I picked up Simon Winchester's paperback from the library that week, and cracked it open—Winchester was a geologist, like my dad, and some of the chapters were a little science-heavy, but I focused on the maps and tried to match the information with my memories of the images from the museum.

Behind me, the door opened then closed, and when I looked up, an older man hovered, one hand on his head, tugging a gray dreadlock, and the other shoved in his pocket.

"I'm guessing you're in the wrong place," he said.

"Maybe," I said, scooting over so he had room to walk past, and then, "No, not really. I'm supposed to be here. I'm looking for someone."

"Isn't it summertime?" he asked. "School's out. Why you reading?"

"I just like it, is all," I said. "I like reading all kinds of stuff," I told him.

"Not me," he said. Another tug on his hair. "Never had the eyes for it. Was born with a bum cornea. The left one, at least."

I nodded, wondering how much longer it would take my friends to finish up inside.

"Thing is, though," he said, "I can see fine with the right eye, so everything's just a little slanted. A little off-kilter. Never been able to ride a bike or drive a car. That kind of thing. Never had good handwriting. Don't really bother me all that much, I just don't like to read. Gives me headaches." Above us, the sky was gunmetal gray as the fog nudged through. "So who is it?" he asked. "Who you looking for?"

I showed him the flyer, but he didn't recognize the photo, so I took it back and shoved it in my bag.

"How long's he been gone?" he asked. "You report it?"

"Fifty-one days today," I said.

"That's a long time," he said.

And I said, "I know. Too long, probably. I should've found him by now." I ripped at the skin on my thumb, tasted the salt of blood.

"You know, kid, some people don't want to be found like you expect they do," he said,

But I shook my head. "Not him. It's not like you think. He didn't choose it," I told him. "He didn't choose to be gone. I'm sure of it."

He eyed me with his hands shoved in his pockets. "All's I'm saying is, it's not always how it seems," he said. "Just because you don't think he chose to take off doesn't mean he's fighting as hard as you are for him to come back. He may have other shit going on."

"That's a jackass thing to say." This was Beckett, standing behind me for who knows how long. "You okay, Callie?" he asked, and I nodded. "Don't listen to this guy," he said when he sat down. "He doesn't know your dad."

Then Beckett told me that Maddie and Rabbit were using his cell phone to call the next few places on our list. "If they have privacy policies, there's no reason for all of us to go," he said. "Maddie offered to drop off the flyers tomorrow, but if we can't talk to the people staying there, if we aren't allowed to wander around and look for him, we're kind of wasting the afternoon."

The dreadlocked man crossed the road, eventually moving out of sight.

"He's not at a shelter," I told him. "Him being at a place like this wouldn't make sense. He's not here. He's not in the city. I can feel it . . . I can tell." I gazed above the buildings on the other side of the street, where the sun tugged relentlessly at the gray edges of clouds.

"Callie."

"I don't want to talk about it," I told him. "Talk about you instead," I said, so he did.

He told me he and Jay spent most of the weekend together. Jay'd gotten tickets for a show at the de Young on Friday night. On Saturday, Jay had taken him to a sushi joint Beck had never been to. Jay had buzzed his hair into a medium-height Mohawk.

"And it doesn't look nearly as lame as you'd think," he

said. "Even though everyone's sporting hawks now."

They'd finally made out on Sunday afternoon, on BART on their way back from Berkeley, where Jay had taken Beckett to his favorite bookstore. Jay tasted like cinnamon and nutmeg from the chai tea he always drank.

"Like a spice rack," Beckett said. "Delicious." He shrugged and slipped his arm through mine. "It's crazy, right? Him working at that coffee shop like he'd been there all along. How come we'd never met him before?"

"So you like him?" I asked, and he nodded.

"Too much, maybe. I like him enough to be nervous about it," he said. "Nervous about how much I like him already."

And I knew exactly what he meant. I'd felt the same way about Andrew Parker. That sure-of-it-at-the-bottom-of-your-gut feeling: trust. An unquestionable faith in a person who hadn't earned it yet.

"I'm meeting him after his shift this afternoon. We're going to the Botanical Garden. Want to come with?" Beckett asked, but I shook my head.

"It'd do you some good, I bet," he said. "Fresh air. Plants and flowers. Nature and whatnot. Come on, you know you want to," he said. But I just couldn't do it.

The last time I'd gone to the gardens was with my dad—it was kind of our place. About once a month my mom got stuck working a Saturday shift at the library, so the two of us would head to Golden Gate Park, where'd we spend the whole afternoon in the gardens. Some days we'd just sit by the pond with our books and a blanket, eat snacks and hang around doing nothing—reading, people-watching, drifting in and out of sleep. Other times we'd hit up a plant sale or a lecture, but mostly we just liked to wander. We'd try to get lost, to see if we could walk our way into a section we'd never seen before or a collection of plants that didn't seem to be where the map said.

"Fifty-five acres," my dad would say. "We'll always find a way to get lost."

He called it a living museum.

"Go," he'd whisper, and then we'd race down the trail toward the redwoods, dodging tourists and women in yoga pants with jogging strollers. Dad favored the tree grove, but I'd always liked the magnolias, the pink and white blooms erupting in late winter.

Next to me, Beck said, "It's a good day for it, look," and he lifted his eyes, so I did too, squinting into the light. The sun had cracked through the cloud cover.

"I should go home," I told him. "My mom could probably use some help around the house. I need to call the coworkers on my list that didn't answer on the first try. And call all the hospitals again. I should go for a run, maybe."

"Runner's high," Beckett said, and I nodded. "When you run like that," he told me, "when you get in the zone, you relax your eyes in a weird way that your body isn't used to. Not with computers and TV and all the other crap we're exposed to all the time. Staring like that, all lazy-eyed when you run, that's what causes your brain to release the endorphins. It's called soft-focus. That kind of relaxation."

He was right. When I ran, I became single-minded, fully immersed in and aligned with the movement, all the noise of regular-life commotion fading away.

"How do you know that?" I asked him.

He shrugged. "Rabbit told me about it that day at the redwoods, after camping. We woke up and you were gone—running. And he said that with your dad missing and all, you should be running as often as possible. The endorphins. That you should be running a hundred miles a day, probably."

"A thousand," I said and leaned my head on his shoulder.

"A million."

"At least," I said.

"Okay, I'll let you off the hook. No Botanical Garden, then. But tomorrow the Boom Boom Room's having an all-ages show, and you're coming with us. No excuses. It's a jazz band, light on the drums probably, but still. It'll be good music for sure," he said. "And Isaac Thompson's in town. I'm betting he'll be there." We were holding hands by then, and he squeezed. "It'd probably be good for you to run into him before the party."

"I guess," I said, and he said, "You know, it wouldn't kill you to have some fun, Cal." And then, carefully, "It's been almost two months. He wouldn't have wanted you to . . ."

"Don't."

"We're going to find him. I still think we will," he said quickly. "That's not what I'm saying. I just mean that you have to keep going. You have to keep . . ."

But I shook my head. "Missing him makes time seem different now," I said. "I don't even remember that first month."

Beckett said, "I don't think you believed it at first. It was like looking for him meant you bought into the fact that he was really gone. It meant he needed to be looked for."

"I guess."

"It's okay," he said, but we both knew it wasn't. Not really. But he said it again. And again. And then he kissed me on the cheek. "'You have got to have something in which to believe.' Eisenhower. We'll find him, Callie. I believe it," he said. "And so should you. Onward." He stood and tugged me to my feet. "Let's check back inside, come on. No sense slinking around out here. It stinks of booze and piss, anyways." He cracked those dimples and picked my bag up. "We'll get out of here and grab some food," he said. "It'll give me more time to convince you to come to the show tomorrow."

After we ate, I took the bus back to my neighborhood, my eyes constantly scanning the city like a searchlight, longing to find him there on the streets, to find him anywhere. I wondered if I'd always be like that, seeking the world for him endlessly, back and forth. Back and forth.

I wanted to stop at the small hardware store at the top of the hill on California Street, and pulled out the list I'd printed off the *L.A. Times* website the night before: "Preparing Your Earthquake Survival Kit." I'd highlighted the items I knew we had at home in one color and the items I needed to buy in another, and then I'd taken two twenties from the savings I kept stashed in my sock drawer. I didn't mind spending my own money on it, figured it was worth it to be prepared. The store was in a strip of shops mostly populated by moms or nannies with strollers and by gym rats grabbing a snack or doing some shopping after a session at the JCC a few blocks down, so I was surprised to run into Andrew Parker when I got off the bus. He was standing outside the Cuban café, holding hands with a girl I'd never seen before, in the predictable uniform of girls from school: skinny jeans, ballet flats, tight T-shirt with a band name on front, and a hip-length cardigan. He turned his eyes away when he saw me but then turned them back, changing his mind, I guessed. The encounter was unavoidable, since he was waiting in line to get on the bus I'd just gotten off of.

"Hey, Cal," he said, and I said "Hey" back, and then we kind of stood there, staring at our shoelaces, or a crack in the sidewalk, or a wad of gum stuck to the curb, or whatever.

But then the girl held out her hand that wasn't holding his hand and said, "I'm Maya. Andrew's girlfriend. From Sausalito, on the other side of the bay," as if I didn't know where Sausalito was, with those huge houses on the water and the ferry that ran from the city to its restaurants and gift shops and day spas.

I shook her hand and said, "Oh, cool," and then I looked at Andrew, who was looking down at his feet again, as if looking at me was too much to bear.

She said that she went to some private school I'd never heard of, and he said they'd better get going since the bus was filling up, and then they were gone. I watched them from the corner as they picked their seats—he let her sit in the window, and she raised her hand and pressed her palm to the glass, smiling as they pulled away.

I arrived home to an empty house.

I'd bought candles, plastic eating utensils, matches, two coils of rope, a manual can opener, a compass, and one of those little portable radios, remembering what I'd read:

"Experts recommend being prepared to be self-sufficient for up to seven days."

I was lucky—since it was summertime, the store had mostly everything I needed, stuff people going camping would want. I decided to use my old suitcase to store the supplies, a pink little-kid thing I would take with me when we visited my grandmother but hadn't been used in years, so I began rummaging through the kitchen cabinet to add nonperishable goods to the bags before I brought them to my bedroom and began assembling the kit. I figured Mom wouldn't notice if the cans of green beans and baked beans disappeared. I would keep the kit in the garage with the backpack—she rarely went down there. And when I turned to start adding the food to the bags, I noticed a box from Powell's Books sitting on the kitchen table, my name and address printed on top.

I'd Googled the photography exhibit when I'd gotten home from the museum that day, and I ordered the book as soon as I found it: *After the Ruins—1906 and 2006, Rephotographing the San Francisco Earthquake and Fire*. It had been published the same week the art show opened at the MOMA, and it included images of all the photos from the exhibit. I hadn't been clearheaded enough to look for it in the gift shop at the museum, so I'd tracked it down online.

I reminded myself that if the photo looked the way I remembered, it wouldn't really change anything. I said that exact statement, "It won't change a thing, Callie," twelve times before I found the nerve to reach for the box.

I knew the man had to be an ancestor, that's all. It was a coincidence. An imagining as I desperately turned something unrealistic into some kind of clue. It was an impossible idea that didn't make sense. I'd been seeing that image nonstop since the trip to the museum and had imagined my father in 1906 trying to make sense of his surroundings just as I'd been trying to make sense of mine since he'd disappeared. Seeing the photo again, even if it looked as I'd remembered—exactly like him—it wouldn't really answer anything. I knew it just as sure as I knew my own name.

I tore into the box and flipped the pages quickly, scanning each image until I found the photo toward the back: IMAGE 8B: "UNTITLED (VIEW OF FIRE DOWN SACRAMENTO STREET), 1906." CELLULOSE NITRATE NEGATIVE, 84 X 144 MM IRREG.

And there in the corner was the blurry silhouette of the man. Dark hair. Small glasses, just like I'd remembered. My heart thumping like a terrible heavy thing. Like a black hole. My brain attempting to attach me to my father through the photo taken a hundred years earlier. I knew it couldn't be possible even as he stood there in the picture, the man who looked just like *him*.

But as I stared at that image in the book, at all those similarities between him and the man in the photo, I couldn't help think that maybe, just maybe, the idea wasn't so crazy after all.

CHAPTER ELEVEN

Fifty-two Days After

06.08.2006—08:22:39

Beckett42: u up?

06.08.2006—08:26:45

CallanP: locked and loaded. about to leave for ur house. why are you awake?

06.08.2006—08:31:12

Beckett42: promised jay id be his 1st customer. want me to bring u something? i wont be long.

06.08.2006—08:32:19

CallanP: romantic

06.08.2006—08:32:52

Beckett42: rudeness

CallanP: im serious. its sweet.

Beckett42: blah blah. coffee w/ cream and sugar?

CallanP: already made mine. travel-mugging it today. thanks tho. about to walk over.

Beckett42: ok forrest gump

Beckett42: still there?

CallanP: yup

Beckett42: leaving the new Strokes album on ur workbench. enjoy.

CallanP: best. friend. ever.

The walk to Lori and Beckett's took a little over half an hour, headphones on and my bell-bottoms skimming the sidewalk. In the summer, the sky arrived in patches of fog sliced by random bursts of sunlight—it's usually colder in June than it is in December, and I loved that about San Francisco, the way we layered our clothes in the summer while the rest of the country shed them in the heat.

My shift passed in comfortable repetition: hammering metal, unstringing and stringing stones and pearls, drilling and hammering again. Lori was in meetings all afternoon, and Beckett stayed at the coffee shop longer than he'd predicted, so I had the place to myself. By two o'clock I'd finished my To Do list and headed out, thinking I'd go for a run or call Maddie to see if she wanted to practice, but Beckett was walking in as I was walking out, and he talked me into going up to the roof deck with him instead.

"Just for a little while," he said. "You'll have plenty of time at home before the show tonight. Doors at nine," he told me. "You're coming with us. No questions asked."

I nodded.

Inside the house, we climbed the stairs to the second floor and then again to the third where the window in Beckett's bedroom opened onto the roof. Planters lined the deck: small boxes Lori nailed together from reclaimed wooden pallets and filled with orange-and-purple-feathered bird-of-paradise flowers. We sat, me in the lounger with my legs stretched out in front and Beckett in the canvas camping chair.

"How was the coffee shop?" I asked.

"Busy," he said. "Too busy to get to talk much, but I like

being there, you know? I read the newspaper and had an espresso. Super-classy stuff."

Since I'd known him, which was pretty much forever, Beckett had been in exactly 2.5 relationships.

Number 1: The summer after seventh grade, just a few months before he came out to me and his family and everyone, kind of, he met Johnny Strickland, a boy two years older and from a different school. They met at Ocean Beach and spent a few weeks together swapping mix CDs and holding hands, IM-ing incessantly and exchanging favorite books, favorite poems, favorite clothes, even. I sort of knew about the relationship while it was happening, knew they were friends and that Beckett had fallen into this weird distant haze all summer. We spent less time together during those months than ever before and I hated it, but I'd always figured he'd end up falling for boys over girls and wanted him to have time to make the decision.

Afterward, when school started and Johnny began his sophomore year while Beck went back to middle school for eighth grade, Johnny ended things over the phone. Told Beck he hoped to see him around, but classes would be keeping him pretty busy that year. He'd landed a starting spot on the soccer team and had plans to try out for the school play. He wouldn't have time to hang around at the beach with Beck and probably wouldn't have time to keep in touch, even. They never actually made out or declared themselves a couple when whatever it was was happening, but me and Beckett counted him as the first in the tally because we both knew Johnny talked him into coming out, even if Johnny never realized he'd done it. That's why Beckett forgave him for breaking his heart in a phone call.

Point 5: Alan Nelson, Alta Plaza Park, the night of graduation after freshman year. First kiss. No real interaction afterward.

Number 2: Jacob Stephenson, his first real boyfriend. Jacob was in our class, a super-nice kid who played basketball and liked to snowboard on the weekends with his family in Tahoe. They'd been pretty good together, but it only lasted a few months. Beckett wasn't really into sports, though we made the effort and went to a handful of Jacob's games. And Jacob had way different taste in music, though Beck dragged him to a few shows at the Independent that Jacob endured with a bored head-nod. It wasn't anyone's fault, not really, and the breakup was clean and neat and just a little bit sad, but for the most part they were still friendly at school.

So even though it hadn't been very long, I could tell it was different with Jay.

"I want it to work with him," he said. "And not because I'm lonely. Because I actually enjoy his company, you know? I'd rather be hanging out with him than *not* be hanging out with him. Except for you and my mom, there's no one else I can say that about."

We talked about the show at the Boom Boom Room that night and about Nothing Right, how we needed to practice as much as possible before the Isaac Thompson gig.

"Have you had any luck?" I asked when he told me he'd spent the day before researching local police reports for info about recent abductions and muggings.

He shook his head. "I couldn't find any patterns," he told me. "I mean, sure, there are purse snatchers and assaults in the city," he said. "But since we found your dad's backpack, it wouldn't make sense to link the disappearance to a mugging. Unless that guy at the construction site knows more than he let on."

I nodded and admitted that I'd gone back to look for the homeless man earlier that week, that I'd taken the bus to the site and searched him out. But he was nowhere to be found. The makeshift tent had been torn down; the stove, sleeping bag, and chair were gone too.

"Why didn't you say something, Cal? I would've gone with you," he said.

But I shook my head. "I thought he'd be willing to give me more information if it was just me instead of a whole group of us," I told him. "It doesn't matter now. I doubt we'll be able to find him again. Plus, you were right—he didn't seem the type to really hurt someone. Rob them, maybe, but that's about it." And from what I figured, getting mugged didn't typically lead to falling off the face of the earth. "What about the abduction stuff?" I asked.

"I found a handful of cases in the Bay Area, but they were all minors," he said. "Plus, most of them were related to domestic issues. Divorced dads trying to move their kids out of state, that kind of thing. Nothing that seemed like it might have something to do with your dad."

I'd researched the statistics too, and even though it was nice of Beckett to make the effort, I already figured my dad's disappearance had nothing to do with a kidnapping or abduction. There was no reason for anyone to snatch him: He was just a normal guy, our family a normal one before the disappearance.

Eventually Beck asked about the Habitat for Humanity program, the first time it had been mentioned since the campsite and the black eye.

"Have you applied?" he asked. "Is this really happening, or is it just kind of happening? You know, like in your head and not actually in reality?" He cracked his dimples. "Because I'm rooting for the latter."

The bass of the neighbor's radio thumped next door, and somewhere in the distance a car alarm shrieked. I pulled my knees to my chest and tucked my Chuck T's under the hems of my jeans. I'd always had big feet, should have been six feet tall, considering the skis I'd sported since sixth grade, one of the reasons I favored wide legs and boot cuts over the trendy skinny jeans most girls wore.

"Well, you have to be eighteen to volunteer," I told him, "so it can't happen, in reality, until October. I can't apply until then, but there are all kinds of things I can start doing now to be a more competitive applicant."

"Like?"

I should've been tutoring ESL students or volunteering at local homeless shelters—both recommendations in the catalog. So that's what I told him.

"You'd be great at that," he said. "You're honest. And down-to-earth. A hard worker. Plus, you're good at making people comfortable. At making people not feel bad about themselves."

It was nicest thing anyone had said to me in a long time. "Thanks," I said.

And he said, "You got it." And then, "Considering everything that's happened, you seem pretty solid to me. I mean, I'm still annoyed about Portland. But I'm also kind of proud of you for thinking of . . . of something different. Something that's more original and maybe more important than going to college right away."

But I didn't feel very solid or stable. I couldn't turn my brain off from thoughts of that photo from 1906, and I felt like the whole summer would be over before I knew it, and that nothing would have changed.

"You know, it's not like you have to make the decision now," he said. He kicked off his sneakers, cayenne-colored low-tops that I'd helped him pick out on Haight Street a few months earlier after Sunday brunch. "College applications will be due around the same time. Early fall? So apply for both. You don't have to make up your mind right now. Jesus, I'm surprised you can decide what to wear in the morning, with all that's happened." His pale toes wiggled while he talked. "There's no harm in waiting. You're allowed to take your time."

That night, I met Beckett and Jay on the corner of Fillmore and Geary, outside the Boom Boom Room, a gritty club I'd been to a handful of times but not lately. It was an all-ages show and the doors opened at six, but we showed up around nine because everyone who went to clubs knew not to show up on time. So we stood in line, waiting to buy tickets and have our hands marked with a gigantic blue underage X. There were high school girls in belted dresses and ballet flats, boys in beanies and vintage T's, and a group of girls sporting gypsy skirts and hippie apron tops. I scanned the swimming mass of skater kids, girls in prairie dresses like Maddie would've worn if she'd come with us, and hipsters sporting trucker hats and old-school sneakers.

"You're looking for your dad," Beckett said to me. "And I pegged you for a pessimist. You're looking for him everywhere we go."

I shrugged, embarrassed to have been caught. "What good does it do? Searching for someone who isn't here?"

"He's not all you have, you know," he told me. "You have me, too," he said.

I nodded and nudged his shoulder with my shoulder before casting my eyes to the ground.

Inside, the room pulsed, the small space packed with people of all ages, from ours to our parents', the heat of the crowd binding to the sticky floors and dark-colored walls. They were in between bands when we got there, and roadies switched the gear onstage from the opener's to the headliner's. The club played a high-strung electronic track as a filler even though the crowd oozed a mellow vibe and the headliner would be, according to their advertisement, "Jazz with a Drip of Funk." We'd been there about half an hour by the time the band sauntered onstage, a trio of lamppost-thin black guys with matching square-rimmed specs and a moon-faced white woman with a short-haired 1920s swoop.

"Y'all'er looking gorgeous out there," she crooned into the mic, wrapping us around her finger in just one sentence. She wore a short, tight black dress, high-heeled red ankle boots, and silver chandelier earrings that spun the lights exactly the way they should have. She was everything you wanted for the lead vocals in a jazz/funk band.

Jay moved behind Beck and placed his hands on Beck's hips, and I suddenly became a third wheel. So I told Beckett

I'd be back in a few and headed to the bar for a bottle of water. And that's where I ran into Isaac Thompson.

"I think I know you," he said.

"Yeah?" I asked, leaning into the wood corner of the bar, sandwiched between a girl who clearly needed a drink and a girl who clearly did not. "I don't know," I said.

He wore all things nondescript: cords, or maybe they were dark-colored jeans, I couldn't be sure in the lighting; a T-shirt, thin and faded, with the white block letters of a band's name, or maybe a music venue I'd never heard of; black tennis shoes, like Vans or Converse, but missing the swoosh or the star. His hair was short, and his eyes were the clear brown I remembered from fourth grade.

"Okay, maybe not," he said. "I'm pretty terrible when it comes to remembering names and faces."

The bartender tapped her blue fingernail on the counter and said, "Whatcha having?" and Isaac asked for a Fanta. Grape. No glass. And I didn't mean to, but I actually laughed out loud, right there in his face.

And then I said, "Make that two," surprising him and me both.

"Like Kool-Aid," he said. "Liquid sugar."

I nodded. "Like Smarties. Or Fun Dip," I said. I'd always loved the tang of the purple and red and orange flavors caked on those white candy sticks.

We waited, me tugging on my gold horn necklace with one hand and rubbing the glass piece in my pocket with the other, and Isaac watching the crowd. Then the bartender with the fingernails gave us the sodas, and Isaac had a credit card in her hand before I had time to argue.

I should have said "Thank you," or maybe "I can pay for mine," but instead I said, "I'm Callie Pace. You were right. We went to fourth grade together," which didn't sound the way I wanted it to.

"I knew that I knew you," he said.

We tried to move out of the way so the people behind us could order at the bar.

"I'm Callie," I said again, and then: "It's not as good as I wanted it to be," motioning to the Fanta after I took a sip.

"You're crazy," he said. "This stuff is like liquid gold." Big smile. A small gap in his front top teeth. Perfect lips.

"Says who?" I raised an eyebrow skeptically, teasing him.

"Says me. But I'm hooked on sugar like these cats are hooked on booze," he said, motioning to the crowd at the bar competing for the bartender's attention. "So are you here alone?" he asked, and then: "Wow. That sounded unbelievably lame. And maybe a little creepy. I didn't mean it as . . . like, a pickup line or anything," his eyes darting around the room, avoiding mine.

But I was smiling. "It's okay." I told him I was there with

Beckett, the guy who made the whole gig thing happen, real-izing as I talked that Isaac probably didn't know I was part of Nothing Right. The loud music muddled things even more when he asked if Beckett was the manager for the guys on stage. So I shook my head and explained about our band and about Beckett's dad working with his dad and being the one who first recommended us, and did his dad always go by all three names because it was kind of . . . you know, not that I'm making judgments, but it *was* a little bit showy? "All three of them sound good together and stuff. But it's still pretty weird, you know? Using them all. All the time," I said.

He laughed. "Are you always so honest?" which for some reason reminded me that part of my job, always, was keeping tabs on Beck.

I told him, "I've got friends up front. Let's go by the stage." Then we shouldered through the crowd, and I introduced Isaac to Beck and Jay even though the music was too loud for them to hear me.

We stayed there, right in front of the speaker, listening to the warm beats of jazz and the milky-voiced woman singing with the guitars and the drums, until set break. I took men-tal notes, like I always did at shows, memorizing the way the drummer played the stand in a swift one-two, one-two to create a metallic sound for the more frantic parts of the songs. And when the band finally stopped, we hung around talking about how great the music was, how perfect and balanced and clean.

"Fresh air?" Isaac asked, and I nodded, but Beckett and Jay said they needed beverages and headed to the bar.

The night air cooled us off as the audience stumbled out of the club and onto the sidewalk. It smelled like clove cigarettes and crowded-concert sweat, and we walked up to the corner and stood under a lamppost, where we could get a good view of everyone hanging around out front.

"I was sorry to hear about your dad," Isaac said as he pulled a pouch of Big League Chew bubble gum out of his back pocket.

I laughed. "Where'd you find that stuff?" I hadn't seen the shredded pink gum since I was little.

"Like I said, I've got a thing for sugar." He unfolded the top and held it out, offering to share, but I shook my head.

"Do you know anything yet?" he asked. "I mean about your dad?" And then, quickly, "That was nosy, I'm sorry. It's just that I read about it in the newspaper when it happened. My mom has the *Chronicle* sent to us in Paris, and I recognized the name. From you. From school."

"No, it's okay," I said. "It's probably good for me to talk about it, I guess."

And then I told him about the photo.

I told him about the exhibit and buying the book and the picture I couldn't stop staring at. I should've told Beckett first, or maybe my mom. Should have taken the book to her so we could have sat at the kitchen table, talking about how badly we wanted an answer, how sharp and huge that wanting was. So huge that I'd started to wonder if I believed in the unbelievable, in a photo from a hundred years ago. But there was something about Isaac—the vague familiarity from fourth grade, but at the same time the distance of all those years and that ocean between his real home and mine. Maybe it was the distance that made it seem safe to share my secret with him.

"I know it's ridiculous," I said. "And I know it's not him. Obviously. I mean, it can't be. But still, I can't get it out of my head. I keep imagining him there, you know? Envisioning him stuck in this other time period as he tries to make sense of the earthquake, of being somewhere he's not supposed to be."

Even as I recognized the ridiculousness of it, I'd allowed the photo from the art exhibit to become some kind of possibility to cling to, a confirmation that my dad was okay. I'd imagined that even though he wasn't home anymore, he was somewhere. Somewhere infinitely far away and absolutely unreachable, but still, somewhere all the same. Aboveground in 1906. Not in *my* world any longer, but in the world, at least.

"I guess I keep envisioning him there because I don't have anything else," I said. "Besides his backpack, the photo is the only clue I've found."

"His backpack? What backpack?" he asked.

So I told him about the man at the job site too, about having to pay to get my dad's stuff back. And he said exactly what he should have: "That's so screwed, Callie. I'm sorry you had to go through that."

He didn't tell me that I'd lost it, that my dad's image in 1906 was impossible. He didn't say I was being crazy or desperate or any of the things I'd told myself a million times since I'd first seen the photo. Instead he said, "I think there are lots of things people will never figure out. Like the Bermuda Triangle or the Great Pyramid of Giza. Seven Wonders of the World kind of stuff. Lots of things don't have a real explanation. Like the sixth sense. Scientists can't actually explain how or why it works, that gut-feeling thing. But it exists, you can't deny it." He kept going: "Or déjà vu. UFOs. And maybe, people who go missing and never get found."

Isaac was the first person who admitted the possibility that we'd never find my dad. For fifty-two days, everyone kept saying we'd locate him eventually; surely we'd track him down or he'd turn up. But Isaac Thompson looked me right in the face and said it out loud: There were people who went missing and never got found. And that meant there was a chance my dad might be one of them. Because the truth was, lots of people disappeared without a trace.

"Maybe time is one of those things too," he said. "The

possibility of parallel universes. Or quantum jumping. We don't really know how everything works. There are tons of things science still can't explain."

In front of the club, the crowd thinned out as people headed inside for the second set, but we just stood there, quiet for a while.

And then he said, "Do you know about the Taos Hum?" I shook my head. "It's this low-pitched sound heard in locations all over the world. Usually only in quiet places, though, in peaceful spots like the Big Island and Taos, New Mexico. They say up to five percent of the population can hear it. A soft drone, this low-frequency noise thing that can't be picked up on recording devices. Some people claim there's a vibration, an actual physical buzz they feel, too." He pulled a receipt out of his pocket and folded his gum in it. "Sorry, that was gross."

I shrugged and said, "What causes it? The noise?"

"Well, that's the whole point. Some doctor in New Zealand recently recorded it. Said it peaked at a frequency of fifty-six hertz. He proved it exists, but there's still no explanation. It's just this phenomenon, you know? With no known cause. Some people blame it on the auditory or nervous system. Others say it's related to the ocean floor, some infrasonic wave thing," he said, and I raised my eyebrows. "I know. I'm kind of nerdy about science stuff," he added.

I wondered if I would have caught him blushing had the light been better.

"Some people attribute it to this thing called spontaneous otoacoustic emissions," he continued, talking faster. "Where the ears generate their own sounds. But the Taos Hum happens in regional clusters, and the ear thing has been recorded with equal frequency in all age groups and locations. Plus, the guy in New Zealand verified its existence. Essentially, there is no answer. An unknown. I think there are lots of unknowns, and maybe your dad going missing is . . . is one of those."

But I didn't want my dad to become an Unknown, and I said so.

"So that's just it," he told me. "Maybe you get to decide. Maybe it's your job to make sure he doesn't become an Unknown. And the earthquake image is a way to do that. What if those things you're imagining aren't just in your imagination?"

I shook my head. "Like what? Like visions or something?" It sounded absurd coming out of my mouth, and I said so. "That's impossible."

Isaac shrugged. "Who knows? Parallel-universe stuff? Another realm or dimension, some other past that's actually happening now, too? And somehow you're tapping into it through the visions. There's probably a better word for it, but all I'm saying is, you don't really know."

"That's insane," I said.

"It most definitely is," he said. And then: "Insane and completely impossible. But maybe not." He shrugged. "Maybe it's totally possible. I'm just saying, if you decide to believe in the photo, then your dad's whereabouts won't be a mystery anymore." And then he said, "And it's not like you have to decide right away. There's no harm in waiting to make the call."

He cracked his knuckles and dropped his eyes like he was nervous he'd said too much.

"Hey, Isaac," I said. "Hey, you," so that he was finally looking at me again when I thanked him.

"What are you thanking me for?" he asked.

"For not making me feel like a crazy person. For letting me tell you the truth. For being honest about the fact that my dad might not ever come back. And even for that gross grape soda."

He smiled, those huge brown eyes staring right at me. "Anytime, Callie Pace, anytime," he said as we walked back toward the club together.

CHAPTER TWELVE

Image 15B: "Untitled (Woman greeting mounted soldier), 1906."
Cellulose nitrate negative, 149 × 84 mm irreg.

He digs for bodies. Tracing voices under debris, he finds a mother and daughter in matching dresses, with high-boned starched collars above dirt-streaked sashes; the two young sons of the owner of the hotel, one alive and one not; and an infant sucking a bottle, sweat-drenched and pink from the heat.

It arrives in waves—the numbness that allows him to work as if the figures in the rubble are not real, not actual fingers and elbows and toes. There are times of mindlessness that come with physical labor, as though he were a machine, iron levers and chain-covered gears lifting the bricks and bodies one by one. And then, unexpectedly, he finds a brass button from a coat painted with blood, still damp and sticky to the touch, and he stumbles away to seek refuge behind a wall, where he retches the yellow bile that has been churning in his gut for hours.

William directs the volunteers, asking the women to tie handkerchiefs around wounds while the men stand under dangling power lines and continue digging.

"Dig," William says over and over again, so that it becomes white noise, a simple tempo marking time while neighboring buildings fall and crumble around them.

The hot stink of smoke weighs on the city while they work through the morning hours, and the man falls into the physical exertion of digging, tugging out bodies, and carrying the dead to one side of the street, leading survivors to the other. Digging, tugging, carrying.

Those who have been rescued cough dust as they rise to stand and eye the chaos. He thinks of wild animals as they claw at him, frantic and hungry for information. "What's happened?" they ask. "Help me," they say. "Find them. . . . My father. My wife. My son is somewhere inside."

It goes on like this until his arms shake and his undershirt drips with perspiration. The sun hovers above them, and each time the wind blows, he can taste it: the smoke and the scent of hair and skin smoldering.

He finds two young girls in the debris, still warm but lifeless, their fingers splayed over their eyes as if they are looking into the sun. The man squats to scoop the first girl from the ground, and he gently folds her hands over her chest, but when he moves to lift her, his arms are shaking too badly.

"I'll do it," William says. "Take a rest."

The man crosses the street to sit and wishes, again, for a jug of water. His palms burn, and when he flips them over, he sees that his fingers are callused and his cuticles are caked with dirt. He imagines he is part of the working middle class, though he can't recall what it is he does for employment.

A woman approaches, retying her white apron around the waist of her long black dress as she walks. Her sand-colored hair has come lose from under her cap, her face is streaked with ash, and her black stockings are torn, but she's beautiful still. The man stands when she reaches him and asks if she needs help.

"I suppose we all do now, don't we?" she says, and then, "Do you mind?" She holds out her hand and he takes it so she can use him to steady her balance as she lowers herself to the curb. "Well, go ahead," she says, motioning next to her, and he sits as well.

"You were in the hotel?" he asks, and she nods.

"I work in the café. The late shift. It's popular with the newspapermen, since we stay open all night," she tells him, and nods to a group of men hovering in front of the hotel, men in suits and dark-colored ties, some with notepads tucked into the front pockets of their jackets, others with their pens and jotters in hand. "The reporters drink and play cards here until five, six in the morning," she says. "It's a good job, the waitressing. Smart customers and insider information about the city if you pay attention."

The man nods as one of the young journalists crosses the street and heads toward them.

"Beatrice," the reporter says, tipping his cap first to the woman and then to the man. "A word? Do you mind, sir? A statement, please?"

"I'm not sure I can tell you anything," the man says.

"You were in the building when the quake hit?"

"No. Not me," he says. "I'm just here to help."

But the reporter presses on. "Your family, then? Are they inside?"

"I can't be certain," he says, recognizing the truth. "I don't remember a thing."

Next to him the waitress sighs. "Leave him be, James."

The journalist scratches on his notepad. "I hear they're setting up a makeshift hospital at Mechanics' Pavilion. You could try there if you don't find your family here." He finishes writing and tucks his pencil behind his ear before turning and crossing the street.

"See them?" the waitress says.

The man follows her eyes to a woman, thin and soft, easily defeated, if he has to imagine a flaw. Next to her a young girl, stubborn and confident in her stance—the daughter, he guesses. The two are at once familiar, and he tries to place them. Neighbors, perhaps, though he's not sure where his neighborhood is, exactly. The wife and child of a friend, maybe.

"I served them hot chocolate late last night in the café," she tells him. "They told me they were visiting San Francisco to see *Carmen* at the Grand Opera House, all the way from Los Angeles. Caruso stole the show, they said. The curtain call lasted twelve minutes."

He watches the woman adjust her flounce skirt and the girl, who has crouched down and is fooling with the tie on her boot.

"I'd bet they hardly remember the show now," the waitress says.

Just before eight o'clock, army troops arrive and instruct the volunteers to clear out of the area. William argues, pick in hand, that there are still people buried in the wreckage. He can hear their voices crying under the debris, waiting. But the troops report fires raging on Sixth Street, and the neighborhood must be emptied. Columns of smoke rise around them as men in military uniforms from the California National Guard ride through on horses, shouting orders.

The man and William are wordless as they walk the city streets under the hot, heavy air.

Eventually William confesses that he looks for his younger brother in each passing stranger. "An artist," William says. "A young man, only twenty last month. A wanderer who was sleeping in a warehouse on Folsom Street, last I heard."

The man nods and wonders how he would describe his own siblings if he were to speak of them to William, but discovers no memory of brothers or sisters—he is an only child, he assumes. He recalls Italian opera music playing during dinnertime while his mother stood in the kitchen, cooking eggplant Parmesan. And Catholic mass at midnight on Christmas Eve, the three of them, he and his parents sliding into a pew and flipping the pages of a hymnbook.

"You'll help me?" William asks as they step out of the street and onto the sidewalk to make way for a collection of army men on horseback. "You'd be willing to help me look for my brother?"

Automatically the man says, "Of course. We'll stick together and keep searching until we find him. You and I both," he tells William.

It is there, in that declaration, that he finds a purpose in the chaos, and in that purpose the man finds his first glimmer of hope.

CHAPTER THIRTEEN

Fifty-five Days After

On Sunday, Beck and I met at Squat & Gobble: He'd spent most of the weekend with Jay, and I'd spent most of mine memorizing the photos from the San Francisco art book and researching the 1906 earthquake online.

"Better," I said when he asked how my mom was doing.

Which wasn't necessarily true, but wasn't necessarily *not* true, either. I wasn't exactly sure how she was doing, because we hadn't been talking as much as we used to—there was a vague and uncomfortable tension lurking at home. When we were both at the house, we mostly watched old movies or hung around the living room, her reading the paper and me reading historical websites.

"It's like my dad being gone dug this weird hole between

us," I confessed as I emptied another packet of sugar into my coffee mug. "Like now that it's not three of us, our family doesn't make sense anymore," I said, realizing that when my mom and I did talk, it was often about takeout for dinner or what time I'd be home after band practice. "It's like we can't figure out how it works with just the two of us."

Before, family rituals went like this: Dinner at six o'clock— Mom at the stove or Dad grilling out on the fire escape, me washing the dishes after, complaining but not really minding it all that much. Saturday matinees—a small popcorn with extra butter for Dad, Milk Duds, Raisinets, and Cokes for me and Mom. Or trips to the museums when nothing good was playing at the movie theater. Bike rides to Ocean Beach to watch surfers catch the evening waves. Or Sunday-morning pancakes with chocolate chips before my dad and I would take one of his motorcycles up north. She opened report cards first, and he helped regulate her new rules if my grades weren't as high as they wanted them to be. He popped the popcorn for movie nights at home, old-school-style, in the frying pan with oil, while Mom mixed the garlic salt and Parmesan and I poured the drinks. On Tuesday nights I was in charge of gathering all the trash in the house, and he'd take it to the garbage can and pull it into the alley, where the trucks picked them up in the morning.

After, family rituals went like this: Footsteps in different rooms and our voices calling to each other from across the house to pick up the phone, turn down the television, or turn in for bed. Lots and lots of delivery food. We missed trash pickup the first two weeks Dad was gone.

"I miss her, you know?" I told Beck. "The normal her, I mean. The normal us. I'll catch glimpses of it sometimes," I said, thinking of the Books Inc. event. "But it kind of feels like work when we're together. Like we're thinking too hard about what to say. And not say. I miss hanging around, talking about nothing, making dinner or running errands. It feels like we're walking on eggshells, and I'm not even sure why. I want to fix it, but I haven't figured out how. It's like I'm not sure who she really is without him," I said.

"She's probably not sure anymore either," he said.

Behind us, in another booth, a baby started crying, and when I turned to the window, I spotted one of the Haight Street street kids setting up camp on the opposite corner. He laid out a patchwork quilt and began unloading his backpack. I imagined hemp necklaces and bumper stickers reading MAKE ART, NOT WAR or RUN, HILLARY, RUN. If my dad had been there, he would have bought the Clinton sticker, not because he liked advertising his politics, but because he had a rule about street kids on Haight: He wouldn't give them money, but he'd always buy at least one thing. That's how I ended up with three Hacky Sacks I never used and nine bootleg cassette tapes of Phish shows I never listened to.

"The roles are all mixed up," I said as Beckett joined the Clean Plate Club with his last forkful of garlic potatoes. "I feel like I should be taking care of her now, but I don't know how."

"But you're trying, right? To talk to her about it?" he asked mid-chew.

"Kind of. There's not that much to say, really."

"Um. Your dad became an unsolved mystery a few months ago. Hello. I think there'd be a crapload to say about that." He reached over and nudged my plate toward me. "Go on. Eat up, waify," he said. "Don't think I haven't noticed you're dropping L.B.s like it's going out of style."

I slid my fists into the pockets of my hoodie and rubbed the piece of glass as I eyed the new hole on my belt. I'd added it that morning with a nail and hammer in the garage.

"You and your mom should be talking about how sad you are. Or how pissed and confused you feel," Beck said. "It's, like, the most dramatic thing a kid could go through, right? It's emotional stuff, and it'd probably be good for you—for you both, really—to talk it over."

"I talk to you," I said, and I could have said, "I talked to Isaac Thompson about it too," but I didn't. I was still trying to decide how horrific of an idea that had been, still trying to figure out how on earth it made sense to me that night to tell him about the photo and the way I'd been imagining my dad stuck in 1906. Isaac probably thought I was insane, straight out of the crazy house. Part of me kept waiting for Rabbit to tell us he'd gotten a call from Philip Cory Thompson saying that he'd changed his mind—he didn't want to hire Nothing Right for the party anymore. I worried I'd put our first real gig at risk by opening my big mouth and spewing my secret to the first boy I'd really noticed since the whole Andrew Parker disaster.

"I will always have an ear for you, my friend," Beckett said. "But you should talk to your mom, too. She's the only person who's going through exactly what you are."

Afterward, I headed to the library on Larkin Street to spend the day researching the 1906 earthquake.

"Errands for my mom. Boring stuff. Too boring to subject you to," I lied to Beckett when we went our separate ways at the bus stop.

I'd been to the library lots of times as a kid with my parents, but besides a few trips for school research papers that required us to use non-online sources, I didn't visit all that often. I'm not sure why—it's a gorgeous building right near the Civic Center, with lots of windows and tables and opportunities for people-watching, which I loved to do. But that day I headed straight for the computers to check the online catalog and start collecting materials. I'd taken my dad's Post-it pad from his backpack and wrote down the location of any book, video, or article about the quake, and after an hour of gathering, my arms shaking under a pile of dusty hardbacks and DVDs, I found a seat by the window, dropped my bag on the carpet, and curled up in the wide armchair to start reading, not sure exactly what I was looking for but certain I was on the right track. Intuition—that gut feeling thing Isaac talked about.

It was horrible, the footage of the wreckage and the stories from those who survived it. All afternoon, I looked through photos, articles, and letters recounting the event. The books were separated into a "Check out and bring home" pile and a "Skip" stack, and then I added all the videos to the "Check out" load so I could start watching them that night. I took notes in the leftover pages of my writing composition book from last semester, the black-and-white-marbled cover ripped and graffitied with Sharpie sketches that matched the ones on my Converse shoes. I wrote down the last names of people who had been there, names from scanned telegraphs and journal entries. I made lists of streets that had been split up the center like a torn piece of cardboard, buildings that had telescoped into themselves, and parks that had served as refugee camps.

I didn't find him there, of course not: not in the video clips or the panoramic images of the aftermath online, not in the black-and-white shots or in the catalogs of names of the deceased and of survivors who recorded their stories.

We were never a family who played hide-and-go-seek. In San Francisco, houses are too small to stay indoors, so we spent weekends on foot, exploring parks and museums, hiking in the redwoods or setting up camp at the beach and watching the surfers. In the city, you have to keep an eye out: stay close at the Farmer's Market and hold hands on the crowded sidewalks; stick together at Golden Gate concerts, the audience dense and hectic, easily engulfing stragglers. Fisherman's Wharf, Ocean Beach, the Botanical Garden, or the San Francisco Pride Parade, the first rule was always "Make sure you can see me." If I could see my father, that meant he could see me. On the playground, in the ocean, in line for candy and sodas at the movie theater. We never hid from one another.

"Make sure you can see me," he'd say. OverAndOverAnd Over every time we left the house.

The night I'd seen Isaac at the Boom Boom Room, he told me there'd be about a hundred and fifty people at his dad's house for the party, and the truth was, Nothing Right wasn't ready to perform in front of that kind of crowd, so on Monday we started a new regimen.

"We have less than three weeks," Maddie said, because they'd decided to have the party the weekend before July Fourth even though Isaac's birthday was June 30. "So every day," she said. "*Every. Day.* We practice every day. Agreed?"

Rabbit and I both said, "Agreed."

We decided to meet at seven every night no matter what—

even on days I was scheduled to work for Lori, or on afternoons Rabbit was in charge of his million little brothers and sisters, or on Saturdays when Maddie had knitting class, something she'd started that summer.

"What?" she said, when she first told us about the course. "It's DIY, and I love that stuff."

Maddie told Rabbit that if he didn't start showing up to practice on time, she was going to stop making out with him, which worked perfectly in terms of motivation, and we aimed to play for at least three hours a night, including two breaks for hydrating and peeing. That was it. No chitchat. No yo-yo tricks. No talking about movies we'd seen or arguments we'd had with our parents. No screwing around.

"This is our main focus," Maddie said, "except for your dad, I mean."

On a good night, this is how it went: Maddie would leave the front door unlocked, so we'd let ourselves in, the sound of her strumming whispered below the floorboards as we walked through the house. In the basement by 7:05, the amp humming and the PA system growing warm. Me behind the drum set, sticks tapping on skin, gently at first, while Rabbit unpacked his gig bag, then hooked up his bass. Maddie, one measure, two, a melody in her throat as she faced me, the mic off and her voice blunted by the sounds of my drums while we warmed up, trying to read one another eye to eye through the thumps and vibrations. Me finding a beat to match her tempo. My foot tapping one-two, one-two by the time Rabbit's guitar joined us. His notes and my beats and her voice . . . and when I found the right roll, I'd open the snare, the sound swelling and the music taking shape just as Maddie would turn away from me, flip on the mic, and begin the first line of the first song of the night. The only hours of the day that felt really good.

Later that week I came home from running to shower before practice and my mom was in the kitchen making dinner, the first time I could remember a home-cooked meal since Before.

"Sit," she said when I came in, so I did.

Eggplant Parmesan and garlic bread, his favorite.

"Is it Dad?" I asked. "Did you hear something? Something's been found?" But she shook her head.

She stood with her back to me as she poured the angel-hair pasta into the colander in the sink, the steam so thick I could almost feel the wet heat from where I sat.

"You look thin," she said. "I wanted to make sure you got a good meal before you left for band practice."

Food hadn't tasted right in a long time. The flavors were too bland, like chewing water, or, at other times, the smells were too sharp, the spices turning my taste buds into ripe swollen wounds or slashing open a headache behind my eyes, a reel of nausea. Sometimes I simply never thought of eating.

"You sleeping okay?" she asked, and I nodded. I'd been sleeping like a rock star, nine or ten hours, though on the afternoons I didn't work for Lori, I mostly slept through the day. It was hard to calm myself down when it was dark out, knowing the nightmares would come as soon as I slipped, so I stayed up reading San Francisco history books and watching videos until the sun rose, and then I'd sleep until four or five(ish) at night. A long run and then band practice. Start all over again.

"You seem distracted," she said. "Distracted and a bit distant. I thought it would be good to sit down for a real dinner together." The pasta went back into the pot and the eggplant and bread came out of the oven as the smell of tomatoes, garlic, and basil filled the space between us.

We sat across from each other, the table feeling huge with Dad's chair empty like that, and she dished the food onto the plates for us both, filling mine with enough food for three.

"That's too much," I said when she dipped the spoon into the pan of sauce and eggplant for the third time.

She shook her head, mumbled, "Sorry." A sigh. A long pause while she watched me push the food around on my plate. "It's just that I fear you're shutting me out, Cal," she said eventually, stumbling on her words a little. "That you're . . . I don't know. That you're pushing me away instead of leaning on me for help."

I wanted to feel completely aligned with her—Beckett was

right, she was the only one who was going through exactly what I was—but there was a vague resentment I couldn't shake. The way I figured it, she should have tried harder to find him once he'd disappeared. She should have done more to fix it.

"I'm not trying to," I said finally. "Trying to shut you out. I've just been busy, is all." I could have told her then about the photo and all the research I'd been doing, but I couldn't bear the risk. Her thinking I'd gone crazy, or feeling sorry for me for being so desperate for an answer that I'd begun to imagine him in another world, another time. That I'd begun to see things in photos that weren't really there.

"It's good you're working and running, still. It's good you've got the band, too." She reached for the pepper grinder. "But I just hope the . . . the distance between us is . . . short-term," she said finally.

The word bounced behind my eyes, unrolling itself. Short-term: a relatively brief period of time. I wondered if Dad being part of us, if our family of three, would eventually be defined as short-term. Or if this gap of life without him would soon be called short-term instead. The difference like air and water, like closed and open.

"I don't know how to fix this," she said, dropping her fork on her plate and looking at all that extra food, and then at the empty chair, his chair, usually clothed by his vest and brown backpack.

"I don't think you can," I told her, and she shook her head, ready to try to change my mind, but I kept talking. "I just mean that the only way to fix it is to bring him back. So I'm trying to do that," and then, "and I'm sure you are too"—a lie because she hadn't done anything really, hadn't searched for him at all, not since she first filed the report with the police. I looked at my fork, the placemat, my hands. "Even if he did come back now, everything's shifted. Everything feels different. It can't really be undone." I raised my eyes to meet hers. "How do you fix fifty-seven days?"

We ate for a while, silverware panning through puddles of sauce. The food was rich and hot and heavy, but I did my best to eat enough so she wouldn't worry so much.

Eventually she said, "I have, you know. Tried to find him. I've read his e-mails for clues, read them all at least a dozen times. I searched through his papers and files, all his things from the office and everything he kept here, too."

I nodded, even though it was news to me. I imagined her digging through his desk drawers and pulling out clumps of hair, fingernail clippings, or old rusted compasses from a hundred years ago, and three thousand pairs of cracked wire-rimmed glasses.

"I contacted his friends, even the old ones I never knew," she said. "Buddies from before we got together. And every other afternoon, at two o'clock, I call the police station for an update, but really just to keep our name in front of them, because they never have an update. They keep saying nothing's changed." She had one hand around her glass of water while the other gripped her fork, white knuckled, but I could see her shaking still.

I thought of the backpack she didn't know about, stashed in the garage. I knew if I told her about it, she'd make me turn it over to the police; she'd always believed in doing what you were supposed to. But it was the last thing he'd left behind, the one real thing that still connected my dad to me, and I didn't want to give it up.

Plus, I knew the statistics: "The federal government counted 840,279 missing-persons cases in 2001. All but about 50,000 were juveniles, classified as anyone younger than 18." The police had their hands full tracking kids. A grown man gone missing after work one day just didn't make the priority list. And I'd run it over in my head a hundred times, all of it—the Post-it notes, the Cliff Bar wrappers, the tube of Chap Stick, and unsharpened pencil—even the ripped transfer ticket. It all added up to nothing. No real information.

My mother sighed. "I know you don't think I'm doing enough. I know that you're angry, and I don't blame you. Not one bit. But it's been the longest two months of my life, Callie. You're not the only one struggling. Lori recommended a therapist. I think I may call next week."

I imagined her biting her fingers off one by one on a

long brown couch while a man sat by a window, taking notes, watching her chew herself like a cannibal. My throat tightened and my eyes filled with wetness—the whole thing was so unbelievably miserable.

"He'd hate it, you know. Us sitting around on hold. That's what I think of most. How he'd want us to keep going, to keep moving forward," she said.

But this is what I knew: He'd never want the two of us at the table instead of three. He'd never want to miss out on people-watching the summer crowd in the Botanical Garden. He'd never want to miss my first real gig with Nothing Right.

"I've seen the flyers you posted," she said. "And I know you and your friends called his coworkers. Danny at the office e-mailed me a while back and mentioned it."

But the calls had gotten us nowhere. Just like the flyers and the trips to the job site and all those stupid homeless shelters.

"That's good of you. Brave," she said. "And stubborn. Determined. You always matched his Taurus sign more than your Libra. Always more like your dad than me, I guess."

I thought of the road trip to Seattle the summer before I turned seven. We'd spent three days driving north, and somewhere along the way my baby blanket, a small yellow scrap of fabric I hadn't outgrown but should've by then, somewhere it'd gotten lost on the road. At a rest stop maybe, it slipped out the door when I was unhooking my seat belt and rushing from the car to the vending machine. Or at a restaurant, an overlook on Highway 1. When we realized it was gone, my mother and father argued: he, convinced we could find it if we only turned around and retraced our steps; she, certain there'd be plenty of places in Seattle to buy a new blanket or, better yet, viewing it as a sign that it was time for me to retire the habit.

"We can't turn around," she said, arms crossed as the three of us stood in a parking lot filled with Mack trucks and SUVs and minivans. "We can't." Poker-faced, but a kind voice when she bent down and said, "Listen, baby, it'll be okay. We have to keep going, though. You'll see. It'll be okay, Callan. Chin up."

In the end, we drove forward, and I wondered, as I sat there at dinner with her, if it had been her turn that time, her turn to make the final call when they disagreed about a decision about me. She was logical and rational, while he'd been an idealist—like she'd said, like me.

"I want to find him too," she said. "You know that, right?"

I nodded. My fingers rubbing, always rubbing the piece of glass in my pocket.

"But I guess part of me, the coward part, worries that having no clues and no information for this long means . . . I guess I'm worried it might mean that he"—her voice bottomed out and she shook her head, letting the sentence fall between us on the table with a weighted silence.

"He's not dead," I told her, and she said, "I know. That's

not what I'm saying. I don't think he's dead either, Callie."

We both knew that if we acknowledged that as a possibility, it would mean we'd given up hope. That we'd been defeated, us and him both. And that wasn't an option.

But her hesitation was written in the zigzag of her eyebrows as she shifted in her seat. She was worried he might have left us. Like everyone else except me, she wondered if he'd chosen it, if he'd actually walked away.

After practice that night, I camped out in my room with *The Great San Francisco Earthquake* again, an hour-long DVD I'd been watching and rewatching ever since I found it at the library. It was horrific, the dust and destruction, the heartbreak of families torn apart when the quake hit. Firestorms raced through the city, and I'd pause the film to study the faces of the survivors riding in horse-drawn buggies, survivors drifting by railroad tracks, and in cars with canvas canopies—rickety windowless vehicles, hardly cars at all. Men in suits and women in long, full dresses stood in front of slanted houses, busted windows behind them and piles of debris at their feet. In the background, the film ran a soundtrack of murmuring voices, a baby crying, a dog's bark echoing like a drum.

And every time I closed my eyes, I saw him there. Clean, sharp images I couldn't shake.

I eyed a train lying next to the track, flipped on its side as if someone had picked it up and set it back down in the wrong place. As if it was were a toy.

For more than two hundred miles along the San Andreas Fault, the crust of the earth slipped as much as twenty-one feet.

It seemed just as impossible as my father leaving for work one day and never coming home.

In addition to all the destruction in the city, eight thousand people were left homeless in San Jose, the same town my dad took me to on his motorcycle one afternoon, so we could spend the day at the Lick Observatory on the summit of Mount Hamilton. He'd always had a thing for telescopes and said if he hadn't decided to pick a job working with dirt, he would have picked a job working with the sky.

The earthquake had been the largest national disaster suffered in a major American city, and I wondered if we were due. How much time, on average, tended to pass between events like that? Like the impact of six million tons of TNT, the video said, twelve thousand times the power of the atomic bomb exploding over Hiroshima. My heart raced as I watched those images while I rubbed the piece of glass with one hand and clutched the remote control with the other.

But then the phone rang, and I stopped the movie, took a deep breath, and reached for the cordless on my nightstand.

It was Isaac Thompson on the other end of the line. And his phone voice mimicked his live voice from what I remembered, only he kept doing this weird thing where he raised his voice at the end of each sentence like he was asking a question.

"Hey, Callie?" he said. "This is Isaac? From the other night? Isaac Thompson?"

"Hey," I said, and he said, "You busy or do you have time to talk?"

He'd gotten my number from Beckett after I'd left the club that night and hoped it was okay that he called. He'd had a good time. Had wondered if we'd run into one another again before his party, but figured it'd be easier to call.

"To make sure that we did. Run into each other, I mean?"

I picked lint from my comforter while he talked, noticing how sweaty my palms were. It had been a while, the inevitable first-phone-call awkwardness thing.

"You still there?" he asked, and I said, "I'm here."

We talked about the show and who'd be playing the Boom Boom Room later that month. He asked about me and about how I spent my time during the summer, but he already knew about the band, so I told him about running to train for the track team and how much I liked seeing the city that way, on foot as I looped through the streets and Golden Gate Park.

"Besides playing music, it's my favorite way to clear my head," I told him.

I also talked about working for Lori, and when I asked about him, he told me he spent three days a week filing records and answering phones at his dad's office. No pay—an internship, he said.

"Worse than boring," he added. "Worse than worse than boring. There's nothing rewarding about it." In France, though, he helped the sound guys at a jazz cub. "It's a real good vibe," he said.

And I wanted, more than anything in that moment, just to leave. To follow him back to Paris and make everything new. Start my travels there. Jazz clubs and coffee shops, cathedrals and bookshops, art museums and the Seine, a water highway always in motion.

Eventually I asked Isaac about his dad's place and what the setup for his party would be like.

"There's plenty of space, don't worry," he said. "Plus, the area we'll use as the stage is in front a wall of windows with a great view. It should make for some pretty good photos. All rock-star-like. It'll be perfect, I promise."

And then, finally, he asked if I wanted to do something on Saturday. "I want to take you to Fisherman's Wharf because it's totally touristy and predictable," he said. "The epitome of tackiness, right?"

I should have hated Fisherman's Wharf. The crowds and overpriced trinket stores and kitschy shops. The tourists who inevitably don't dress warm enough for our city, who tugged crying kids behind them on leashes, their SLR cameras hanging around their necks or their compact digitals tucked into fanny packs, wearing San Francisco sweatshirts bought right there on the corner. But in truth I loved Fisherman's Wharf. I loved the people-watching and the smell of the boiled crabs drifting from the seafood stands, the sound of the cable cars dinging over the noise of the crowd. I even liked the Ripley's Believe It Or Not! Museum. It was my embarrassing secret—I liked it just as much as the out-of-town gapers did. Not that Isaac could have known that.

But I'd already started sharing my secrets with him by then, so I said, "Oh yeah? Fisherman's Wharf, huh? I love that place," hoping he could hear me smile through the telephone wires.

"Yep. Crab chowder in sourdough-bread bowls. An Alcatraz tour with those germ-infested earphones and all. The works. I like to make sure I get a full dose of sightseeing when I'm here every summer."

I glanced at the TV screen, the sepia photo of a gigantic building burning, and I decided that Fisherman's Wharf was exactly what I needed. I hadn't planned on it, and he probably hadn't realized it, either, but in some strange and surprising way Isaac Thompson knew that I needed to be rescued. Even if just for a day.

CHAPTER FOURTEEN

Sixty-four Days After

The next week was clean-the-jewelry week at Lori's, so we spent my Tuesday shift in her kitchen, a large room with a countertop wrapped around the perimeter and a freestanding island in the middle. She stood at the island and unpacked and wiped down all the pieces, inspecting them for any damage or wear and tear, while I stood at the sink, dropping each piece into a Tupperware of diluted lemon-scented ammonia to soak. I used a toothbrush to scrub the stones, and then I'd rinse and lay them on the runner of dish towels spread on the counter. She'd inspect them again to make sure nothing needed to be run through twice. It was good: Because we'd known each other for so long and didn't mind working in silence, there was no pressure to chat. Before, that is.

"You seem a little better today," she said, and I said, "Yeah, I guess."

I'd been thinking of Isaac when she said it, and then I felt immediately crappy for thinking of Isaac instead of thinking of my dad. But when I thought of my dad, I felt worse than ever, so it was kind of a no-win situation.

She passed me a handful of bracelets, her signature piece, the metal twisted and wound with wire that was threaded with different patterns of stones and pearls. Each pattern had a name: Compassion, white coin pearls and crystals; Peaceful, turquoise and corrugated beads; Dance, amazonite discs and long, flat freshwater pearls. It was the clasp that people loved most about the bracelets, though—a custom twist thing she'd come up with when she first started working as an artist, a design that made it easy to put the bracelet on yourself so you didn't have to ask your husband or boyfriend or whoever to help you. I guess that was a huge deal for some women, the appeal of being able to put on your own accessories. People went nuts over that clasp. And she made all different sizes, so you could always find one that fit right, small wristed or big-boned, Lori made sure everyone could wear her work. She was smart that way, and thoughtful.

She wore a tank top and one of her long hippie skirts that day, and it was hot in the kitchen even though we had all the windows open, so she pulled the bottom up and tied it in a knot at her hip while she talked. "Your mom told me about you taking a year off after graduation to travel. You're thinking of volunteering with Habitat?" she asked. "There are a lot of people in the world not nearly as fortunate as us, and working for an organization like that is a noble choice."

I nodded and said "Thanks," but really I felt like a con. When I'd been thinking of the international programs, I'd been thinking of myself, of how great it would be to be far away, doing something no one I knew had done. I hadn't really been thinking of the people who needed help—hadn't thought of them first, at least.

"I just haven't found a program at any of the state schools that I'd want to study, you know?" I said, hands unhooking each bracelet before dropping them in the solution. "And then I was thinking, if I don't know what I want to study, maybe I shouldn't be going to college yet in the first place. Why rush getting there if I'm not sure what I'll do once I arrive?" I swished the Tupperware liquid around and picked up the toothbrush to begin scrubbing.

"You can learn a lot by traveling, Callie." Lori had a fistful of earrings in her palm that she held up to her face as she squinted. She shook her head and said, "These have faded. The store must have been displaying them in direct sunlight." And then, as she began popping off the backings and dropping them into one bowl and the earrings into another, she finished her first thought with, "You can also learn a lot in college. Even in colleges that aren't in Portland."

I told her it wasn't about Portland. "It's weird. Initially, it was about wanting something totally different than"—I motioned with the toothbrush to the space around me—"this. But then this"—repeat motion—"became something different when my dad disappeared." I tried to think of a way to explain the simple fact of just wanting to go. That maybe there didn't need to be Some Big Concrete Reason. Maybe I just wanted to move to another country because it would mean moving to another country. It would mean exploring something new.

I'd finished rinsing the bracelets and was waiting for the next batch to clean, a collection of necklaces she eyed one by one with her magnifying glass. "I just want to . . . broaden my worldview," I told her, wondering if I'd lifted the phrase from one of the pamphlets or websites. "I want to live in another culture. I want to be somewhere completely unfamiliar and exciting. I think it'd be good for me. To see other places."

"Preaching to the choir, Cal. It's your mom you've got to convince," she said.

Isaac picked me up on Wednesday around noon, but in a city where most kids don't have cars, "picking me up" meant taking the bus to my house, meeting me there, and then paying for our bus fare to Fisherman's Wharf. He looked good, like he tried a little but not too much. He wore his dark hair short, a nice break from the floppy mess a lot of the boys in school sported, and product free, no gel or any of that sculpting cream stuff. He'd picked a gray T-shirt with something written in French on it worn over a black thermal long-sleeve and the kind of jeans that were sort of casual but nice-looking too, not sloppy. Black tennis shoes and a metal bracelet. Simple. He smelled spicy when I opened the door, like cedar or sage, and I was glad I'd stopped in the kitchen and put a few drops of vanilla behind my ears before he came over. A trick my grandmother taught me when she decided I was old enough to start thinking about things like smelling nice.

I'd ended up picking my wide-legged jeans and flip-flops to wear, but I borrowed a shirt from Maddie, a white short-sleeved peasant blouse she said was too hippie for her style. And I made sure to shower early enough in the day so that my hair was dry and I could wear it down.

"Hey, you look great," Isaac said when I came outside after he'd rung the bell.

I mumbled "Hey" without looking at him and forgot to say "Thank you."

We walked toward the bus stop and he apologized for not having a car. "Maybe on the way back I'll spring for a taxi," he said. "You know, upscale-like."

But it was no big deal—I liked riding the bus—and when

we took our seats, he let me have the window, like he knew that's what I wanted even though I hadn't said so. Except for a few teenagers in the back, it was mostly empty, since it was still business hours.

We sat about six inches apart, me looking out at the street at first, trying to think of and failing to find something interesting to say, but he nudged me eventually and said, "Don't look so serious. This is a fun thing. It's just me."

Just me. But it was too soon to know what that meant. He was the kid who had moved away, and even though we all pretended we knew him well enough to report I.S.s with authority and imagine what his life was like, the truth was, I didn't know him at all. *Just me.* Sitting six inches to my left with those perfect brown eyes. I wiped my palms on my jeans and tried to smile.

He'd been kind of quiet back in fourth grade, but he must have grown out of it because he took the lead and filled the time talking about how bad work was that week—"like slit-my-wrist boring"—and how his dad had left that morning for a business trip—"it's nice to have the house to myself sometimes." He told me he hated the time difference between Paris and San Francisco and that he didn't get to talk to his mom as much as he'd like to during the summertime. "She's nine hours ahead of me, so when she called this morning, I was eating breakfast and she was already finished with work for the day. Isn't that weird?"

Every so often, he'd do this funny thing and crack his jaw when he ran out of things to say. He'd open his mouth so wide I probably could have seen his tonsils if I was sitting in front of instead of next to him, wide enough for me to think of cartoon characters like the Muppets or the Road-runner if his beak came unhinged. I'd hear the pop, a small air-filled explosion inside his mouth, and then he'd close his lips. Maybe he had that TMJ thing my mom got sometimes when she was super-stressed-out. But I figured it was a nervous habit, which made him seem less intimidating. Either way, I liked how I could smell the cinnamon toothpaste on his breath when he did it.

It was the contradictions I noticed the most: the way he'd say something with confidence but then look insecure, doing the jaw-pop thing or lowering his eyes and fidgeting his fingers in his lap. The brave way he reached out to brush the hair from my face once we got off the bus and stood on the corner, deciding which way to go, but how he was too shy to hold my hand when we started walking.

I noticed the steaming smell of crabs as soon as we were on the sidewalk, the afternoon sun and summer crowd warm-ing the air on the wharf.

Somewhere nearby, the Hyde Street cable car bell rang, and Isaac said, "See that there? That bell is exactly why I make sure to do one grossly touristy thing in the city each time I'm here. Not everyone gets to hear a cable car ding in the middle of the afternoon on a Wednesday."

We walked past cheap souvenir stores and street performers doing magic tricks or playing music for money, food vendors using metal tongs to lift huge white crabs from pots of boiling water. A man painted gold from head to foot stood on an overturned bucket, miming and posing for photos as tourists took pictures and dropped change into a black top hat in front of him. We made our way to the bay to check out the view and the hordes of sea lions lazing on the wharf, even though we'd both seen them a bunch of times.

As we navigated the crowd, I bounced my eyes from Isaac to the swarm of faces drifting in the opposite direction, always looking for my dad. Ever since the photo at the museum, I'd been spotting him all over the city. Not *him*, but someone who looked close enough to shoot a jolt through my body for at least a few seconds before the person would turn and I'd see that he was a teenager in a puffy vest or that the man I'd been staring at didn't even wear glasses.

The first time it happened, I was in CVS with Beckett buying snacks by the bus stop in my neighborhood before we headed to Hippie Hill. A man in the greeting card aisle. The thing was, my dad never would have bought a greeting card at CVS. He didn't believe much in those long-winded sentimental poems you'd find in those cards. If he wanted a card, he'd make his own, basic notes on folded pieces of graph paper from work or, when I was little, marker drawings on stolen pieces of construction paper from my craft sets. I knew he'd never be in that spot in that store on that day, but it didn't stop me from calling out his name. I shouted, "Dad!" and when the man turned, it was someone who really looked nothing like him. Reddish-blond hair and round in the middle, a button-down shirt and leather loafers. Except for the glasses, he was nothing like my father. The whole thing was pretty humiliating.

Eventually, Isaac bought us sourdough-bread bowls of clam chowder, and we walked down the waterfront to Pier 39, where we had a perfect view of Alcatraz.

"This okay?" he asked, and I said "Absolutely" as we sat on a bench facing the bay.

The food came in cheap square paper to-go carriers, and I tried to balance the bread bowl with one hand and spoon the chowder with the other without spilling it, all the while paying attention to what Isaac was saying and looking only somewhat— if possible, not totally—awkward.

"I bought tickets for the 3:50 ferry out to Alcatraz," he told me. "I guess I should've asked how late you wanted to stay out. It's about a three-hour thing—total, I mean—but I figured if you were tired of me by then, you could just wear the headset for the tour and pretend we weren't together." He smiled, and then the smile changed quickly to anxiousness and he added,

"Not together, I know we're not together-together, but you know what I mean," and I nodded. "That was awkward," he said. He told me he'd gotten the full Alcatraz package, the one that included the boat trip and the headsets and a souvenir map. "Go big or go home."

"It sounds great. A full-on gaper experience," I teased, and then I had to explain that gapers were what we called the tourists in the city. Because they wandered around, staring and pointing, with their mouths hanging open. He liked that, and I liked the sound of his laugh.

He told me about going to Alcatraz when he was a little kid and said he didn't remember much except that he'd been disappointed that there wasn't any food. "They told me it was an island, and I guess I'd thought it had some kind of fair or festival with rides and prizes or something. I'd expected funnel cakes and cotton candy. I'm pretty sure I threw a tantrum and we had to catch an early ferry back."

It was nice that he talked so much, because it gave me the chance to watch him. He had short eyelashes the exact same color of his hair, and he often talked with his hands.

"I like this," he said, and reached over, not touching but almost touching the horn pendent around my neck. "What does it mean?"

So I told him about my grandmother in Chicago and how I'd been missing her more since my dad disappeared. "She was his mom, and it's been like a weird chain reaction," I said. "I think of him all the time, but I think of her more now, too." He nodded. "She used to wear this when I was a kid. It's an Italian symbol, to keep away the bad spirits."

In front of us, a woman walking her dog stopped to answer her cell phone. The pier was crowded with shoppers and street performers and tourists wandering around.

"What about this?" I hooked my finger under his bracelet, his skin against my skin for a quick second before I leaned back.

He popped it off his wrist and handed it over. "Guitar strings," he said. "A girl in one of the bands that plays at the club where I work makes them. Cool, right?"

I couldn't tell what bugged me more, that Maddie and I hadn't thought to do that—making jewelry from old guitar strings was just our style—or the fact that he was wearing a bracelet some other girl gave him. Some girl in a band in France.

But then he said, "You should keep it. It goes with your whole"—he raised his hand and waved it around or toward or at me—"your whole thing."

"And what thing is that?" I said, catching an edge in my voice.

"No, it's a good thing. The music thing. The not-looking-like-a-clone-of-everyone-else thing."

"So I look weird?" I asked.

"That's not what I meant. I should stop talking," he said, but then he kept going: "You're just different, that's all. I noticed as soon as I saw you at the club. You don't worry about what everyone else is doing or wearing or whatever. It's a good thing."

I tried to hand the bracelet back, but he wouldn't take it. "Keep it. Really. Every time you look at it, you can remember how I acted like an idiot on our first date," he said, and smiled.

The water was rough on the boat, and about four minutes into the ride Isaac said, "Maybe I didn't think this through," his face shifting to a pale cream instead of his usual honey brown.

"Do you get seasick?" I asked.

"I'm not sure. I guess we're about to find out."

He'd let me pick the seats when we first got on, and I'd chosen the best ones, near the front where the boat was open and we could see the ocean and the island getting closer as we moved toward it, but I told him it would be better to sit where he couldn't see the water if he wasn't feeling well, so we moved to a back bench in a corner. I started digging in my bag for gum, remembering my grandmother's trick about peppermint calming down an upset stomach, and when I told him what I was looking for, he pulled two Peppermint Patties out of his back pocket. He handed one to me and tore the wrapper of the other one with his teeth before popping it into his mouth.

"You're like a walking vending machine," I said.

"You say that like it's a bad thing."

We hit a wave or some kind of bump in the water and he gripped the edge of the seat, white-knuckled and eyes closed.

"Try not to think about it," I said. "Think of something else." I almost told him to count backward from twelve, but I figured that would sound weird, so instead I said, "Tell me a story."

"Maybe you could do the talking for a little while?" he asked, but I said no, it would be better if he was the one talking.

"If I'm talking, you'll still be distracted by the motion," I said.

And that's when he told me about the underwater power plant.

Isaac said that PG&E was in the middle of planning a huge launch of wave farms, turbines under the sea that used the ocean's currents to generate electricity.

"Tidal power technology," he said. "The Electric Power Research Institute recently identified the bay as one of the world's best candidates for electricity generation using tidal power technology." PG&E was planning to put up $1.5 million to help fund a test site. "This huge study is supposed to start next year. My dad told me all about it."

"So there'd be windmills? Along the floor of the bay?" I

thought immediately of my dad, of how much he'd love the idea.

"Turbines, yep. Maybe one day," he said. "Soon, probably, if the study works and they can prove it would be a reliable source of electricity. And that it doesn't harm the sea animals." He smiled that smile that shot waves through my belly. "Can you imagine? We'd be up here fishing off charter boats or swimming at Ocean Beach. Kayaking or windsurfing or whatever. And down there there'd be turbines churning on the ocean floor, making electricity. It's amazing, right?"

By the time he finished telling me about the underwater energy plant, the boat ride had ended and his face looked the right color again.

Alcatraz stopped operating as a federal prison in the early 1960s, but it was a big historical draw for the city, and I'd been to the island before—as a kid with my mother and Beckett and Lori one summer afternoon when they were trying to think of interesting things for us to do. But that had been in fourth, maybe fifth, grade, and everything looked smaller and more remote than I remembered. We walked past the residential apartments where the family members of guards and other employees of Alcatraz had lived; we saw the warden's house, the guard tower, and the power plant, too. The walls were cracked and the grounds had grown messy and wild, the whole place feeling like a ghost town. We wandered through the recreation yard and tried to envision what it would've been like to be able to see the city from the jail yard, so huge and alluring just there on the far side of the water, and to know you were super-close but endlessly and impossibly far away.

We picked up our headphones from the desk in the front of the cell house and started our audio tour. The recorded voice directed us around the prison building, explaining the history, its words intercut with stories told directly by the guards and inmates, or maybe just actors pretending to be them. It walked us through the rooms and cells, the space feeling tight and hot, and told us about the elaborate escape plans that never worked and the one that came close, the one that resulted in the Battle of Alcatraz. We watched as other tourists took turns standing inside the cells, their hands on the bars looking out while friends or family members snapped photos from the other side: "behind bars" pictures taken at Alcatraz.

It was dark and cold out by the time we got in line to wait to get back on the ferry.

"Pretty great, right?" Isaac asked, and I nodded. "It's good, I think," he said, "to remember how many different ways people live out their lives." Then he popped his jaw.

My thoughts seemed blurry, caught between being there with him and being inside those headphones, hearing the noises of cell doors creaking and the voices of inmates. And before I'd even decided to do it, I took his hand in mine. Just like that, it felt so much better and more interesting and more real than anything that had happened between Andrew Parker and me.

The ferry warmed quickly with the heat of all the passengers, and we slumped on the bench in the back again, our hands incessantly touching: thumbs rubbing palms, fingers tracing lines. And I felt him everywhere, in a million different places, my heartbeat swooshing between my ears as if I'd been running for hours.

The Ready.gov earthquake preparation website talked about the importance of fastening all your bookshelves to the walls, so after work the next day I stopped by the hardware store to buy the necessary equipment, figuring it would be easier if I just did it myself and didn't try to explain to my mother why I'd decided it needed to be done.

- Place large or heavy objects on lower shelves.

- Store breakable items in low, closed cabinets with latches.

- Mirrors, pictures, frames, and other hanging items should be secured to the wall with closed hooks or earthquake putty. Do not hang heavy objects over beds, sofas, or any place you may be seated.

I planned to reorganize my bedroom accordingly, but first I had to buy drywall anchors and hooks, a stud finder, and long, fat nails, all stuff I hadn't found in the garage when I'd looked earlier that week.

The hardware store sat in a strip of shops a few blocks from my house, squeezed between a Laundromat and an eyeglass shop and a few doors down from an amazing-smelling bakery that sold the best macarons I'd ever had. I decided that was just what we needed, my mother and I: macarons. Brightly colored cookies, the perfect blend of almond and sugar flavors. Coconut was Mom's favorite, but I liked the burgundy-tinted raspberry ones. We used to do that sometimes—eat dessert before dinner, just the two of us after school before my dad got home from work. Other times she'd slip me a biscotti or a freshly made cannoli she'd picked up from the bakery near campus.

"Don't tell your dad," she'd say, and I'd eat it while she finished cooking dinner and we waited for him to come home. I hadn't thought of that in forever.

And that's where I saw Jay, *Beckett's* Jay, kissing another boy. A boy that was absolutely not Beckett, kissing a boy outside that bakery that smelled like chocolate and butter when you walked past.

Jay had one hand tucked into the back pocket of the boy's corduroys, and his other hand was on the boy's waist as their mouths, fused and ravenous, tugged at one another. Like they were eating. Or auditioning for a B-list movie, one of those films where you can tell that the actors are trying too hard. Mouths open and eyes closed, their hands running all over. It was definitely *not* the first time they'd kissed. I stood there, watching as one hand moved from a back pocket to a neck, as palms ran over shoulders and fingers dug through clumps of hair.

The other boy noticed me staring when they pulled apart and said, "What? Jesus."

Then Jay saw me too, and his face dropped, like a chin-on-the-pavement kind of dive. And he said, "It's not what you think"—that predictable sentence that proved the exact opposite.

But I turned away before he had the chance to say anything more, taking off down the street with that plastic bag full of disaster relief tools slapping against my leg as I ran.

PART THREE

SUSPENSION OF LAW

Image 17B: "Untitled (Remains of drugstore, location unknown), 1906." Cellulose nitrate negative, 132 × 84 mm irreg.

They walk, he and William, through streets covered in ash as the wind tugs the smoke around them like a second skin.

"The pavement opened in front of me," William says again. He says the weather that morning had been unusually clear, no fog. "I should have known something was amiss." Shaking his head, eyes to the ground. "I'm a lawyer. It's my job to notice clues."

The man nods, though he admits, "I can't remember the earthquake. I remember fruit on the ground and waking in the street. The fire and the pavement cracked like broken glass." He raises his hand to his head and finds a tender spot just behind his left ear, a swollen knot he hadn't noticed before. He rubs the small mass, and when he pulls his hand away, the specks of a new scab are plastered to the pads of his fingertips.

"It will come back to you," William says. "You must have fallen when the shaking began. Hit your head, perhaps. Give it time."

They stop in the street to exchange news with others about the collapse of buildings and the makeshift construction of relief camps, the squatters in vacant lots scrawling names and notes on papers and posting them on walls or trees.

"Drugstore up the road is being pillaged for medical supplies," one man tells them. He clutches spools of gauze and bandages, and his pockets bulge with bottles of pills. "Best get it while you can," he says over his shoulder as he moves away.

"Can't blame them, I suppose," William says. And then, "Henry, my brother, he suffers from shortness of breath sometimes, palpitations in his chest. A doctor recommended opiates and bromide salts, which have helped. But I fear for Henry. For what he must be feeling now. For what he must be feeling in *this*." He waves his hand in the air.

The man searches for words to ease William's worrisome mind, but his thoughts are interrupted by distant thunder . . . no, not simply thunder, a physical shaking as someone in the road yells "Aftershock!"

He and William jolt, bumping into each other as they scramble. There are cries and shouts and the clapping of hooves, hundreds of pounds of weight storming through the streets as a stampede of horned cattle tears toward them down Market Street.

"Move!" the man shouts as he grabs William's arm and yanks him out of the way.

The animals are crazed, slamming against each other and stumbling through piles of debris. They topple wooden beams and crash into buildings, wild and rough, fleeing down the sidewalk and through the street.

A woman tries to dive out of the way but falls, and a steer crushes her shoulder. She writhes on the ground as bystanders hurry past, trying to escape into doorways, some jumping for fire escape ladders hanging from the sides of buildings.

"What should we do?" the man shouts, but William's mouth is slack-jawed and speechless, his eyes wide.

There are gunshots—one, two, three—and the sound of animals wailing. Half a block down, a warehouse collapses onto the thoroughfare, burying most of the herd and crushing them onto the pavement. Fallen cornices pierce the longhorns, catching and crippling the cattle, slicing into legs and leathery bellies. More shots are fired as the animals thrash under the debris. Those still running amok bellow and fall, and those trapped under the wreckage are put out of their pain as bystanders load and reload their pistols.

In front of them, a steer charges toward a saloon on the opposite side of the street, chasing a white-haired man running for shelter. At the doorway the gentleman turns, a gun suddenly in hand, and he shoots. The animal drops to the ground, howling as William and the man dodge through the crowd. A second shot is fired just as they reach the saloon, silencing the animal's cries, close range. At their feet, the wound drips blood from between the cow's eyes.

"There was nothing I could do," the shooter says when he turns to William and the man. "You saw . . . there was no time to think. He would have crushed me." He is crying, and the man ushers him into the saloon, out of harm's way.

"It is over," the man says as he waits for the gentleman to stop shaking. "You're okay now."

Once the animals have moved on, the men return to the streets and find the remnants of a battle scene: bodies and the metallic stink of blood; men and women ripped open by the longhorns; fallen animals, some dead and some not, some crushed under parts of the warehouse and others slaughtered in the road. They move away, heading south, silent and slow.

"Vaqueros," William says eventually. "The cattle must have escaped from their herders after the quake."

"I don't understand," the man replies, blinking grit from his eyes.

"The Mexicans drive beef cattle to the city stockyards in the south once the inbound ships are unloaded. They must have fled the docks in the chaos after the quake."

• • •

They switchback the streets, north to south, down one block and up another as they stop to help where they can and gather information from others also on foot. It seems that hours pass in this way.

A family of seven drag suitcases through the middle of the road, fleeing to the Ferry Building, at the foot of Market. The mother holds a baby, and the father carries a young girl on his shoulders; the child's legs are bare under her pleated skirt, and her socked feet thump against her father's chest with each step. Three other children trail behind.

"We want out," the father says. "A second shock will surely hit tonight. Oakland," he tells them. "I hear there's help across the bay."

The heat intensifies, and the city becomes more deserted as the firestorms rage. The smell of smoldering wood meets them at every turn, but still they walk on.

They are told that marines, the National Guard, the navy and army are moving through San Francisco. Cadets from the University of California. Someone they meet on the sidewalk says Mayor Schmitz has issued a "shoot to kill" order.

"Chaos," one woman says. "Men are being murdered in the streets."

They pass a liquor store with shattered bottles leaking from cardboard boxes strewn in the debris. The man eyes the broken glass of the storefront and searches the room behind it: Shelves hang half hooked to walls and a countertop lies collapsed on the floor.

A young man skitters through the store and their eyes meet. "Did you hear?" he calls to them. "The police are confiscating all the alcohol. Pouring it in the streets to reduce the risk of mob violence. It'll be streaming through the gutters soon." He takes one last bottle and meets them on the sidewalk. "No harm done," he mumbles, and then crosses the road.

Earlier that afternoon, they heard news of camps being built in Golden Gate Park and Jefferson Square, and, realizing that the square wasn't far, they agreed that would be their destination.

At a nearby intersection, they stop to speak with a fireman. "Valencia Street shifted to the east," he tells them as he wipes soot from his face and smears the ash with sweat. "All the lines snapped . . . water, gas, electric. The College Hill Reservoir is emptying fast. We'll be out of water before the night ends."

"And if we're looking for family?" William asks. "Where would be the best place to find information?"

"Golden Gate Park," the fireman says. "The city released records there, a master list from the registrar that families can check. We're trying to keep track of those reported as deceased and those who have survived. I've heard there are plans to begin hauling lumber into the park on Friday. To build structures in

the camp. No telling how long people'll have to live there."
He wishes them luck before rushing toward Eighteenth Street.

"The square tonight and Golden Gate Park tomorrow, then," the man says, determined to help William find his brother. As they walk on, he is reminded of his thirst again, and as he brings a finger to his lips, he thinks of sand.

CHAPTER SIXTEEN

Sixty-nine Days After

The decision to tell Beckett about seeing Jay kissing another boy wasn't really a decision at all. There was no two ways about it. I knew he would want to know—no one likes to get duped.

On Sunday, Maddie requested an all-day practice since the party at Isaac's was only five days away, so I bailed on the Squat & Gobble ritual and told Beck I'd meet him at Ocean Beach afterward.

"I'm sorry I've been so busy," I said when I called, "but there's no way I can blow this off."

He sighed, and I imagined him on the roof deck on his cell phone. "'There is no pleasure in having nothing to do,'" he said. "'The fun is having lots to do and not doing it.'"

But I told him Maddie would kill me if I showed up late again. Wednesday was bad enough—by the time Isaac hailed a cab and I got to practice, it was past ten o'clock, and she and Rabbit had called it a night.

"What time does she want you there? I'll eat fast," he said. "Like a vacuum. You won't even notice I've eaten at all. Just give me an hour. One cup of coffee."

"No can do. But after practice, I promise, I'll meet you at Ocean Beach around five."

"It was Andrew Jackson, by the way," he told me. "You didn't even ask. . . ."

But I was already saying, "I have to go," and dropping the phone on the cradle.

We played for over two hours before we took our first break, but I was thinking too hard and couldn't get in the zone. The more I tried not think about Isaac or Jay or my dad, the more I focused on the music, and the more I focused on the music and what I should have been doing with my hands and my feet, the worse it got.

"You're four beats too fast," Maddie said when she stopped singing mid-song and turned to face me. "What's going on back there?" she asked, but I just shrugged. "Let's take ten to regroup," she said.

I didn't feel like telling them about the scare I'd had that morning and explaining why I couldn't get my head on track, so I just nodded.

I'd been calling the local hospitals every few days to check and make sure no one with my father's name had been admitted, and that morning, for the first time, they asked me to repeat myself. Twice.

"Hold, please," the woman said eventually.

I'd clutched the phone and counted backward from twelve at least seven times as I sat on my bed. It wasn't even one of those hold systems that played classical music to calm you down. Just white noise.

"Pace?" the woman said when she came back on the line. "And you're his daughter?"

For seventeen years. *The apple never falls far from the tree. Birds of a feather flock together.*

"He came in last night," she said, and behind her I heard a telephone ringing and voices talking.

My heart was in my throat then, a gigantic thumping thing shutting down my airway.

"Adam Pace, right? Looks like he arrived around midnight."

I made her repeat it three times—Adam, she said, *not* Aaron. It wasn't my father after all, but it had taken me almost an hour to stop shaking.

• • •

Ocean Beach runs about four miles along the west coast of the city, but our favorite section was at the bottom of Golden Gate Park, south of the Cliff House near the Beach Chalet. In the summer it's cold near the water, which mostly keeps tourists away, and Beckett and I liked to hang out there and watch the waves as often as we could. It wasn't the cleanest spot, because lots of people brought their dogs there to run and didn't bother picking up after them, so you had to be careful where you stepped. The homeless liked to hang out there, and you had to dodge trash and bonfire debris when you walked in the sand, but it was our spot, it just was—we'd been meeting there ever since we were old enough to catch the bus by ourselves, and it'd always been one of the best places to clear my head.

I found him sitting on a log, brown blanket spread out at his feet, and he said, "You, my rock star friend, are twenty minutes late."

"It didn't go well," I said as I sat down, stripped off my Chuck T's and socks, and dug my toes into the sand. "Practice, I mean."

In front of us, a couple threw a Frisbee for their golden retriever, his fur knotted and wet. The woman was wrapped in an oversize sweater and wore brown-and-white pinstriped leggings, and the man sported a small navy coat with brass buttons running up the front. We watched for a while as they took turns with the disc and chased the dog toward the waves, but really all I could see was Jay kissing that boy in front of the bakery.

"Did you get brunch?" I asked Beck, and he said, "Nah. I hung around the house with my mom most of the day and talked on the phone with Jay. He was stuck at work, but it was pretty slow. Slow enough for him to call and ask me to keep him company. We talked so long, I swear I thought my cell might melt in my hand."

That was my opening. Right there. "So, about Jay. There's something I need to tell you." Or "Oh, that's nice he called. I guess he finally got that other kid's tongue out of his mouth long enough to remember he was dating *you*." Or maybe I'd start with "You're not going to like this, Beckett, and I hate to be the bearer of bad news, but I promise it's going to be okay."

Because it would be. He'd been through worse by then. Like the time Lori found that lump and we had to wait three days for the results, even though it ended up just being some weird cyst thing that wasn't anything at all. Or when his cat died when we were in ninth grade, the one they'd had since before he was born, the one that used to sleep at the bottom of his bed and warm his feet—he always said Turquoise was my stiffest competition for first chair as best friend. Those were real-life things, but he and Jay had only known each other a few weeks. That's what I kept telling myself. Rose-colored-glasses-phase stuff, and even though the news would be a buzz-kill at first, in the long run I knew he'd be glad that I'd told him.

Opening Number Two: "I know Isaac Thompson's party will be mostly kids from our school," he said. "And I know Jay's older and everything, but I asked him to come. He said he'd have to meet me there, though, so I was thinking I could go with you. I could be your first roadie. That'd be good, right?" He'd dropped off the log and was sitting with me on the edge of the blanket by then, and he raked his fingers through the sand while we talked.

I should have said, "No. You need to drop that kid like a bad habit. He's not what he seems. He doesn't deserve you." But instead I told him sure, he could ride with us; Rabbit was going to drive all the equipment over around five, then come back and pick up Maddie and me.

Opening Number Three: "Cool. Because I really want you to get to know him better," he told me.

I know him better than you think.

"I know it hasn't been that long, and I know this is totally gooey and lame, but I feel like he gets me, you know?" he said.

Gets you in trouble. Gets you and another boy too.

"It's really important to me. For you and him to be friends. I've got a good feeling about this one, Cal."

Behind him, a few hundred yards down the beach, a man walked by the edge of the water. He was barefoot and wore baggy cargo pants and a white long-sleeve, his tangled hair blowing and overgrown just like my dad's might have been if he hadn't gotten a trim since we'd last seen him.

Opening Number Four: "I want to hear all about your trip to Alcatraz," Beck said. "I was thinking it might be something fun that Jay and I could do sometime."

He was in that annoying phase where his brain relentlessly drew a line between any tiny thought straight to Jay, this boy he believed he was falling in love with, this boy who, meanwhile, was probably making out with other boys all over the city.

I hooked my finger under my guitar-string bracelet, running it back and forth on the steel as I spoke. "Beck, listen," I said. Twelve, eleven, ten. "There's something I need to tell you," I told him. Nine, eight, seven.

I didn't want to break my best friend's heart, and it wasn't fair Jay had put me in that position. Jay, with that ridiculous Mohawk. Jay, who worked in a coffee shop and probably rode a fixie bike like every other wannabe hipster. Give me a break.

"But it's not like it's the end of the world or anything," I told him. Six, five, four.

I was supposed to be the one who protected Beck and made sure nothing got in the way of what he wanted. But I was also supposed to be the one who always told him the truth. It was like an unspoken pact, non-negotiable and binding.

"Just remember that. Promise me, okay? That you'll remember it's not the end of the world?"

His eyes narrowed and shifted away from mine.

Three, two, one.

But he interrupted me, saying, "Wait," and I followed his gaze to the barefoot man, who was much closer by then, facing the water, but with his profile in plain view. Black wire-rimmed glasses. His nose the opposite of my mother's and the one I'd always wished I'd had instead of hers. Of all the men I'd seen those months in the city, this one was the closest. Close enough that Beckett saw it too.

I stood up, called "Hey," just like I had in every nightmare for the last sixty-nine days. He turned and knocked the wind out of me when I saw it wasn't him.

Beck moved his hand to my foot and squeezed. "Sit down, Cal," he said. "It's okay. Just sit down."

It struck me then: the impossibility of finding him. Like the Alcatraz prisoners who had tried to chip through the wall with spoons—that's what I felt like I was doing. The thought hit me square in the jaw—odds were, I was never going to see my father again. Not the real him. I might find him in impossible photos or the profiles of strangers, might have visions of him stuck inside century-old scenes . . . I could spend forever looking, but it had been too long and he'd left too few clues—no clues at all, really. The truth was, the chances of me finding him were flatlining.

I sank to the blanket, gasping for air, scrambling for the twelve breaths I couldn't catch.

I didn't end up telling Beckett about Jay. Instead he put his arm around me until I stopped crying, and we lay on the beach on that dirty brown blanket counting birds, counting clouds, counting all the different bands we hadn't gotten to see live yet but wanted to. Eventually I calmed down enough to realize I should probably head home. It felt like days since I'd seen my mom, between band practice and running and her work schedule, and I suddenly wanted to hear her voice in our house. I needed something familiar, something I could trust.

Back at home, I pulled out the stack of California earthquake books and struggled to get some reading done, but I was too distracted. I tried the books I'd checked out from the science section too, disaster relief books and ones exploring theories about time warps and black holes, but that didn't work either. And then I was in the closet, taking down the shoe box next to the translation dictionaries, the shoe box I kept those homemade cards from my dad in. I dumped the box onto the bed, pushed the books aside, and read and reread his notes, the neat scientific handwriting—printed, never cursive, and always lowercase.

happy birthday to my favorite daughter. A recurring joke, since I was his only one.

to the kid i like the most—proud of you on fifth grade gradua-

tion day. He'd given me a copy of the *Children's Encyclopedia of American History* that year, a huge hardback I'd spent hours looking through.

"I like what you've done," my mom said from the hallway, where she slumped against the doorframe. "It looks good. That in particular." She nodded to the framed photo of the Chicago Theatre—it had hung above my bed, but I'd moved it to the other side of the room when I'd rearranged the furniture and fastened all the bookshelves to the wall near my reading chair. "It's better there. Gets more light near the window," she said.

My mother's hair was pulled into a perfect ponytail, and I could tell she'd been out walking because her cheeks were pink, like sliced strawberries. She did that sometimes, took the bus instead of driving and got off five or ten blocks before our stop. "Head-cleaning time," she called it. "Walking off the cobwebs."

She eyed the cards on my bed. "I always loved his hand-writing," she said. "Thought he should be a teacher, with that kind of print." She picked one up, and I almost stopped her, thinking they were mine and not something I should have had to share, but then I realized maybe she needed them as much as I did.

"He never was very good at telling jokes," she said.

what type of music do mummies listen to? wrap music!

Her eyes had those puffy purple half-moons under them,

and I wished I'd stopped for macarons after I left the beach. We could have shared a box before dinner.

"You want anything in particular for dinner?" she asked, reading my thoughts, almost. "I feel like cooking tonight," she said, and I told her anything sounded good to me.

"Something hearty, then," she said decidedly. She poked me in the belly. "I worry about you," she said, "all skin and bones these days." And then she picked up *Organize for Disaster: Prepare Your Family and Your Home for Any Natural or Unnatural Disaster*, by Judith Kolberg.

"I was thinking we should have a plan," I told her as she flipped through the pages. "They're called Family Communication Plans. So we'd know how to find each other if we aren't together when something happens," I said. Our school had sent home outlines of those kinds of plans after 9/11, but that was years ago. I wanted one for now. One that would make sure I could find her if a quake hit and we were on opposite sides of the city.

It had started to rain outside, the drops drumming against the bay window.

"You shouldn't have to worry so much," she said, and swapped the book for another one of the cards. "It shouldn't be like this. You should be out having fun, not reading old notes from your dad."

But I told her I liked reading his letters. "I know I'm not remembering him right anymore. Like I remember the good stuff only, and part of me hates that," I said. "I want to remember that he was terrible at telling jokes, you know?"

have you heard about the explosion at the cheese shop in france? everything is covered in de brie!

"He slurped his soup through his teeth," she said. "Do you remember?"

I did—it was something I hated, like the sound of nails on a chalkboard.

"He did it on our first date. French onion soup. I remember thinking he seemed like a good guy but that it would probably never go anywhere. Someone who made so much noise when he ate," she told me. "That's how stupid I was." She pinched her lips together, drawing in air for that whoosh noise until I started laughing. "I ended up falling in love with that dumb little gap between his two front teeth, and the soup thing turned into no big deal. It's funny how that happens."

She didn't end up making dinner after all. We ordered in instead and took turns reading the cards with the jokes out loud while we waited for delivery. She even used funny voices for some of them, which I never would have expected in a million years. Then we put all the notes back in the box and gorged ourselves on broccoli-and-corn pizza, both of us eventually falling asleep on the couch in the living room, with *Splendor in the Grass* playing on the TV, a teenage Natalie Wood flickering on the screen.

CHAPTER SEVENTEEN

Image 36B: "Untitled (Earthquake refugee camp in park), 1906."
Cellulose nitrate negative, 84 × 146 mm irreg.

"I feel as though we've been circling the same ten blocks for hours," William says, "yet each time we cross Sacramento Street, it has changed." He pulls his handkerchief from his pocket to mop his forehead again. "Do you pray?"

The man admits, "I can't remember ever doing it. Though I wouldn't say I never have."

"If there's ever a time to start . . . ," William begins, but his voice drops as they walk on.

The hunger erupts just as they make their way into Jefferson Square at dusk while the sun lowers itself into the city. It is a violent steady thing, the yearning in the man's belly as they walk, and he realizes he has no recollection of the last time he ate. His stomach cramps as he wipes his shirtsleeve over his forehead. A dirt path carves its way through the center of the park and a string of benches lines the walkway, while groups of men, women, and children clutter the grass. He searches their faces for something familiar, his eyes desperate and easily distracted. Stumbling, his legs shake as they navigate the mob.

Coffee, he thinks, black and thick to wake him; warm pieces of fresh bread and sharp cheddar cheese. But it is water that he needs most.

Wagons and wheelbarrows filled with supplies and personal belongings are strewn throughout the camp, and he watches as, nearby, a handful of men shed their coats and hats and attempt to create some kind of shelter from strips of lumber and soiled sheets taken from building debris. He eyes the constructions—barracks or tents on wooden platforms for housing, small shacks scattered in a haphazard configuration on the grass. A large sign reading COMMITTEE FOR HOUSING AND HOMELESS leans against a tree, and next to it a young woman in a bulky feathered hat pulls blankets from a stack at her feet, handing them out to anyone who requests one. Perhaps that is something he can do: volunteer for an organization such as this. He begins to approach the woman, but stops when William tugs the sleeve of his coat.

"I know him," William says as he starts across the path toward a man perched near a tree. "He is the cousin of a partner at my firm. Franklin!" he calls.

Introductions are made, and as they shake hands, Franklin asks the two, "Are you hurt?"

This is a recurring question the man cannot find an honest answer for. He is not physically hurt, but disorientation engulfs him like a casket—his memory is torn and touseled, and the not knowing is impossibly painful.

Franklin tells them that his wife and son accompany him, though they are searching the tents for family and friends. "My mother-in-law," Franklin says as he pulls out an engraved silver cigarette case. "She lives alone in Hayes Valley, but by the time we got to her neighborhood, they weren't letting anyone through." He shakes his head. "Old Mill?" he asks as he lights the cigarettes and hands them out so that all three men have smokes clamped between fingers or lips. "Did you hear about the Hayes Valley fire?"

That morning a woman began to cook breakfast on the stove, not realizing that their chimney had collapsed during the quake.

"Ham and eggs," Franklin tells them as the smoke unfurls from his mouth. "There was no water to fight the flames." He says, "Here, let's sit," and motions to a set of brown luggage trunks with brass fittings stashed beneath a nearby tree. "The winds have been blowing," he says. "And the fires swept over St. Ignatius Church and the college, too. Just heard the last of City Hall has collapsed." He smokes and flicks ashes as he speaks, quickly, his voice barely above a whisper. "The fire jumped Market Street. I can't imagine she made it out of the area. Ruth, my mother-in-law, that is."

The three pull on the cigarettes, though the man's throat burns and his eyes sting as he does so; he must not be a smoker. Eventually he drops it to the ground and stamps it out with his foot.

"Most homes have them," Franklin is saying. "The chimneys of furnaces fueled by wood and coal. Turns out they're promoting the spread of the fires just as much as the wind is."

The man has seen dozens that day, chimneys that have crashed through roofs, crumbled to the floor, and torn holes through homes as they fell, and he imagines families in their beds that morning, crushed by the collapsed flues.

"It's happened all over," Franklin says. "I'm guessing it's happened to Ruth, but Emma wants to see the lists. She says she has to see Ruth's name on one list or the other to believe it either way. Says if she can't find the information here, we'll leave for Golden Gate Park tomorrow to check with the registrar. That's the best you can do, I suppose," he tells them. "Seek some kind of proof."

They talk of the Mission District, where the tenements folded like accordions. South of Market saw the worst of it, the tightly packed wood-framed constructions making for fast fuel.

"They say the police are starting to shoot those trapped

in the wreckage," Franklin tells them. "Shooting them to put them out of their misery."

The man thinks of the slaughtered longhorns, killed because their fear and confusion turned them wild.

"With the instatement of military rule declared, there's been, in effect, a suspension of law," Franklin says. "Who's in control? No one, as far as I can see."

"Do you know anything about the volunteers?" the man asks. "I would like to help somehow." He turns to William. "Once we find your brother, I would like to volunteer." He imagines pumping water and operating hoses to douse the flames, helping maintain order in the camps, and participating in the reconstruction of the city. There is comfort in the vision of working with steam and water, pumps and levers and tools.

"Surely you can find information in Golden Gate Park," Franklin says as he scans the crowd. A pause and a sigh. "Where will we all go? Where will the food come from, and where will we sleep?" he asks. "I can't imagine how long it will be before the city feels normal again."

Jefferson Square grows into a carnival of grief and confusion when night falls: Hungry children are tucked into makeshift tents; candles are lit as locals walk the lawn, calling for those still missing; fistfights erupt over food, over park benches, over blankets, over jugs of water and packs of matches.

The man and William walk through a tent of survivors being treated for injuries and find no familiar faces, with the exception of a woman William purchases milk from at the grocery and a young teenage boy he once met during a trial. They ask the nurses about William's brother, but there is no information.

"He must be growing desperate," William says while they scan a list tacked to a tree next to the medical tent. At the top, it reads *Deceased*. "Nighttime was always difficult for Henry."

They walk Laguna Street as the evening wears on. They have no shelter, no water or food; the benches have been claimed hours earlier, and the sky grows dark.

"My house collapsed before I had time to think," William says, apologizing. "I should have grabbed blankets. Should have packed a bag with food and filled jugs of water."

They pass a man playing a washboard, the hat at his feet collecting change; next to him a woman and young girl are curled under a blanket, with a small dog tucked between them. There are bonfires, NO PEDDLERS signs leaning against white-sheeted teepees, and children careening through the darkness as they bump into one another, laughing.

He sees her then, a teenage girl with dark hair, light freckles, and a profile that at once feels familiar as panic streams within him. She is alone and walking quickly through the crowd, with a loaf of bread tucked under one arm. He bolts, leaving William as he follows her, two syllables pulsing up his throat but having no form, no name to match the beats. One-two. A name he has said a million times, it seems — loudly in daylight to get her attention in a crowd; softly in a bedroom to calm her to sleep. He desperately tries to find the letters that make the name he knows but cannot trace, the name he can use to call her to him. And then she stops at the corner of Turk Street, looking both ways and running her fingers through her hair, slowly enough that he is upon her.

Catching his breath, a three beat sigh: "Ex-cuse me," he says.

But when she turns there is no recognition between them, nothing but shadows at their feet.

"I'm sorry," he says. "I thought you were someone else." Though he can't imagine who.

She nods and crosses the road. She is out of sight by the time William reaches him.

"I thought . . . ," he says, the words unnecessary as William pulls the man into his arms. The man's face is wet as he stands there on the sidewalk with a stranger who has become his clos-est friend. And William says over and over, "It's all right. It's all right. It's all right."

CHAPTER EIGHTEEN

Seventy-four Days After

It took us less than half an hour to figure out that (1) because we had never gigged before, we had never noticed we didn't own gigging essentials like cases to transport our equipment, and (2) Rabbit's car was ten sizes too small to fit everything in it, which meant that (3) we'd have to load the stuff Tetris-style, but either way, (4) we'd have to make at least one more trip than we'd planned for, so (5) we were running late for Isaac's party before we even began getting ready.

We loaded Maddie's stuff in the car first, along with whatever parts of the PA system we could fit, then we moved my bass drum to the front passenger side, and I seat-belted it in. Rabbit had directions to the house and figured Isaac would help him unload the car while Maddie and I finished packing up the rest of the equipment. Since Isaac worked at a club setting up the stage, he'd be able to unpack the gear and get things organized while Rabbit came back for the second carload.

"Handsome," I told Beckett when he showed up around five. He sported a charcoal pinstriped suit, the pink-and-black paisley bow tie my parents gave him for eighth-grade graduation, and black high-tops. And he'd done something to his hair, something that made it a little bit crispy.

"It's not too much?" he asked, and I said, "Absolutely not."

He kissed me on the cheek. "Thanks, Callie."

And then I thought of Jay and that other boy kissing, and my heart plummeted.

Beckett took a look around the basement, at the half-packed equipment and power strips strewn about the floor, at the cymbals, the tom-toms, the snare drums, and the stands. "Well, this looks like a shit show," he said.

"That's helpful." Maddie stood at the top of the stairs, and she threw an empty cardboard box at us. "Keep at it," she said, and then disappeared.

"It'll be fine," I told him. "It'll be fine."

Rabbit showed back up around six, just an hour before we were supposed to start playing, but the three of us had packed up the rest of the gear by then and were waiting on the curb when he pulled up.

"I'm impressed," he said.

"Don't be," I replied. "You're going to have to make one more trip after this one. There's no way we're all fitting in that car with the rest of this stuff."

Beck left with Rabbit to help unload the equipment at the house, and then he planned to come back with Rabbit's Volvo to pick up Maddie and me while Rabbit finished setting up the stage with Isaac.

After they left, Maddie and I went inside to take another look around and make sure we hadn't forgotten anything, and then we changed into the dresses she'd picked for us to wear to the party. Hers was short and black, with a million little straps crisscrossing down her back. She pulled on her black ankle boots, immediately transforming her look into rocker chic, then she told me my dress was hanging on the back of the bathroom door. She'd chosen a strapless navy-blue one with an empire waist and a loose, flowy skirt, which would work well, since I had to sit with my legs splayed open while I played the drums. It was shorter than any dress I'd ever worn, which had me worried, but when I pulled it on and looked in the mirror, I knew it was exactly what I was supposed to wear for our first gig.

"It's good, right?" she asked when I came out of the bathroom and she checked me out.

"It's perfect," I told her, and she said, "I thought so."

Then she went to the fridge, an energy drink for her and a bottle of water for me, and we crashed on the couch while we waited for Beck to come back for us.

"It's going to be a good party, right?" she asked hesitantly.

"A great party," I told her. "No questions asked."

"Are you sure he said a hundred and fifty people? There's no way he has that many friends. The kid doesn't even really live here."

"But that's what we want. We want a lot of people there," I said, trying to sound convincing.

"I'm worried we won't be good enough. That all this work has been for nothing," she admitted.

"Are you kidding? We're ready," I told her. "We're absolutely ready for this." I had my bag of drumsticks at my feet, and I reached down and counted them. Again. I only used wood sticks, Vic Firths, and that bag was the one thing that actually made me feel like I belonged on a stage, in a real show.

"You don't know this yet," my dad had told me when he came home after work with the bag—a gift, he'd said, "just because." "But drumsticks break. And fly out of your hands when you're onstage," he said. "Especially when you're nervous and all sweaty-palmed. Real drummers bring a whole bag of sticks to shows."

He'd bought me twelve pairs, my lucky number, and a navy-blue canvas bag to hold them—his way of proving he believed in me and in the band, in my commitment to turning Nothing Right into something real.

"I'm proud of you, you know," he'd said, and then he'd tapped his forehead against my forehand and smiled.

By seven(ish) we were all at Isaac's, but so were a whole slew of kids from school I recognized and a whole slew I didn't.

Rabbit and Isaac and a man I assumed to be Philip Corey Thompson were waiting on the curb by the valet stand—the *valet stand?*—when Beckett parked in front of one of the nicest houses I'd ever seen.

"I feel like the Fresh Prince of Bel-Air," Beckett said as we looked up the sloped driveway toward the house, which sat behind a plot of lawn that was too green to seem real.

There was a balcony on the top floor facing the street, and a group of kids in cocktail dresses and suits stood watching the road or each other, probably. I spotted Jay, and a few girls from my English class too. But then Isaac was knocking on my window and opening the car door, and he became the only thing I could see: He wore a tuxedo, a real full-on tuxedo, with a navy-blue cummerbund and tie.

"Hey, look, we match," he said when he saw my dress, and then he reached down and helped me out of the car. "I figured go big or go home, right? I actually kind of feel like a penguin, or the maître d' at a five-star restaurant, but my dad talked me into it. It's my birthday party, and when else would I get to wear this ridiculous getup?" And then he did that jaw-crack thing, which for some reason made me feel better about being so late and so nervous about playing in front of all those people.

Isaac introduced us to his dad, who seemed nice enough and not as scary as a man who used three names all the time could be, and then we headed inside to help Rabbit and Isaac finish setting up. The first floor was where they were throwing the party—there were bedrooms upstairs and a full basement below, Isaac said—and we plunged head-on into the crowd, a shiny black Lab waiting at the door.

Isaac bent down and scratched behind the dog's ears. "This is Loki," he told me. "And this, Loki," he said, "is the infamous Nothing Right." He told us his parents bought Loki in a last-ditch effort to save their marriage, but when things didn't work out they'd decided the dog belonged in San Francisco with his dad, even though it broke his fourth-grade heart at the time. "Who does that, you know? Gives a kid a dog, then makes him leave it behind and move to the other side of the world? It was for the best, though," he said. "Because those first few trips back and forth were kind of rough on me, going between Paris and here and not having any friends in the city. It was good Loki was waiting for me every time I got off that plane."

He showed us around, which took about two seconds because the first floor didn't actually have any walls and was this big sprawling space, with the kitchen linked to the dining room, which opened to the main living room, where we'd be playing. There was a bar set up at the gigantic counter island in the center of the kitchen area, and behind it a man and woman in matching white button-downs and black pants poured drinks. I recognized the woman—Jayne Watson, who used to cut her own bangs over the bathroom sink during lunch period. She'd been a senior when I was a freshman, and we'd been in the same art class, where she made the most amazing water pitcher I'd ever seen. When she caught me staring, she smiled and I waved.

A handful of grown-ups mingled in the dining room area with Isaac's dad and a woman with long red hair, but for the most part the crowd was our age and a little bit rowdy, drinking and eating from the bar and a food buffet that had been set up in the dining room.

Isaac held out a ceramic bowl and said, "Keys?" to Beckett, who was standing next to me. "My dad figured someone or other would smuggle in booze, so at the end of the night, if you want to drive home, you have to get the keys from him. A pass-his-test kind of thing," he explained.

Beck said, "Fair enough," and dropped Rabbit's key chain into the pile.

It turned out one of Isaac's dad's friends from college was visiting from Los Angeles, where he played the drums in a seventies cover band, and by the time we got there, he and Isaac had already set up most of the equipment. "Hudson," he said, and held out his hand as we stood near the stage area, which was, just like Isaac said, in front of a wall of windows facing the most amazing view of the Golden Gate Bridge I'd ever seen. "Just let me know if you want me to adjust anything," he added.

We were pretty close to being ready, so I sat at the drum set and tweaked the stands, the ride cymbal, the snare, and the hi-hat, trying to get everything to feel just like it felt at Maddie's for practice, but something was off-balance. I counted backward from twelve as a crowd began forming in the living room, eyeing us. Rabbit was warming up and Maddie was in the bathroom, and I watched, trying to hold down the vomit, as Beckett and Jay stood by the bar, their hands touching each other incessantly. Andrew Parker was there, too, with his new girlfriend from the bus stop, and when he caught me looking at him, he gave me an exaggerated thumbs-up and mouthed "Good luck," which was kind of cheesy but nice all the same.

"What is this?" Maddie asked when she came back and was standing in front of us.

"What is what?" Rabbit said.

"This. You being to the right of me. You're always on the left," she said, her voice rising.

"There's no plug on the left," he told her. "Not my fault, boss. I have to plug in, and this is where the socket is."

"But it won't feel right," she said, and he said, "We've got no choice."

Then Isaac's dad was there too, saying that it would probably be a good idea if we got going. The music was supposed to start—he glanced at his watch—a while ago, and the neighbors had only agreed to loud noise until eleven thirty.

"Almost ready," I told him.

"Find an extension cord and move to my left," Maddie told Rabbit.

"There's no time," he said. "This is fine."

"Here's the deal," I said, lowering my voice. "This setup *is* different than how we practice. But this isn't practice, it's a real gig. So different is inevitable. And that's okay. Because this is our chance." I paused and we looked at the room where, I bet Isaac had been right, about a hundred and fifty people waited for us to begin. "This is our chance to show them that we're good. Really good. Good enough to be here."

I slid one hand into Maddie's and the other into Rabbit's, and then they did the same, so that we all held hands in a circle.

"I don't feel so good," Maddie said. "Woozy, like. And shaky."

"It's just nerves," I told her. "Adrenaline. We'll use that

nervous energy to show them how kick-ass we are."

Next to me, Rabbit nodded, even though Maddie looked pretty pale all of a sudden. "Your heart's just racing too fast," he said.

"My whole body's racing too fast."

I told her to take a deep breath. To take two, three, four huge inhales.

But she said, "I don't think I can do this."

"You *are* doing this," I told her. "You already are," and I pointed to the crowd. "Look, they're waiting for us. For Nothing Right. Which means we're already the band gigging at Isaac Thompson's birthday party. You're already doing it."

I squeezed her hand, and she whispered, "Three, two, one."

And then I kicked off my shoes, because I always played barefoot when we practiced. And Rabbit pulled out his yo-yo and did a quick Sleeper, because that was his lucky trick, the first one he learned when he got sober. And Maddie blubbered her lips in this weird way that made a funny motorboat sound because it was something she'd been doing since she was little girl whenever she was nervous.

I took one last deep breath and a long, hard look at them both and said, "Okay, let's do this." And then we started playing.

CHAPTER NINETEEN

Seventy-four Days After

The thing about being in a band, for me at least, is that the words to the songs disappear altogether and you actually stop hearing the music when you play. On a good night, the best kind of night, it's not the sound that drives the music, it's the racing, the beat and thump behind your eyes, running through your arms, throbbing in your legs, even in your bare feet on the pedals. It's the way the chords build before they drop into the chorus in a one-two hit, the curved thump of the bass note, the rush and pulse of the most important line of lyrics.

When you're a musician, you don't listen to the music with your ears, you sense it all over. It's touch—it's not really sound at all.

. . .

The room buzzed when we started, the audience settling in and warming up. They swayed at first, heads nodding and muscles unwinding as they found our rhythm.

Left, left. Right, right. Drill the snare.

I caught Isaac's eyes during the second or third song and thought of the ferry ride, his skin under my fingertips.

Left, left, right, right. Tap the cymbals.

I watched Beckett and Jay standing by the front speaker, swigging from blue Solo cups and playing PDA, but I shifted my mind away from them.

Left, left, right, right. Push the tempo.

Someone turned the lights down and I closed my eyes, sensing the pulse of the crowd, our sound building faster, louder, cleaner, and crisper.

When I looked again, the audience was dancing with fists pumping in the air, with the surge of adrenaline and the frenzied vibe of everyone in the room feeling and doing the same thing. I could feel the drums in my gut, the snap of stick against skin, as our sound came crashing over them.

I'm not going to lie, we botched a handful of rhythms during the first set and obliterated the sixth song when Maddie lost track of the lyrics and turned to me halfway in with that desperate end-it-as-soon-as-you-can look. But we never stopped playing, a huge accomplishment since in practice you can stop and start over whenever you want. And when we finished the last song before our set break, the crowd went nuts. Like rip-roaring, whistle-blowing wild.

"We're gonna take a break," Maddie purred into the mic as she shifted her weight onto one hip and popped her left motorcycle boot out in front of her. "Come on now," she said when they booed. "Keep your shirts on, we'll be right back."

The set break began with an explosion of "ThatWas Amazings" as me and the rest of Nothing Right huddled around, high-fiving and half hugging, attempting to play it cool but too amped to be nonchalant. We rehashed all the good stuff, like when Hudson dropped a beer bottle on the tile floor in the kitchen during "Body in My Basement" and the crowd started shouting like it was the Super Bowl. Or when my drumstick flew out of my hand during "Finding Wild Acres" because my dad had been right, they fly out of your hand all the time when you're sweating during a gig, and Katie McCrae picked it up and raised it into the air just as Jose Lopate lifted her onto his shoulders, chicken-fight-style.

"What about Maureen Green?" Isaac said when he was next to me. "Did you see her dress fall down?" he asked, and then, quickly as he winked at me, "Not that I was looking."

We had seen it. Everyone had seen the strapless dress drooping as she bounced and jumped and gyrated, and then, finally and inevitably, it had slipped down her chest, flashing anyone who was looking. Maureen Green, the girl with the high-pitched voice who was gossiping in the restroom as I sat in the stall and listened to her say, "I bet he's no more missing than he wants to be."

Beckett made his way to the group of us, his breath hot and boozy as he told us what rock stars we were and how great we sounded. "Just like I knew you would," he slurred.

Someone put on the Ramones and the crowd drifted onstage to talk to us while others wandered onto the balcony or toward the food table to munch. Their voices were hoarse and their eyes were bloodshot, sweat-slicked hair and smeared mascara, but they couldn't stop talking about how great the show was. *Our* show.

"Half an hour?" Maddie said, and Rabbit and I nodded, and then the two of them headed into the dining room to check out the table of snacks. Someone had told us there were bacon-wrapped dates. Someone said there were sliders and mini-cheesesteaks.

"You hungry?" Isaac asked me, but I shook my head. "So I can steal you for a few minutes? I want to show you around the house," he said. Then his hand was in my hand, that electric wave pulsing between us.

I couldn't find any words, so I just nodded.

We shouldered through the crowd to the upstairs, where the noise of the party shifted into a blur of voices punctuated by bursts of laughter. He showed me his father's study first, a massive office space facing the water, and we stood next to each other behind the gigantic oak desk and in front of the wall of windows, pressing our foreheads and fingertips against the cool glass. I thought of my dad first, wondering if he was down there somewhere. Maybe he'd spent the day wandering the Marina neighborhood below us, or maybe he'd walked the beach, looking out at the bridge.

"Look," Isaac said, and pointed. "Alcatraz. Right there."

"You think if there were still prisoners there, they could see us from the courtyard?" I asked. "During yard time, when they got their ten minutes a day outside?"

"The lucky ones could see you," he said.

It didn't seem all that far away, the small island anchored out there in the bay. The sky was shadowed in dark pinks and grays by then, and the bridge looked more amazing than I'd ever seen it look before.

"Sometimes I forget, you know?" I said. "That not everyone gets to see this all the time."

As much as I resented the fact that San Francisco was the city that took my father away, I also knew there were a million people out there who would have loved to wake up here every day, like I got to.

Isaac was nodding. "That's why I let myself be a tourist at least once every summer," he said. "To remind myself. I feel that way about Paris when I'm there, too. It's like with school and work and everything else—I forget to see it sometimes. To actually see the city."

"We're spoiled," I said. "Everyone is, kind of. In one way or another. I think that's how it is everywhere. Like no matter where you live, it becomes normal. And no matter how normal it is to you, it's new and amazing to someone else."

I remembered visiting Chicago as a kid, staying with my grandmother in Berwyn but going into the city to see the Navy Pier or Millennium Park. Granny and I would take a day just the two of us, and we'd spend the afternoon at Lincoln Park Zoo. Somehow the buildings in Chicago seemed bigger and more mysterious than ours, the stores filled with more interesting things. We'd catch a game at Wrigley Field, and even though my dad had taken me to see the Giants lots of times by then, seeing the Cubs was more exciting. I couldn't believe that he'd actually gotten to grow up in Chicago. But standing there with Isaac, looking out at the Pacific and the bridge stretching toward the redwoods, I figured lots of kids who visited my city couldn't believe there were people like me who got to grow up here, too.

Next to me, Isaac slid his hand back into mine and tugged me toward the door. "Onward," he said.

By the time we made it to his bedroom, my heart had finally slowed down from the gig but had sped up all over again when I realized where he was taking me. He opened the door and moved out of the way so I could go in first.

"Voilà," he said. *"Mi casa es su casa."*

He'd strung Christmas lights from the ceiling, tons of them, the only lights on in the room, and when he followed me in, he loosened his tie and lit a stick of incense that was sitting on his nightstand. There was a desk with photos and concert ticket stubs tacked on a bulletin board above it, and the walls were covered in movie posters and a huge world map. But it was the books I couldn't stop looking at—books *everywhere*. Stacked into a makeshift table and piled on his dresser, where most kids would have had a TV or leftover dishes from late-night snacks. There were heaps of them, crawling up the walls by his bed; by the doorway; by the reading chair, where the pile was tall enough to reach the bottom of his Beatles poster, which was hung next to the floor lamp.

"Like most bedrooms, I guess," he said.

"Right," I said. "Except for the fact that your bedroom is actually a library."

He laughed. "Except for that."

He sat on the bed and I sat next to him, nervous a little, but knowing there was nowhere else I'd rather be.

"Bookworm," he said, and shrugged. "Now you know my secret."

I picked through the stack on his nightstand: *Extremely Loud and Incredibly Close*; *White Teeth*; *Slaughterhouse-Five*;

The Hotel New Hampshire; The Perks of Being a Wallflower.

"I got really into it after we moved," he said. "Reading, I mean. I guess I was lonely, you know? I didn't know anyone in Paris when we got there, and when I came back here that first summer, it seemed like all my friends had found other friends. It's not like you can call someone up and ask him to meet you for lunch or go for a hike when you're in the fifth grade. You're still just a kid, but you're too old for play dates, for your parents make sure you have friends." He cracked his jaw. "It was a tough few years. So I read. A lot."

I realized that even though Isaac had always intrigued my friends and me, we'd never actually gotten in touch with him when he was in town. We never invited him to hang out with us, never included him when we went to parties or met up at Hippie Hill or Haight Street. We'd built him into some kind of alluring idea, an enigma, really, but we sort of forgot he was just an awkward kid like the rest of us.

"Don't get me wrong. The music stuff is important to me too," he said. "I love my job, helping a band prep for a show. There's nothing like it."

And I suddenly pictured him a million miles away at the end of the summer, setting up the stage for someone else, some random band in Paris instead of my band in California.

"And I love watching *you* play," he said, his hand on my leg, tracing circles just below the hem of my dress. "But it's not important to me the way it's important to you. Books are. They're what I like the most." Then he tilted his head and smiled. "What I *liked* the most until you, that is."

I was smart enough to know that Isaac had probably shown lots of girls his room before, had maybe even used the same line on them: "Until you." But it didn't really matter, because being with him felt good. It felt easy and exciting at the same time, comfortable but different than being with any other boy. It just felt right.

Slow hands and eyelashes on my cheek when he kissed my nose, my mouth, my neck. He lifted my hand, kissed the inside of my wrist and bit at the guitar-string bracelet, smiling with his eyes locked on mine before he moved back to my lips. His fingers gently tugging through the tangles in my hair and sending goose bumps down my spine. Slow and cautious and sweet. Below us, someone dropped a glass or a bottle and people whistled and cheered, but they all sounded so far away. My lips were on his cheek—the coarse stubble and smell of cedar—on his neck behind his ear to make him laugh, and finally his lips again, more serious by then. I was lit up, like his skin made my skin a million times more sensitive. His hands on my waist and my palms on his shoulders, pulling him closer. Our mouths quicker, lips wetter, as I leaned against him and we both fell back onto the bed, laughing a little, but not stopping.

And then footsteps. And voices in the hallway. I thought first of Philip Corey Thompson and all three of his names, the whole of him bursting through the door and catching us. But then the worry dropped away as I recognized the voice and the rise and fall of the words.

"Caalll-ie . . . Caalll-ie?"

So I pulled away from Isaac and whispered "I'm sorry" before kissing him quickly again and calling out, "I'm in here, Beck. Here."

Beckett was drunk—I knew it as soon as I saw him. He and Jay were bumping into each other as they stood in the doorway, and when Beck finally started talking, it sounded like his mouth was full of glue.

"Ooooh, man," he said. "God, Cal, I'm sorry," seeing us on the bed, breathing hard. "I didn't know you were . . . didn't know you two . . ."

"It's okay," I said quickly.

He kind of looked like a little kid, disheveled and disoriented, which was almost endearing. But then I moved my eyes to Jay, Jay with his stupid Mohawk, in his tiny hipster T-shirt, with his smug little smile as he leaned into Beck like he actually deserved to be hanging out with my best friend.

So I said, "Are you okay, Beck?" and even though he nodded, I told him, "No, you're not. You're wasted. How did you get so drunk?"

He said, "Jay brought the booze. Snuck in a flank in his hoodie."

Next to him, Jay was laughing. "A flask. You mean a flask," he said to Beck, and I said, "Classy. Way to get him slammed, Jay," but Beck was shaking his head.

"No, I'm fine," he said, swaying a little. "Really. I just need the thingamajigs. The whatsits."

Jay laugh-whispered something I couldn't hear, and then Beck took exaggerated care to straighten his bow tie—his jacket was who knows where—then he slowly put his hands in his pockets and tried to stand up straight and serious, a last-ditch effort to pull himself together.

"The keys," he said. A laugh, high-pitched and mashed with a hiccup or a burp, I couldn't tell which. "I need the keys. For, like . . ." He slid his hand in Jay's hand—Jay, who still had not said one word to me since the bakery sidewalk sighting. "The keys to the car. We need some time alone," Beck said definitively.

"You've got to be kidding me," I said. This was why he needed me? Because he wanted to hook up with his slimeball boyfriend? I looked at Jay, but Jay looked at the floor and next to me, Isaac stood up.

"My dad's got all the keys," he told them. "And I hate to say it, but I doubt he'd be willing to give them to you guys, since you're . . . well, you're shitfaced."

But Beck was shaking his head. "That's where you come in, my friend." He pointed and wobbled his finger at me. "You're sober, right?"

"There's no way I'm getting the keys from Isaac's dad so you and this loser can go make out in Rabbit's car," I told them, realizing, as I said it, that in Beckett's mind there was no reason in the world I should be calling his boyfriend a loser.

Beck said "Whoa," and I said "Sorry," and he said, "That's pretty harsh, Cal," and Isaac asked me, "Are you okay?"

Isaac being another person who had absolutely no idea that Jay was a complete fraud.

I was counting back from twelve, like always, and when I hit zero I asked if I could talk to Beck alone. And then it was just me and him in Isaac's bedroom, which had, I swear, only five minutes earlier been the best place in the universe but now suddenly felt toxic and claustrophobic.

Beck stood next to the book table and stumbled with his words. "Look, I'm sorry I interrupted your . . . but it's not like I'm asking . . . it's not like a life-or-death . . ." And then, a little quieter, "I mean, I really like him, Cal. It'd be nice if you made an effort."

It was absolutely the worst time to do it, with him being drunk and the band probably wondering where I was so we could start the second set. With Jay and Isaac maybe standing right outside the door, waiting for us—listening, even—and Beck with that woozy I-might-just-need-to-puke look creeping across his face as he leaned on the book table, which wasn't really a table, just a pile of hardbacks, so that he almost fell over when it swayed.

It was worse than the worst possible time, but I sat back down on the bed and said, "He's cheating on you, Beck. I saw him with another guy. Kissing some boy in front of the bakery in my neighborhood. The one with the good macarons." And it was like once I started talking, I couldn't stop, so, with my eyes on the floor, I kept going: "And it wasn't even like he apologized. He saw me, I mean. When I saw him. He didn't even come clean. I kind of thought that if he told you first, then maybe he wasn't such a sleaze, but he didn't. He didn't tell you at all. He acted like everything was fine. And you seemed so happy that I just couldn't be the one to say it. I tried at the beach—I swear, I was going to tell you everything—but you just kept talking about how important it was to you that he and I got along."

"When?" he said. "When did you see him?"

"Last week."

I figured he'd be angry. Angry at Jay, obviously, but maybe also a little angry at me for not telling him sooner, and then for telling him like that. I thought he'd get mad and then he'd probably ask for another cup of whatever it was he'd been slugging all night, concede the fact that his new boyfriend was, in fact, a total moron, and finally collapse next to me on the bed. I was ready to say all the right stuff. I wanted to tell him that Jay wasn't good enough for him anyway, that Jay was too old and too trendy, that his jeans were skintight and his T-shirts too small. That in a few weeks we'd laugh about the time Beck dated that guy who actually had a Mohawk. We'd stop going to the café—the lattes were too expensive and the line was always long—and who needed Jay, anyway? Beck would find someone a million times better in half a second once word got out that he was single again. And I figured it would take some convincing, but eventually he'd nod, let me kiss him on the cheek. Maybe we'd stay in the bedroom for a while longer, listening the crowd downstairs, and then he'd be . . . well, I figured he'd be okay.

I did not figure he would turn his eyes to me and say, "You are a selfish brat, Callan Pace. And you're totally full of shit."

"What?"

"You heard me—it's not true. You just made it up because you've been jealous ever since Jay and I got together."

"Are you kidding me? Please tell me you're kidding me," I said.

He was standing in front of me by then, looking down and spitting a little when he said, "What I'm trying to saying is . . . What I . . . I just mean this thing with me and Jay is real. And making up some lie isn't going to stop it."

"It's real, huh?" I asked, standing then too. "As real as him climbing all over some other guy's face in the middle of the street? I saw it, Beck. I was there. Why would I make that up?"

"Because your summer's been shit so far," he said. "Because you haven't found your dad and you aren't allowed to apply to the school you really want go to. Because you haven't had my unadvisable attention since I started dating Jay, and you need that . . . you, like, totally need that. You're angry for all kinds of good reasons, and I get that, Callie. But you can't do this. You can't take it out on me."

"Undivided," I said. "Undivided attention, moron."

"Whatever."

"You're not even making sense," I said. "Look, I know you like him and this whole thing sucks. But that doesn't mean it's not true. Ask him, Beck. See what he says."

"You're just trying to break us up. So I'm miserable, just like you are. So we're on an even playing field, like always. So you can have me back as your sidekick, always on call."

"Why don't you dry out a little, and then we can talk this over?" I said.

And he said, "Whatever," and then, just before he stormed out of the room and slammed the door like the drama queen that he was, he called me a jealous asshat.

The second set did not go well.

Beckett and Jay were nowhere to be found, so even though I shouldn't have cared, I was pretty distracted. My head was pounding so bad by the time I sat down behind my drums, I wasn't even sure I'd be able to play. Rabbit suggested we begin with some covers, but we'd lost most of the crowd by then—a lot of the kids had gone home or had gone to different parts of the house to make out or play cards or whatever. Isaac stood up front during the whole second set and pretended we were doing great, even when one of Rabbit's strings broke and we had to finish Porno for Pyros' "Pets" without him, which sounded terrible. So we made it a quick set and called it a night, agreeing to pretend the second half of the show never happened.

"You sure you're okay?" Isaac asked for the third time once we had finished and were packing up the gear.

I nodded yes but said no. "It's just this thing with Beckett," I said, knowing I was being short with him but not knowing how to fix it. I was tired and hungry—one hundred percent deflated.

I called my mom around midnight from Isaac's landline. The gig was great, I lied. We were all really happy, and could I please spend the night at Maddie's since we were celebrating? In truth, I just couldn't imagine going home and having to answer her questions about the party. Or worse, her being already asleep and having to face a quiet house.

"We're leaving now," I told her. "Rabbit's driving. Everything's fine," I said.

I was asleep in the backseat, my head knocking against my snare drum, by the time we pulled out of Isaac's neighborhood.

CHAPTER TWENTY

Seventy-five Days After

I slept a toss-and-turn dreamless sleep and woke on Maddie's couch in the basement to her phone ringing that high-pitched loop OverAndOverAndOver again. I propped myself up, groggy and a little bit light-headed, my muscles sore.

The ringing stopped just as Maddie said, "'Morning, sunshine," her voice rising from the floor, where she was tucked into a green sleeping bag.

"I feel awful," I said, as a headache slammed behind my eyes. "Like I slept on my cymbals. Like I ran a marathon."

"The life of a rock star," she said. "We forgot to eat dinner. Plus, you refused to wear earplugs." She stretched her arms over her head and moaned. "And I don't know about you, but my shoulders feel like they're on fire. Who knew moving band equipment was so taxing? I guess I'm supposed to get in shape before our next gig."

She was right—my body ached and my ears were ringing as I worked my way through the memories of the night before. I thought about kissing Isaac first. And then about the fight with Beckett.

Maddie was up and stuffing her sleeping bag back into its sack. "Brunch, right?" she said. "ASAP. I'm starved. Let's call Rabbit and see if he'll pick us up."

I nodded, and then the phone started again, so I said, "Not it," and she said, "Me neither."

"Where's your mom?" I asked, and she told me her mom was at work.

But the ringing wouldn't stop, so eventually Maddie crossed the room to grab the phone, an old see-through handset she'd won in third grade selling magazine subscriptions. It lit up when it rang, and as kids we loved inspecting all the parts, the wires and circuit boards and levers; we'd try to guess which piece would move when we punched the buttons. We'd used it for prank calls when were in elementary school, then first calls to boys we had crushes on when we were old enough.

By the time I was up on my feet, she was holding the phone out toward me.

"It's Beckett."

The first thing he said was, "I'm not talking to you, just for the record," and I said, "Okay," and then he said, "But your mom called my cell. She said she tried Maddie's a bunch of times but no one answered. She sounded pretty upset, Cal. You should probably call her back."

"Upset how?"

"I dunno. Like crazy upset. Just call her, okay?"

She picked up on the first ring—the first half ring, really—and I knew right away she'd heard something about my dad.

"It's me," I said. "Is everything okay?"

I was back on the couch with the cordless, and Maddie was upstairs taking a shower so I could have some privacy while I made the call.

My mother cried that quiet kind of cry, muffled by her attempt to sound brave and in control.

"Where are you?" she asked.

I told her I was still at Maddie's. We'd slept late. We'd ignored the phone. We'd heard from Beck. "Is everything okay?" I asked again.

Outside the basement window, voices spoke Spanish on the street, the quick words flicking off their tongues and seeping through the walls. Laughter and low tones before the sound of laughter again.

"Mom? Is everything okay?"

"Yes," she said, then, "No. I'm not sure."

And then everything slowed down—the voices as they drifted up the street, the sound of the shower running as the water slid through the pipes above me. A bus as it brought people to and from Saturday morning brunches or coffee dates.

And finally, my mother's words, sluggish and mangled as she said, "The police called, Callie. They found a body." Then even slower, crawling through the wires from her phone to mine. "A man," she said. The syllables hopeless, like a whisper of the final verse of the saddest song ever written. "Dark hair. There were glasses, too. Black wire frames. Near the body."

I imagined white teeth and bones.

I listened to her crying—the pitch of her inhale and the sigh of her exhale; the white noise in the breaks of her voice; the way she started to say something, and stopped. A dampness in her throat.

"I'm going to the coroner's office," she said eventually. "And I want to go alone."

"Where?" I asked. "They found it where?"

"Dolores Park."

Dolores Park near SoMa, near his last job site.

"Callie, it doesn't mean that it's him," she said, the slow-motion giving way to a quickening in her voice as she breathed in, desperately trying to convince me—to convince herself too, probably. I imagined her at the kitchen table, wiping her nose on her sleeve and chewing her nails. "It wasn't . . . the body wasn't . . . the face was too . . ."

"Don't," I said.

"I just mean that they couldn't be sure," she told me. "It wasn't . . . clear. They're running tests on his hair and finger-nails now."

His hair, tangled and overgrown if he hadn't gotten a trim since we'd last seen him.

"Come home," she said. "Wait for me here, and I'll call you as soon as I know anything. But I want to go alone."

Before: On the Saturday after my very first gig, he would have been home, waiting for me.

"How'd it go?" he would've asked as soon as I'd made my way to the kitchen.

He may have been eating a snack, a clementine with slices of sharp cheddar cheese, a glass of chocolate milk, maybe.

No, that wasn't it.

Instead, he would have said, "You were amazing. My little girl, holding her own in a band," because he never would have missed the gig. He would have been there even if I hadn't invited my parents to come watch me play.

We would have sat at the table, rehashing the night, and then I would've asked him to make me a grilled cheese sandwich. A little mayo, a slice of avocado, and lots of butter in the frying pan.

He would have told me I kicked ass and wouldn't have mentioned the lousy second set. Halfway through the sandwich, he might have reminded me that anything worth doing takes time to do it right. Each gig would get better; the music would become more consistent. He would have said that he was proud of me.

After: The house was empty when I got home, just a note on the counter in my mother's cursive: *I'll call as soon as I know anything. Stay home. Love you.*

She said to wait at the house for the call, but I couldn't possibly wait there, so I tied on my sneakers and decided I needed to run. Shorts, long-sleeved T-shirt, halfway out the door when the phone rang.

"Are you okay?" Maddie asked when I answered. "You were gone when I came back downstairs."

My heart popped beneath my breastbone, OneTwoOne TwoOneTwo. The kitchen had grown inexplicably small as I counted down the seconds until I could get out of the house. I needed air. Movement.

"I had to come home," I told her. "But I'm on my way out for a run."

I couldn't say the words yet, not aloud. A body in Dolores Park. I cut her off quickly when she asked about my mom's call and told her I'd left because I didn't feel well.

"But now you're going for a run?" she asked.

"I'm fine," I said. "Really."

She asked again about my mom's call, but I was telling her I had to go, already hanging up the receiver before she had a chance to say good-bye. I headed out the door and caught the Divisadero bus to Fell Street, my 8.67-mile loop.

I skipped the stretching and started into the park, past the Conservatory of Flowers and out toward Stow Lake. As I ran, I told myself everything I could remember about my dad, afraid it was the last time I'd be able to think of him while still hoping, still having the chance to see him again. His allergy to shellfish. The slurping soup sound and the peanut butter toast for breakfast. But I needed more than that.

On Saturdays they closed the main road that ran through the park so there were no cars, but the streets were crowded with rollerbladers and couples walking dogs, people drinking coffee and wandering the grounds like everything was normal.

A body. A man's body. In Dolores Park.

I thought of how much it hurt my feelings when he'd take his motorcycle out on the weekends without me, wanting a day to himself and the freedom to ride without having the worry of his kid on the back of the bike. He'd be gone for hours, alone, heading north toward the redwoods. Or sometimes he'd go with a friend, Roland, the guy my dad bought bike parts from when his motorcycles needed work. He'd come home with sunburned hands, smiling and feeling "like a million bucks," he'd say, hurting my feelings even more. I remembered the way I'd sit in my room, waiting to hear him pull into the garage, angry but waiting for him still.

I passed the de Young museum and then Lloyd Lake, my fists pumping and my heart racing as I dodged tourists taking photos, a man walking with headphones over his ears, and a woman on her cell, talking too loud. I passed boys in skinny jeans and sunglasses. Girls in long skirts clutching cardigan sweaters around their bodies, the cool air of the nearby water spraying wind-blown bursts through the park. And I just kept moving.

The thing is, when a person goes missing in a small town, telephone trees are set in motion, calling the community to action. Phones ring and news spreads lightning fast between families, down main streets and country roads, through church basement meetings. The talk passes between women ordering meats and chesses from the deli counter at the local grocery. The story spreads through department store aisles, from mouth to mouth to mouth, into living rooms, until everyone—gas station attendants and schoolteachers and tellers at the bank—until everyone knows.

And then they find him.

I'd seen it in movies and read it in books set in small towns. In the end, the locals pull together, hold a late-night vigil with candles and posters and flyers, and then they find the person who's gone missing.

But in a city—even a small one like ours, which is only seven miles by seven miles—that's not how it works. The *Chronicle* might run an article buried on page 6; the local news station might cover it on the evening show, prime time. But even so, no one will respond. A city is too busy to slow down enough to save a man like my dad. And in that way, San Francisco failed me. The city that my parents swore was the only place on earth they could ever live. In the end, that city bailed on my family and didn't find him quick enough.

I pounded past the Disc Golf Course and then by Middle Lake, north again at the fork. Sweat dripped down my back as last night's mascara ran into my eyes, burning my vision with brown charcoal smears, but I kept running. I ran through a leg cramp and ignored the racing in my chest. I just kept going.

And the way he always let me win at Scrabble, even when I was old enough to know better. That had always bugged me too. Like letting me win was a way of showing me that he cared about me, when really I'd wished he'd just play fair and honest. I wanted to lose if that's how the score turned out— that would have been the best way for him to show me respect. He shouldn't have faked it and ignored the chance for triple word scores when his turn came so my name always ended up circled in red ink on the scorecard. *Winner* he'd write, with a check mark. Like I believed him.

And what about Elizabeth Martin? Elizabeth, who was twenty years old and sleeping in the bed with her mother when the earthquake hit in 1906. The two of them clutching each other at five in the morning, imagining the end of the world happening on Wednesday, April 18, as their bed slid around the room like a boat at sea, whipping from one wall to the other like a kite caught in the wind.

That's what family really is—holding on in the worst situations. Not up and disappearing.

April 18. The same day my dad went missing. Seventy-five days ago, counting the day he vanished. Which I did.

My feet pounded the pavement and my head throbbed as I passed the Beach Chalet, but I kept running, the water just there on the other side of Highway 1.

I thought of the man I'd been envisioning all those weeks—the man from the photo, navigating the destruction of the earthquake in a 1906 version of my city. I wondered if it was him and if it was possible that the images were more than just strings of imaginings I'd tied together. My dad rescuing survivors from the debris and helping strangers track down family members, befriending those still struck by the shock of the earthquake and providing some kind of comfort. He would have been great at that.

The temperature dropped then, the air cooled by the ocean, with the salt and the wind rocking off the Pacific. And the thumping between my ears grew louder than it had ever been before as I pushed forward, off the path and over the grass, longing for that water, wanting the ice of it on my legs, my arms. The way it would numb my skin, my fibers, my cells.

The thumping grew even louder than those waves on the other side of the highway, louder than the honking horn when it came, louder than the sound of tires shrieking against asphalt in front of me as the car kept getting closer, closer, closer.

The pain that came next—the metal-slamming thrust of a million pounds of weight trying but failing to slow down, to stop before it was too late—the pain wasn't tangible at all. Instead it was sight: slices of white icicles in frozen waterfalls; white waves out past the sand. Whitecaps breaking against one another, the peaks and crests foaming and frothing just out of reach. Honey-colored sand. The midnight black of highway asphalt and the silver of the car's bumper. And then, finally, darkness.

Heat blanketed me when I woke—red heat streaming across my face as I lay on the pavement, heat throbbing down my shoulder and firing through my leg. I heard voices, but far away and foggy under sirens, the whooshing in my ears, and someone ScreamingScreamingScreaming like I'd never heard before. I wanted to tell them to stop, the noise was too high, too loud, and too much, but when I tried to speak, nothing worked the way I wanted it to, and I realized the screams were mine.

Voices calling out numbers, strong arms lifting me up and placing me down, the cool metal of scissors slicing through my clothes before the shutting of a door and the rocking back and forth beneath me. There was blackness; quiet, finally; sleep maybe; and then a crowd of faces I didn't recognize. Cream-colored walls, but not just cream, stripes of blue, too. Specks of green.

Someone said, "Can you hear me? You're in the hospital, hon. You're okay," and then it went dark again.

Whirs and rhythms of machines: thump, beep; thump, beep. One, two. Someone clamped a mask on me, a thing that smelled like my mother's cleaning supplies. A mask for breathing. So I went to the ship, that ship underground at my father's job site in SoMa. And I tried to rescue him. Him on the stern in a hard hat, and me with my mask, wearing my blue party dress. But I'd arrived too late, because the crane released its big crane arm and slammed me in the chest. One two, one two, one two.

Beeping and ticking and cold liquid ice flushing through

my arm. Daylight outside a window, the clouds a calm-looking cream. Nighttime and daylight and nighttime again. The headache from the morning, the headache from all the days I'd ever had a headache in my life. And that violent heat streaming across my face that never stopped. Like white lightning.

My mother standing over me as she brushed her fingers along my arm. Her in a chair by the window. Her in the doorway, sitting on the bed, standing by a machine with thin tubes that stretched like tentacles to who knows where.

My father was there also, but not *there* there—somewhere else where I couldn't quite see him clearly. He slumped, a thin shadow, in a sepia-colored park as men in uniforms passed by. His suit, two sizes too big, as he reached into his jacket pocket and pulled out a perfect piece of clear cut glass, triangular, jagged on one side but smooth on the other two.

In and out of sleep for days, it seemed, and then, finally, groggy while my mother helped me shower at the hospital, helped me dress, and helped me into a wheelchair once I was discharged to go home. I awoke in a car, nighttime and bleary from pain pills, lying across the backseat with my leg a million pounds heavy and my face throbbing, still, with bloodred heat. A radio played something strong with horns, as if the jazz music were tapping inside my head. I counted the drumbeats and searched for the rhythm to anchor me in the car, inside something real, but the trees passing in the window above me were blurred and watery. I closed my eyes and focused on not getting sick as the metallic tang of nausea fought its way out of my stomach and into my chest, up to my throat.

I tried to talk, but my face felt boarded up, like a plank of wood, and what I said ended up sounding like "Hmmhhmm."

"Baby," my mother said.

I leaned to turn on my side so I could see her, but my body wouldn't work right.

"You're okay," she said. "Stay still. We're in the car. Almost home. I'm taking you home," she said. "You're okay."

"Hmmhhmm," I tried again. "Wssss it hmmmm?"

"No, baby," she said. "The body wasn't him."

CHAPTER TWENTY-ONE

Image 6B: "Untitled (View of fire downtown), 1906."
Negative of unknown film type, 132 × 171 mm.

In the morning they leave for Golden Gate Park.

"I can't stop thinking of that woman," the man tells William as they walk. "Such an embarrassing mistake. I keep searching for an explanation, but there is nothing." He touches the scab behind his ear, still tender and swollen.

Next to him, William plunges his hands into his pockets. "Have faith and your memory will surely return soon."

Clouds of smoke rise from the city, and while they walk the man notices that the uppermost billows are sunlit as the air warms and the morning temperatures climb. The roads are obstructed by debris and caravans of carriages, buggies, and dog carts, even, families and their servants trying to escape the city or to make their way to the camps in the parks to find those still missing. News of food rations and shelter in the Presidio and Golden Gate Park had spread quickly the night before.

It takes hours to reach the park, and when they arrive, it is a mass of large white marquee tents; shelters typically used for lawn parties or entertaining are now being used for lodging and protection from the smoke. Many of the wealthy have hired help to haul their household goods in wagons, and their camps are easily identified by the rocking chairs and wooden tables set up out front, where women in long corselet skirts and large hats pour cans of milk into glasses for the children at their feet.

"The registrar list?" the man asks one of the mothers. "Do you know where we can find it?"

She says their station is located near the garden, so they move in that direction.

The man spots Henry—William's brother—first, and though he doesn't recognize Henry in any way, he is overtaken with an instinctive feeling that this is the boy they have been searching for. The young man stands on a tree stump, reading to a small crowd; one of his eyes is bruised and swollen, his waistcoat soiled with ash and mud, and his pants are torn at the left knee. His right arm drives his fist upward with the beats of the words, while the other hand cradles a book as he reads from its pages. The group in front of him sways and calls out, or rather calls back to the refrain of the poetry he recites.

The man thinks of church first, and then of school. Of some kind of lecture he attended in his youth.

He points, and then William is upon the young man, hungrily tugging on a shirtsleeve, pulling his brother down from the stump and into his arms. He rocks back and forth, with Henry enfolded in his embrace. "You disappeared," he says. "How could you do that to me? How could you . . . ," scolding the boy one moment and then thanking God the next for finally having found him.

It is a beautiful thing, this reunion grounded by years of memories shared between the two, but the man slips away, giving William and the boy privacy as he moves toward the large white registrar's tent. In the line stretched in front of it, he spots a blank-faced man with a young child in his arms. The toddler cries quietly, her pale hair drifting lose from her cap as the father mummers "Now, now" and "Hush, hush."

Heat blankets the park as a teenage boy walks up and down the line, selling jars of water. The man is surprised when he checks and finds that his pockets are empty, that somehow he is without identification, cash, or even a handful of change. He sheds his coat and unbuttons the top of his dress shirt, taking inventory of his clothes, searching for clues embedded in the fibers. No monogram marks his lapel, no embroidered handkerchief is folded into his breast pocket.

William and his brother approach, William calling out and

laughing, as if he has just stumbled from a saloon, though Henry's face is locked, his eyes downcast and his body tense. Introductions are made, hands shaken, backs and shoulders patted.

"He's fine, just look at him," William says, nudging Henry forward. "He's here. And he'll be just fine now." He looks at the man: "Thank you for helping me find him."

The man smiles but can't withdraw his eyes from the father in line with the small child.

William explains that Henry was walking the streets when the quake hit. He had been to an art show the night before and couldn't rest, so he wandered up Russian Hill to view the sunrise.

"I found shelter at a friend's," Henry says. His hand shakes as he wipes sweat from his brow. "We were forced to evacuate early this morning, though—everything south of Washington is now gone."

William shakes his head. "No need to think of it," he says. "We're together now, and that is what matters most."

In the line, the child has begun to cry and the father moves the girl from one shoulder to the other. But the wails grow louder. Eventually, he turns to those standing behind him; "Hunger, I suppose," he says, apologizing. "She's not been fed since dinnertime last night."

The line advances, and a jolt of heat pours through the man's body, electric and tingling. His coat drops from his fingers as he watches the father and child shift forward.

William picks the coat up from the ground. "We'll search for water now, my friend. For something to eat," he says softly.

The man's knees buckle and he stumbles, but William catches him by the elbow and says, "It's all right," once, and then again—finally, a third time. "We're here," William says. "You're okay."

But the man is shaking as the father with the child stands at the front of the line, speaking in a hushed voice to a pair of women sitting behind the table.

Henry rocks back and forth. "Would you like to get in line?" he asks the man, and then, to William, "Does he want to check the lists for his family?"

"Do you have family to check for?" William asks. "I should have asked sooner. Are there names you would like to inquire about?"

But still the man cannot speak.

"Breathe," William says. "Lets find somewhere to sit. Let's find some shade."

The man's hands burn and his feet are numb. He watches the father and child as one of the women behind the table shakes her head, while the other pushes a stack of papers aside and draws up the list, using her finger to scroll down the names. The toddler keeps crying, and the father mumbles, "Dear God, dear God."

A long pause and then, finally, a rustle at the table. The women are smiling, nodding their heads, as one of them says, "Yes, yes, she is here, she is fine. Her name is right there, in the 'Survived' column."

The father takes one of the women's hands and brings it to his lips, thanking them over and over and over again.

The thumping between the man's ears dims, and the temperature drops as the air is cooled by a wind rocking off the ocean.

"Do you have family to check for?" William asks again.

The man shuts his eyes, knowing suddenly that yes, he does have a family somewhere in the city. A family longing for and looking for him, a family he is bound to. But the names are lost and the images he sees are mere shadows, vague outlines of silhouettes he can't quite make out. A wife. A child.

"I'd like to help," he says carefully as his purpose becomes clear. "To join those working to reunite the survivors," he tells William. "That there," he says, pointing to the man with the toddler, who now kneels with the little girl, rocking her in his arms as tears stream down his cheeks. "I'd like to help make that happen as best as I can for as many people as possible. For those still searching for family."

And next to him William nods as if he understands that this ambition will now define the life of his friend.

CHAPTER TWENTY-TWO

Seventy-nine Days After

I'd been in the hospital for three days, and the night my mom brought me home, when I asked what had happened, she called it a mishap.

"You were running," she said. "And they couldn't stop in time. A mishap." She pulled the covers up to my chin as if I were a child and ran her palm over the wrinkles in the blanket. I noticed her nail-bitten fingers shaking. And then she leaned over the nightstand, poured two pills into her palm, placed them on my tongue, brought a glass of water to my lips, and said, "Just sleep."

In the morning, I woke to the cadence of sidewalk traffic outside the house: dogs barking, buses stopping and starting, voices laughing, and there, just behind the noise, somewhere a few miles away, I imagined I heard the ocean.

"You're awake?" My mother stood in the doorway. She wore jeans and a red V-neck sweater and was barefoot, with her hair pulled back in a ponytail, no makeup, but somehow more beautiful than I'd seen her look in a long time.

I raised my hand to my face, the burning having shifted from red to pink, but a rich pink still, and she said, "Don't. It'll be sore to touch for a while now."

My fingers ran over the ply of hospital gauze, and, under- neath, my skin throbbed.

"Road rash," she told me as she sat on the bed, nudging my hand away from my cheek. She smelled like the lavender lotion she used, and a bit like vanilla, too, my grandmother having taught her the same trick she taught me. "It'll heal before you know it."

My left leg was set in a cast that ended mid-thigh, and I wore a matching cast from my right wrist to the elbow. My mother told me the pill bottles on the nightstand were pain medicine and antibiotics for my abrasions.

The car that hit me—the couple heading north toward Sonoma who didn't see me run past the Beach Chalet and push off the path—was the second half of the accident that broke my leg, shattered my wrist, bruised my shoulder, and left me covered with severe lacerations on the right side of my face from skidding over the highway.

I was the first half of the accident.

I hadn't been wearing headphones with the music cranked, and I wasn't talking on a cell phone—typical excuses for that kind of accident. There wasn't a reason in the world that I darted in front of the car—not one that made sense, at least. I'd simply been running too fast, distracted by my thoughts. In the end, it had mostly been my own fault.

"I'm so sorry," I said. "I don't know what happened."

She adjusted the pillows so I could sit up. "It was someone else," she said. "In Dolores Park. I told you last night, but I didn't know if you remembered."

Someone else that was not him, which meant he was still missing.

"I was thinking of him," I told her. "When I was running. Thinking of all the things I didn't like about him when he was here."

She smiled. "Like the toothpicks? The way he'd use them at the restaurant instead of waiting until we weren't in public? Most people use them in the car, on the drive home."

"I'd forgotten that," I told her. I leaned for the cup of water on the nightstand and saw the guitar-string bracelet and the piece of glass from the job site resting next to it.

"The hospital gave me the bracelet," she said. "And I found the glass in the wash. For some reason I thought it might be important."

I picked up the piece of glass and rubbed it between my fingers. "I realized I'm angry, you know? I've been working so hard to distract myself from missing him that I didn't notice how angry I am. At him for letting it happen and for leaving me behind, and at me for not being able to find him. At . . ." I hesitated. "I've been angry at you," I said, "and I'm not even sure why."

She'd cleaned my room while I was at the hospital, and my books from the library about 1906 were stacked on my reading chair, along with the photography book from the art exhibit. She'd also organized the earthquake DVDs on my desk and picked up all the clothes from my floor.

"You've been so worried," she said, drawing my eyes back to her. "About disasters and emergency plans, all these what-ifs that I don't have an answer for. It's not healthy, Callan. It's not fair, and I don't know how to fix it. I don't know how to stop you from worrying so much."

"It's okay," I told her, but she said, "No, it's not. And I know I've put a lot of pressure on you. School, track, and college prep. And this thing with your dad . . . it's an impossible thing for someone your age to accept."

I'd gone back to the library and made copies of the photo—I'd blown it up one, two, three hundred percent so I could look closer at the man who looked just like him, and I wondered if she'd seen the copies when she'd cleaned my room, the sheets of blurred images tucked inside the book. I wondered if she'd seen him there too, or if I was the only one.

"Being a parent is the most difficult thing," she said. "It's like playing with magic—there are so many things you have to trick yourself into believing."

"Like what?" I opened my palm and held it out to her so she could take the piece of glass, which she did.

"Mainly, you have to trick yourself into thinking you have some kind of control, that you can protect your child."

She held the glass up to the light, and I wondered if she could feel what I felt when I held it—that soft vibration and warmth.

"But it's there all along, that truth that you can't stop bad things from happening. There's too much of it, the possibility of pain. But as a parent, you have to convince yourself that you can prevent your child from having to face it, that you can guarantee they'll make it through unharmed." She shook her head. "The One Great Lie parents must tell themselves every single day." She put the piece of glass back on the nightstand. "Because if you don't believe you can protect them, if you don't think there's a chance, then being a parent would be an impossible thing . . . It would be senseless, an impossible and unbearable thing."

We listened to the sound of ringing down the hall, and I realized she'd turned the volume off on the phone in my room. Eventually, the machine picked up in her bedroom— my father's voice still, the same recording I'd played a million times when she wasn't home. It was the only way I could still hear him.

"I miss him," I said. "His voice. His . . . everything."

"I know you do." And then, "I realize I don't have a monopoly on missing him. I know it's been just as hard on you as it's been on me. He was my best friend, Callie, and I'm guessing he was your best friend too."

I realized that even though losing my dad was by far the most terrible thing I could have had to endure, I had no idea what it would be like to lose a husband, that one person you picked to be a part of your family, your greatest ally. I looked at my mother and knew she'd been just as lost as I had those past months.

"But we can't keep doing this," she said as she ran her fingers over my cheek, pressing lightly on the gauze. "Running in circles like this. I could have lost you," she told me, her eyes filling with tears even though I could tell she was trying not to cry. "That's not something I'd be able to handle. I couldn't go on if something . . . It's just not an option," she said finally. "I miss him. But I've been missing you, too." She kept going: "I know I'm not supposed to admit it, that I should be stronger. But I need you. I need you to be here. To be *present*. We won't survive this if we keep shutting each other out."

I thought of all the hours I'd spent practicing with Nothing Right after my father disappeared. The long shifts she'd taken at the library and the afternoons I'd spent running in the park. The brunches at Squat & Gobble and the meetings with my friends at the cafés. Her, silently passing me in the hallway, quietly drifting through the house. And all that time I'd spent looking for him, never once explaining to her what I was doing. Not once asking for her help.

"You can't keep worrying about bad things that may or may not happen, studying disasters from a hundred years ago," she said. "He wouldn't want that. I know it, and you know it too."

She hadn't found the photo, then—or if she had, she hadn't seen him there. My mother believed I was reading about the earthquake and watching the videos because I'd been worried it could happen to us. Maybe I had been.

"So I'm thinking that's what we use to make it okay," she said. "Us missing him so much. Knowing that we're both fighting the same thing, even if we miss him in different ways. What if we use that common ground to build on something new? To work on *us*? Our relationship?" Her eyes were pleading.

It was one of those moments that are so horribly beautiful, an unbearable truth there in the middle of everything: Because he was gone, we needed each other more than we'd ever needed each other before.

"We're going to be okay," she said.

And a terrible sadness poured through me, because what she meant to say was "We're going to be okay without him."

I wanted to believe her. Even as my heart was breaking, I wanted to believe that she was right.

It took over a week for my shoulder to heal enough so I could start using crutches to get around the house, and I mostly spent the time holed up in my bedroom, sleeping and watching old movies with my mom. I read all the back issues of *Rolling Stone* I'd been ignoring since I'd started studying the earthquake; then I read my dad's copies of *National Geographic*, which actually weren't boring at all. I read about Lake Powell in the Southwest and about the Irrawaddy River in Myanmar. I studied photos of a sixteen-hundred-year-old mummy unearthed in Peru and thought of all the other boats or bones or relics that might be buried under our city. Eventually, I ran out of magazines, and my mom brought me the stack of college catalogs she'd been collecting "just in case," so I looked them over and tried to imagine hanging out at the beach near UC Santa Barbara or going to concerts at the House of Blues near UCLA. I also reread all the Habitat for Humanity pamphlets and talked my mom into spending an afternoon on the computer with me, researching the different countries where they had programs for long-term volunteers.

"Only the safe spots," she said. "No war zones. No drug lords or prostitution rings," she told me, kind of being serious but also laughing when I rolled my eyes.

It felt like an unspoken truce. Like we both agreed to consider all the options.

And then, eventually and inevitably, I pulled out the photography book and looked at the picture I'd found my father trapped inside. I studied the image—the buildings with their fronts ripped off and strewn in the street, piles of wood and plaster spilling into the road. At the top of a hill, a group of women in floor-length dresses stood below a lamppost, their hands perched on their waists with their backs toward the camera. On the other side of the street, a handful of men sat in a collection of folding chairs, also peering down the hill at the tall buildings on fire. They wore dark-colored suits and old-fashioned hats. Sacramento Street near Powell.

And the man, a blurry silhouette. Impossible to know his height or the true angles of his face, but undeniably familiar.

I thought of my mom then, of her damp eyes when she'd said she could have lost me.

It's a treacherous and wondrous thing to be needed, to be loved by and linked to another person's happiness so severely. And it had been completely my fault, the car accident—it hadn't been a mishap at all. I'd run into oncoming traffic because I'd been locked inside my head, inside myself. And my mother deserved better than that. She deserved a daughter who would work as hard as possible to keep that need and loving safe, who would protect that back-and-forth reliance on family.

I looked at the photo and ran my fingers over the man's face. The grainy cracked pavement at his feet and his eyes tilted toward the city streets.

"It has to end here," I said.

CHAPTER TWENTY-THREE

Ninety Days After

Isaac called every morning, and Maddie and Rabbit dropped off flowers and mix CDs one afternoon while I was resting, but I didn't want any visitors until my face was healed enough for me to take off the gauze. The skin was stretched and swollen, a raw, puffy pink that softened a little each day, but the head-aches were relentless, and at nighttime I had to take the pain pills so I could sleep through the itching and not scratch off the bandages. When the sores were ready, I used vitamin E, popping the gummy liquid from the capsules and applying it with my fingers. And I took the antibiotics religiously, so that when I went for my follow-up a week after they'd sent me home, the doctor said eventually my cheek would look just like it always had.

"Keep treating it the way you are and it'll be light scarring at most, I bet," he told us. "The kind of thing that would only be noticeable if you sunburned. I can refer you to a plastic surgeon in a few months if it still isn't healed, but I doubt that will be necessary." He wrote something down and then closed my chart. "You're lucky, you know that? It could've been worse," he said.

Beckett ended up being the first person I saw after the accident, besides my mom. He showed up with a bag of to-go boxes from Squat & Gobble hanging from his wrist and a cup of coffee in each hand.

"I come with a peace offering," he said as he stood in the doorway. "Zorba the Greek and the Mama Mia. Am I allowed to come in?"

I nodded. "Absolutely."

I was in the reading chair with my laptop, watching *Sid and Nancy*.

"You look . . ." He eyed the casts, both of them, the sling I wore for my shoulder when I wasn't practicing with the crutches, and finally my cheek, the sores still pink and prominent. "Let's be honest. You look like you got reamed by a car on PCH."

He started unpacking the food on my bed as he talked. "I called, you know? I mean, I know that you know. Your mom took a million messages, and told me she was telling you." He opened the boxes and handed me plastic silverware, restaurant napkins, and my paper cup of coffee. "And I totally get why you didn't want to talk, but then I figured if I just showed up and knocked on your door with my tail between my legs, then you'd have to let me in, right? Especially if I brought food."

He sat on my bed with his Styrofoam container and I stayed in the chair with mine, and he told me that Maddie and Rabbit were officially together together, which I already knew, and that someone took a video of Nothing Right playing the gig, which I hadn't heard about, and he could e-mail it to me if I wanted him to, because it'd been making the rounds with the kids from school and everyone was still talking about how great we'd sounded.

"Minus the second set," I said. "I'm pretty sure the second set was awful. Like record-making horribleness."

But he shook his head. "Not that anyone's saying."

"I'll take it," I said. "I'll be happy if no one mentions the second set ever again."

And then, halfway through my crepe, Beckett finally said, "I'm sorry I was such an asshat that night. About Jay and all the other stuff I said too."

I shrugged. "Water under the bridge," I told him.

"Yeah?" he said. "Really? Just like that?"

"Well, some pretty major things happened since then." I

nodded to my collection of beat up and broken bones. "You know, perspective-changing stuff and all. So I figure life's too short to spend time harping. Besides, it's just not that fun being mad at your best friend. I tried."

"Wow. That was like, Mother-Theresa-noble of you."

"And don't you forget it," I told him, and then scooped a huge piece of cheese-covered eggplant into my mouth. "So you talked to Jay, then? He came clean?"

Beckett took his last bite, licked his fork, and closed the box. "Coming clean isn't exactly how I would describe what happened." He reached for a fistful of my fries. "When I heard about the accident and all, I was crushed, you know? I mean, your mom told my mom everything as it was happening, and I knew you were going to be okay, but still. You probably don't remember it, but I came to see you at the hospital. I'd never seen anyone so messed up like that, Cal," he said. "I mean, you looked so close to being dead, you know?" He closed his eyes and shook his head as if wobbling the image away. "So anyway, it'd be really cool if you promised to never get hit by a car again. It was like, really rough on me," he said, smiling.

"Done and done. I will never get hit by a car again."

Then we hooked fingers and shook twice, pinkie-swear-style.

"Perfect. I feel much better already," he said, stabbing at a piece of my crepe. "So I was upset. And I felt like crap that we'd been fighting and hadn't gotten the chance to make up before the accident. Guilt and regret—all that messy stuff. Plus, Maddie and Rabbit were spending all this time together, like 'couple time,' since they'd made it official and all. Yada, yada, yada . . . I was bummed, so I went to find Jay, because he'd been working a lot since the party. A *lot* a lot, and I wanted him to make me feel better. I'm pretty sure that's what boyfriends are supposed to do?"

I nodded and he leaned over again, but I said, "Here, just take it, I'm done," and handed him my container of food.

"So I went to the coffee shop to let him cheer me up. But I showed up unannounced."

"Unannounced," I repeated. "As in, he wasn't expecting you to be there."

"I think you can imagine how things went from there," he said. "That guy, the one you saw him with outside the bakery? He had a safety pin through his lip, Cal. And a leather-studded collar. It was just too much."

He dipped the fork into the dollop of sour cream and wiped it on a fry. "My boyfriend, my *ex*-boyfriend, is officially a cheating, lying dillhole. And I'm an asshat for drinking so much and for not believing you when you tried to tell me, for saying all kinds of weird things that didn't make any sense. End of story."

"I like that," I said. "Dillhole. It works."

He sighed and dropped the fork, closed the container, and moved it aside so he could lean toward me. "'I have tried so hard to do right,'" he said, "but I totally screwed up."

I leaned forward too, as much as I could with the casts and the sling and all, but I leaned forward enough so that I met him halfway and we could hold hands.

"Grover Cleveland," he said. "Well, not that last part. That was all me."

The next morning, when Isaac called, I asked if he wanted to come over. "As long as you promise not to call me Scar Face or something, I'm officially ready for visitors."

I took a shower with the help of my mom, the whole plastic-trash-bags-wrapped-around-my-casts-chair-in-the-tub debacle, but I cleaned up okay, put on normal clothes—not just pajama pants and a T-shirt—and asked her to comb my hair and help me with my toothbrush.

"So he's Philip Corey Thompson's son?" she asked. "*The* Philip Corey Thompson?"

I nodded and looked at the ceiling like she told me to while she penciled my eyes with her eyeliner. I'd never worn the stuff before, but I figured the more attention we put on my eyes, the less attention there'd be on the cuts on my cheek.

"He's not pretentious, though," I said. "Actually, his dad, *the* Philip Corey Thompson, is pretty normal too. They just have a bigger house than most people. With views of the ocean like you've never seen before. But that's about all."

"And you like him?" she said.

"Yeah. I think I like him a lot," I confessed.

"Okay, you can look down now," she told me. I looked at her in the mirror and at myself, eyeing her nose and then mine, small and ski-sloped, and her freckles, too.

"Not bad, right?" she asked, and I nodded.

"No complaints," I said.

By the time Isaac showed up, I was on my bed, looking almost like a normal person and scanning my Spanish dictionary, thinking that if I ended up traveling, I wanted to work in Central or South America. I listened to my mom let him in and, holding my breath, to the two of them introducing themselves and making small talk in the hallway. And then he was in my doorway, looking just like I remembered, only better. His hair seemed a little longer, and I swear I could smell him from where I sat, the soap and spices I'd noticed that first date at Alcatraz.

"Hey, you," he said, running his eyes over me. "I'm so sorry this happened."

I started to lift my hand to my cheek but stopped myself. "I know. I mean, thanks," I said. "I actually feel a lot better. Believe it or not, this is an improvement," I told him, miming a Vanna-White–style presentation with my non-casted hand.

"I brought snacks," he said, pulling a bag of candy from behind his back. "Okay, so it's more for me than for you, but so it goes."

He dumped the boxes of Lemonheads and Milk Duds and Fun Dip onto my bed and then scoped out my room, stopping to stand by my bookshelf for a while, running his fingers over historical novels and biographies. "I'm a firm believer that the easiest way to learn about a person is to study their bookshelves. It's the most honest glimpse into who they really are." And then he was on the bed, sitting gently before he tapped the cast on my leg and said, "No signatures. Now, that doesn't seem right."

I found a Sharpie in my nightstand and handed it over so he could start sketching. "No peeking," he said, and then he nodded to the dictionary. "*¿Como está?* How are you holding up?"

I felt the pressure of his hand on my leg, even under all that plaster. I leaned forward, grabbing his attention when I wrapped my fingers around his wrist so that he had to stop drawing.

And then he kissed me. That no-rush, slow kind of kiss, like we had nowhere else to be. I loved that.

We talked about the party and the band, and then he asked about the dictionary, and I told him I was doing research for after graduation.

"I want to take a year off to travel," I told him. "I think I might apply for a volunteer program with Habitat for Humanity. An international program for six months or so, maybe a year."

He didn't knit his eyebrows together skeptically or say, "Wouldn't it be better to go to school first?" He nodded like it was the best idea he'd ever heard. "I think you'd be amazing at that. You'd kick ass in a program like that, and you shouldn't feel guilty about wanting to travel and explore the world a little before going to college."

And I couldn't help it, it just seemed like it was sitting there between us, since we were talking about making plans, so I asked, "What about you? I kind of get the feeling we're not supposed to talk about the fact that you leave for Paris next month, but it's there, you know? And I can't help but think about it."

He said that he had until the end of the summer and always left the last week of August so he'd have a few days to settle in back at home before school started. "Home," that's what he called it, and I wondered how I'd been such a moron, to let myself fall for someone who lived on the other side of the world.

"It's okay, though," he said. "I like this," he told me, waving his hand in the space between us. "And I like e-mail. I actually like writing letters, too."

"Oh yeah?"

"Old-school-style. With a real pencil and everything." He moved his hand to my hand and pulled me in, kissing me again. "I'm an excellent e-mail and letter writer," he said. "You'll see." He tilted his head, looking at his drawing on the cast, and then lowered the Sharpie back down and kept going. "My dad's been bugging me about sharing time on the holidays. Sometimes he comes to France for a week or so after Thanksgiving, but I know he'd rather have me here. Maybe I'll come back for Christmas." He moved his hand out of the way and said, "Voilà," showing me the sketch.

A girl with long dark hair and light freckles, a backpack on her shoulders and a small tom-tom drum in her hand. Hightop tennis shoes, a zip-up hoodie. Behind her there was a trolley car, and in front of her a trolley stop. At the stop was a boy who looked just like him, waving. A little farther down, closer to my ankle, he'd drawn the Golden Gate Bridge and Alcatraz just on the plane of my foot, and then he'd signed his name in small square print, his handwriting just like my dad's.

"I love it," I said.

We hung out for a while in my room, and then I admitted I'd had ulterior motives when I'd asked him to come by.

"I like the sound of that," he said, kissing me again, but I pushed him off playfully.

"I was wondering if you would help me." I nodded at the stack of books piled in my reading chair. "I'm twenty days overdue, and after seeing your room, I kind of figured a trip to the library would be right up your alley."

He went to the stack and started sorting through them, flipping through the history books about 1906. "So there's still no information about your dad?"

"No trace. No nothing." He had the photo exhibit book in his hand, and I said, "That one's mine. The rest I want to return. All of them need to go back."

He nodded. "And that means . . ."

"It just means that maybe I failed, you know? That I couldn't find him, couldn't figure it out. Maybe because I didn't try hard enough or couldn't think of The One Great Thing that would unlock all the answers." I shifted so that I was sitting on the edge of the bed, and he sat down next to me. "Or maybe it's not my fault. Not my failure at all. Maybe you were right and it's just one of those things—those mysteries that can't be explained."

"Like intuition."

"Like that Taos Hum thing. Exactly." But then I shook my head. "Except not exactly. That's not good enough for me. I know myself better than that, and I know I won't be able to stop looking for an answer until I *have* an answer. I don't think I can accept my father as an unsolved mystery. He's better than that. And I'm too stubborn."

He nudged me with his shoulder. "A fighter. That's what I thought. So, what then?"

"Things will never go back to normal until I know what happened to my dad, so I'm deciding to believe in the photo from 1906. I'm making a choice."

I drew in my breath, waiting for him to tell me I was crazy, for him to stand up and leave, maybe to laugh and say it was the pain meds talking. But he didn't say anything, so I kept going.

"And I know it doesn't make any sense. I don't even believe in time travel or time warps or whatever. But I have to believe in this. So I'm deciding that's where he is. Because at least it's somewhere. I'm deciding he's there, and that he's safe, and that maybe even, on a good day, he's doing something he believes in, something that makes him happy. I imagine him helping out, volunteering or working with some kind of organization. It would be just like him to take that on. To spend his time trying to help others."

Isaac reached up and stopped my tears before they rolled down my cheeks.

"I know it's crazy," I said. "But it's the only thing I have. And this way I can move forward. No matter what happened to him, that's what he would have wanted."

Isaac was nodding, but then he said, "I don't think things will ever go back to normal either way, though. I don't mean to be argumentative, but the thing is, you have to make a new normal now, right? You kind of already have. I mean, since he's been gone, you've become a more dedicated drummer. You played your first gig. You changed your plans for after graduation." His hand found my hand, and he moved them to his knee. "You met me and we started this . . . well, there's this thing between us now, right? Everything is different. You've already created a new normal."

Just like he did when his parents split up, I guessed. Or like Rabbit did when he got sober, or Maddie when her dad left. I realized we were doing it all the time. That there was no such thing as a permanent normal. And maybe that was a good thing.

"So it ends here, with my choice to believe in the photo," I said. "It ends with us returning the books. No more researching. And less worrying, too. Less harping on things I can't control. And more paying attention to what's happening *now*."

He kissed my hand. The inside of my elbow. My cheek. "I like the sound of that." My nose and my eyelids and my mouth, too. "So we'll return the books today?"

I nodded and kissed him back.

CHAPTER TWENTY-FOUR

June 21, 2007

> "I and this mystery here we stand."
> —Walt Whitman, *Song of Myself*

I think of him, still.

Not all the time, not like before, but always in crowded places, like when I waited for Isaac's plane to land at SFO in December. The coming and going of family, of loved ones arriving from far away or old friends departing with long embraces, foreheads pressed against foreheads and hands squeezing hands. I always think of him in airports.

And I think of him at every gig we play—not the small house parties but at the real venues, the getting-paid gigs at Cafe Du Nord, Slim's, and finally, the weekend after our graduation, as the opening act at the Boom Boom Room. With the stage lights on, it's hard to see the faces in the crowd, and sometimes I let myself imagine him there. His proud eyes and his mouth slightly open, his head nodding to the sound of our music.

I think of him when I run in Golden Gate Park on a busy day and on lazy afternoons when Beckett and I visit the Botanical Garden.

And I imagine him in the aisles of the music store each time I need new drumsticks. I remember him knowing long before I did that Nothing Right wasn't just a fleeting whim, that music would become the thing that anchored me, the one thing that made me feel absolutely complete.

"Looks full," my mom says from my doorway as she eyes my suitcase and the pile of travel-size lotions and shampoo bottles that still need to be packed.

"Hey, there."

She smiles. "Hey, there yourself." She's in the room then, moving the Spanish dictionary out of the way so she can sit in my reading chair. She cut her hair last month, the shortest I've ever seen her wear it, but the layers make her look younger and spontaneous, less weighed down. "Think you have everything?" she asks.

I know that I don't—I couldn't possibly, no matter how long I stayed in this room packing—but I tell her yes, and even lift the large yellow mailing envelope up to show her as I lower it into the suitcase. The envelope is full of college catalogs and applications to three music programs in California that I'll apply to this winter.

"What time do you arrive?" she asks, and I tell her, for the hundredth time, that I'll land in Paris the next morning around ten. Isaac will be waiting at the airport, and then I'll fly to Peru a few days later.

"*¿Estás lista?*" she asks.

Are you ready?

"*Tan lista como siempre estaré.*"

As ready as I'll ever be.

But mostly I think of him in that photo, and of the city beyond its edges. The community of men and women rebuilding their San Francisco, just like I had to rebuild mine when he disappeared. When I envision him there, he's never alone. He is surrounded by friends, good-hearted people who have taken him in and made him a part of their world. I imagine him there, imagining us, him with a vague but valid sense of a family far away who never stop remembering and missing and loving him. And I imagine that feeling brings him comfort, somehow.

Acknowledgments

I began writing *Invisible Fault Lines* in Portland, Oregon in 2012, so I am especially grateful to Wordstock Literary Festival, David Levithan, and Burnside Brewing Company; you may not have known it, but you sowed the seeds.

The historical elements of this novel were crafted through a combination of research and imagination: *The Great Earthquake* and *Firestorms of 1906* by Philip L. Fradkin; *A Crack in the Edge of the World* by Simon Winchester; and *After the Ruins, 1906 and 2006, Rephotographing the San Francisco Earthquake and Fire* by Mark Klett with Michael Lundgren, essays by Philip L. Fradkin and Rebecca Solnit and an interview with the photographer Karin Breuer (organized by the Fine Arts Museums of San Francisco and published by the University of California Press Berkeley); and *The Great San Francisco Earthquake*, and film written and produced by Tom Weidlinger, as seen on Public Television via the American Experience series, WGBH Boston Video. In addition, I would like to acknowledge Melba Pattilo Beals, who served as the inspiration for the author and civil rights activist in chapter ten.

I am incredibly thankful to have had the opportunity to

work with David Gale and the generous, insightful team at Simon & Schuster BFYR again. Thank you, Liz Kossnar, Justin Chanda, Kristen Vossen, Hilary Zarycky, Heather Faulls, Martha Hanson, Katrina Groover, Katy Hershberger, and Chrissy Noh. Handing this manuscript over to you felt like sending it home.

No author could navigate the publishing world without his or her agent, and I am ridiculously fortunate to have had Gail Hochman in my corner for the last eight years. Her honesty and enthusiasm have made my work stronger, my determination fiercer, and my successes even sweeter. Special thanks to Marianne Merola and Jody Klein, as well.

Invisible Fault Lines would not have come to be without the invaluable support, guidance, and inspiration of my models, mentors, and writing communities: Jill McCorkle, Steve Yarbrough, Stephen Cooper and the University of California, Long Beach MFA faculty, Jocelyn Johnson, Hope Mills, Aaron Weiner, and George Kamide (who allowed me to borrow his memories from his high school rock star days), James River Writers, WriterHouse, the Key West Literary Seminar, and the Taos Summer Writers' Conference. I am also thankful for my students and colleagues and their endless encouragement, particularly those who I have worked with at the University of Virginia, James Madison University, and the University of Nebraska, Omaha.

Thank you, especially, to Judy Blume—no author could hope for a more compassionate, inspiring role model than you.

I am also thankful to Astrid Decker, who took care of my baby when I needed to take care of my book.

This novel, like all the novels that have come before and will come after, belongs to my family, the Madonias, the Lomases, and the Gordons. From day one, my mother and father fostered a love of storytelling and the strong belief that if you want something bad enough, anything is possible. The rest of you were there to catch me when I stumbled and to encourage me to continue on.

And finally, my favorite partner-in-crime, Chris Gordon: You make the work more rewarding, the celebrations more joyful, and the challenges easier to bear. Thank you for everything you do, for me and for our family—this journey wouldn't be nearly as wonderful without you by my side.

If you enjoyed
Invisible Fault Lines,
turn the page for a peek at
another book by Kristen-Paige Madonia

MY MOTHER GOT HER THIRD TATTOO on my seventeenth birthday, a small navy hummingbird she had inked above her left shoulder blade, and though she said she picked it to mark my flight from childhood, it mostly had to do with her wanting to sleep with Johnny Drinko, the tattoo artist who worked in the shop outside town.

"Stella-Stella," he said when we entered. He sat in a black plastic chair in the waiting area, flipping through a motorcycle magazine, and he looked up and smiled. Big teeth, freckles, alarmingly cool. "Good to see you."

He put the magazine down as the bell above our heads dinged when the door closed behind us. He was tan and toned and a little bit sweaty, and he wore a dirty-blond ponytail that hung to his shoulders. His sharp eyes were so blue, I thought of swimming pools and icicles the first time I saw him. My mother told me about Johnny Drinko after he gave her the orange and blue fish on her hip, but I'd expected him to be as unlikable as the other burnouts Stella hung around with back then. I had not expected *him*.

"And you brought your kid sister this time." He winked at her, and I popped a bubble with my piece of pink Trident, listened to the hot hiss of the tattoo needle inking skin somewhere inside the shop.

The hummingbird was Stella's third tattoo, but it was the first time she let me come along, so she was nervous, her hips shifting from left to right inside her tiny white shorts. It took a lot to make her shaky, and I could tell she wanted a beer or maybe a highball of vodka, but I knew she'd go through with it since I was there watching. Once she made her mind up, there was no going back. It was one of the things I liked and disliked about my mother.

"Lemon's my kid," she said to Johnny, and she tucked a panel of frizzy bleached hair behind her ear.

She'd gotten a perm a few weeks earlier and was still adjusting to the weight of the nest hovering above her shoulders. It was the first and last perm she ever got, but I'll never forget the vast size of her head with her hair frazzled and sprung out around her face like that.

"I figured it'd be good to bring her along, let her see how much it hurts," she said, and I thought of our argument the week before when I announced I wanted a tattoo of my own.

"Like hell," she had said when I told her about the sketch of the oak tree I found in an art book at school. We were in the apartment, and she was making baked chicken for dinner. Again.

"You have two," I reminded her.

"I also have nineteen years on you and my own job." She peeled back the skin of the bird's breast and shoved a pat of butter underneath.

I rolled my eyes. "I've got my own money," I said, which was true. I'd been saving my allowance and slipping five-dollar bills from her purse when she wasn't paying attention.

"You're not even seventeen yet, and I'm your mother. No. Chance. In. Hell," she said, and she put her hand up like a stop sign as if directing traffic, signaling that the conversation was indisputably over.

Johnny Drinko wiped his palms on his jeans and ran his eyes over the curves of my body. "Lemon, huh? How'd you get a name like that?"

And then my mother used the laugh she saved for men she wanted to screw when she wasn't sure they wanted to screw her back. "Look at her." She nudged me forward toward him. "Sharp and sour since the day she popped out."

It never ceased to amaze me that she insisted on using this line for explaining my name, when really we both knew she picked Lemon on account of her obsession with the color the September I was born. She was a recreational painter, and each month she randomly selected one shade to use as the base for all her work. September of the year I was born was the month of Lemon, a muted yellow paint she found in an art store when we lived in Harrisburg.

Johnny Drinko sat down behind the cash register and lit a Marlboro Red while my mother leafed through binders of tattoo sketches. The shop smelled like plastic wrap and cigarettes and sweat, and I could feel Johnny watching me from behind the counter, so I cocked my hip and put my hands on my waist, reciprocating.

I'd lost my virginity that spring to a senior at school, and even though we only did it four times before he got suspended for selling weed at a soccer game, I considered myself to be experienced. The first time the pothead and I tried it regular, the second time he did it from behind, and the last two times he used his tongue first, so even though I was just getting started, I thought I knew what felt good and what didn't. I'd learned enough, at least, to recognize that a guy like Johnny Drinko could teach me all the things I still wanted to learn.

I moved next to his chair and looked at the photos taped on the wall behind his head: Polaroids of bandanna-wearing bikers and big-haired blondes with crooked teeth showing off sharply inked dragons and crosses on forearms and ankles. "Roughnecks" we called them, the townies who never left town, never went to college or got a real job, the grown-ups who never grew up. There were also photos of sports-team emblems tattooed on fine-tuned athletes and pictures of girls in low-slung jeans sporting new tramp stamps: fresh flowers and vines inked at the base of their spines. Aerosmith played from a set of cheap speakers mounted on the wall, and a fan blew warm air inside from a corner by the window while Johnny leaned over a leather notebook sketching a tree with long-reaching roots and thin, naked branches.

"You going to the race next month?" he asked me.

I shook my head, and behind us my mother said, "Oh, I think I like this one" to no one in particular.

Stella and I lived in a small city in southern Virginia that had a NASCAR racetrack built on the outskirts of town. We'd been living there for over a year and a half, and race weekend happened twice a year, but the closest I'd come to going was parking with the pothead in a cul-de-sac near enough to the track that we could listen to the buzz of cars between beers and awkward conversation.

"I must have inked a hundred NASCAR fans last spring. This one guy had me do a foot-long car driving up his back. It was pretty cool, really." Johnny nodded to the photos on the wall. "I did a good job."

I shrugged and popped another pink bubble, my trademark gesture that fall. My mother called the habit white-trash, but my friend Molly-Warner read an article in one of her magazines about the importance of drawing attention to your lips when flirting with boys, and she insisted we follow the rule.

"His old man had been a racer, got killed back in '81 in a crash," Johnny said between drags off his smoke. "That tat was really important to him."

I could see the black ink of a design inching up the back of his neck, and I suddenly wished my mom wasn't there so I could reach over and take a drag off his Marlboro. I needed my mouth around the tight white tube where his lips had just been. I was looking at him, and he was looking back, but then a woman with bright red hair pushed aside the white sheet that separated the waiting area from the tattooing room, spoiling the moment. She had wet, glassy eyes and a square of Saran Wrap taped below her collarbone.

"All good, Suzie Q?" Johnny asked, and they moved to the register.

"It's a keeper." She smiled at him and then at me.

I nodded like I knew exactly how it felt to walk into a room without a tattoo and to walk out of the same room permanently adorned. She shifted her attention back to Johnny, who was eyeing her with a slick smile slapped across his face, and I had a quick but detailed vision of them screwing in the truck bed of a white pickup. She was on top, bucking back and forth with her palms pressing into his chest, and his eyes were closed while his body pulsated beneath all that pumping. He might have liked it, or maybe not. I couldn't decide.

My mother called my name then, and I looked up and winked at Johnny before I turned away from him, checking to see if I could get his attention the same way Stella and the redhead had.

It took about twenty minutes for Stella to settle on the hummingbird, then she handed Johnny the sketch and leaned over the counter where he sat. "You mind?" she said, and she took a smoke from his pack. I thought of her mood swings back when she quit and the nervous way she used to chew her fingernails. She caught me watching her when she brought the Marlboro to her lips. "See something you like, kiddo?" she asked, and then she followed Johnny Drinko to the customers' chair behind the white sheet.

The other tattoo artist, a man with a thin black braid, finished cleaning his gear while Johnny completed the stencil and poured ink into tiny white paper cups sitting on the stand next to his chair.

"I'm taking lunch," the other guy said, and he pulled off a pair of pale blue surgical gloves and tossed them into the trash.

And then it was just me, my mom, and Johnny Drinko squished inside the heat of the tattoo room.

That was the third town we had lived in since we'd left Denny, and I liked it best, because of the low mountains and the sticky summers and the way our apartment smelled like fresh bread all the time, since we lived next to the sub shop by the mall. It was a rough ride to get there after the six months at the Jersey Shore with Rocco from the pool hall, and I was glad to be in Virginia, where my mom seemed calmer and the men she dated were quieted by the innate laziness of a small town. My best friend, Molly-Warner, had a car and a fake ID, and we had spent the summer making out with boys from school and smoking cigarettes at the public pool in town. I'd finally found my lady curves, as Stella called them once while watching me under raised eyebrows, and when school started that month, Molly-Warner and I would head to the neighborhood park after class and spend our afternoons in our bikini tops, lying out, reading books, and gossiping about our teachers, our classmates, the latest school scandal. Stella liked to take her notebooks up to the Blue Ridge Parkway on the weekends to sketch split-rail fences and ragged farmhouses she'd paint back at home. It was the first time I felt like we were ready to put Denny and Rocco and those last years behind us, and I hoped we stayed in town until I finished high school. It was my senior year, and I was sick of moving boxes and cheap motels and having to make friends every time my mom picked a new place for us to live. I needed to finish driver's ed. I needed to stay in one place long enough so I could recognize the faces in the crowd when graduation finally happened. I'd finally found a group of friends, mellow kids like me and Molly-Warner who partied a little but also knew how to keep out of trouble, and the librarian at school liked me enough to drop the late fees I'd accrued over the summer. Plus, Stella had a good job working in the jewelry department at J.C. Penney, and I could tell she liked the cheap rent and the apartment that smelled like bread too.

Johnny Drinko was pressing the hummingbird stencil against my mom's skin when she licked her lips and said, "Get me a mint from my purse, Lemon. I need something to suck on."

It was not the first time I'd watched my mother throw herself at a man. She'd been throwing herself at men in each town we passed through ever since we left Denny after the black eye. She was pretty and thin and wore cute clothes, and after all the drama when she and Denny split up, I was just glad to see her back on her feet. I knew she liked the game—the chase and the satisfaction of getting what she wanted—but there was something about Johnny Drinko that made me nervous, something I sensed right away that day at the shop. He was mysterious like he had a secret, and controlled like he knew what he wanted, and that had me worried. If Stella wanted him and he didn't want her back, if the game lasted too long, she'd walk away. While we'd been living in Virginia, things had finally evened out, but I was constantly afraid she'd get bored or, worse, vulnerable, and I knew it would be someone like Johnny Drinko who would send us moving again.

I used to tell my friends my mother was made of metal and glass. She was smooth and sturdy on the surface, but there was always that part in danger of shattering, a childlike aspect that never disappeared. I resented that unpredictability and tiptoed around the threat of her cracking apart, of her dragging us out of one city and into the next.

"Let's motor," she said as she took the breath mint from me, sucked it between her lips with a smile, and settled into the chair. Then I watched Johnny Drinko ink a perfect permanent hummingbird above her shoulder blade.

A trip across the country . . .
to find the missing pieces of her past

"Her writing is luminous, her voice original,
and the journey she takes us on compelling.
What a thrill to discover this talented writer."
—Judy Blume

It seems too good to be true when Daniel Tate—missing since he was abducted at the age of ten—turns up six years later and is reunited with his overjoyed family.

It's perfect. It's a miracle. Except for one thing:

He isn't Daniel Tate.

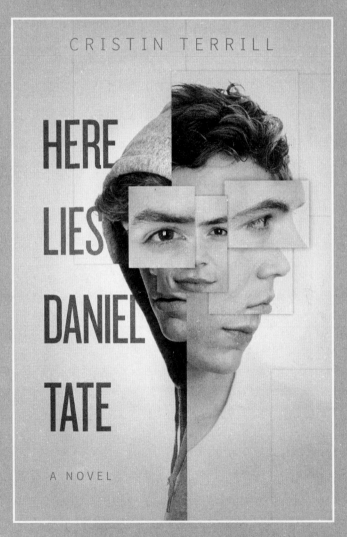

CRISTIN TERRILL

HERE LIES DANIEL TATE

A NOVEL